REFLECTION IN THE SHADOWS

OLIVER & VASQUEZ
BOOK ONE

CHRISTOPHER H. JANSMANN

Ephram Cotte
& Company
PUBLISHING

ISBN: 978-1-960914-23-1 (Kindle Edition)
ISBN: 978-1-960914-24-8 (Paperback)
ISBN: 978-1-960914-25-5 (Hardcover)

Library of Congress Control Number: 2025906570

Printed in the United States of America

For Paula:

My perfect match – no deity needed.

BOOKS BY THIS AUTHOR

OLIVER & VASQUEZ

Reflection in the Shadows

SEAN COLBETH INVESTIGATES

Blindsided

Outsider

Downhill

Duality

Bewitched

Vengeance

Solitude

Belie

VASILY KORSOKOVACH INVESTIGATES

Pariah

Peril

Ditched

Bygones

Focus

Requiem

CONTENTS

ONE

Dropping onto the cool metal of the shipping container, Ocelot was forced to take a moment to clear his head; the vertigo that always accompanied the use of a mirror portal never seemed to get any easier to handle, despite assurances to the contrary from the adept that had trained him. Taking a deep breath to steady himself — and sending up a fervent prayer that his swimming vision would settle down quickly — he let his enhanced senses go to work filling him in on his surroundings. There was a slight breeze on the warm Southern California evening carrying with it the overlapping scents of diesel fuel, rusting metal and, oddly, someone's backyard barbecue; off in the distance, the cringeworthy screeching of brakes being applied announced the arrival of yet another freight train to the intermodal yard, one of many that would pause just long enough to exchange containers similar to the one he was crouched upon. Shipping was big business, which meant efficiency was the order of the day; any loss in time getting goods to their destination meant a commensurate decrease in profits for the massive conglomerates involved. Cocking his head slightly, Ocelot caught the wheels of the security SUV as it rumbled over the gravel a hundred meters behind him; nodding slightly — and glad to see his vision had stabilized — he crept to the edge of the container and watched as the rental cops slowly continued on their patrol, oblivious to what was hovering just above them.

Right on schedule, he smiled to himself. *I'll have to thank my insider for their accuracy.*

Looking out across the massive rail yard, he squinted slightly into the darkness as he took his bearings. The massive rail yard was cleaved in half by the mainline shared by the two major freight railroads that dominated that part of the country; sidings splintered off to either side of the double tracks like some sort of genealogical tree gone mad and were filled to overflowing with an eclectic collection of rolling stock. Boxcars that had seen better days stood tiredly in one section, anointed with graffiti picked up somewhere along their travels; in another, plump tank cars huddled close together, bearing strange markings warning of the exotic chemicals they were transporting. On the side where he was crouched, rows and rows of flatbeds had been arranged on tracks that had massive gantries above them; shipping containers in gaudy colors were even at that late hour being hoisted off the rails and moved into the storage area beyond. Glancing behind him, Ocelot narrowed his masked eyes when he realized just how big a task he had ahead of him, for the shipping containers were stacked seven high and stretched away from him as far as he could see.

Taking another deep breath, he found the worst of the vertigo had finally dissipated; after scanning to ensure the security patrol had moved far enough off, he swung over the edge of the container and momentarily clung to the side, then dropped the few meters to another that was beside and below it. Crouching slightly, he scampered to the edge while he sorted through the spells he had considered for that evening; unsure of what he was going to face — it was his first time out solo, after all — he'd been a bit aggressive about memorizing just about anything he thought would have come in handy, which meant he was slightly overwhelmed by the choices. Ocelot felt a wave of anxiety rising within him, and tried to tamp down the self-doubt that always accompanied it.

Get a grip, he thought to himself as he looked across the canyons of sheet metal before him. *They need you, and there isn't much time to waste.*

Closing his eyes, he steadied himself for a moment and was rewarded when just the right one popped into his head. Smiling slightly, he whispered the words he knew so well to the wind, then opened his eyes and waited for the magic to work. It wasn't long before the faintest of vibrations reached his attenuated ears; cocking his head, he focused on the rapid fire *thumpa-thumpa-thumpa* coming from a heart filled with terror then leapt from where he'd been kneeling to land on the gravel below in a crouch. Pausing briefly to gauge the proper direction, he felt his own pulse quicken as the predator within him took over; sniffing the wind again, he broke into a full sprint, fully embracing the hunt.

Slowly the sound of that panicked heart grew louder in his ears; the faster it raced, the harder Ocelot ran, darting down one row of containers and then across to another, all the while feeling like he was running out of time. If the information he had intercepted earlier that day were to be believed, the precious cargo he was seeking was slated to be sent far, far overseas; the fear of allowing it to leave had been enough for him to risk exposing his presence. If there had been a singular lesson all of the adepts had literally pounded into him during those long years of training, it was the need to remain shrouded in the darkness that protected him and all that had come before; working from the shadows could effect great change, for sure, but as he raced across the uneven gravel of the lot, he knew this was one time when a bolder approach was more than warranted. At least, that was what he continued to tell himself; if he were wrong — well, it would be one hell of a front page for the *Orange County Register* in the morning, wouldn't it?

Behind him came the rumble of an approaching semi-truck, its massive wheels crunching their way across the surface where so much commerce had been stacked. His senses told him the source of the heartbeat was dead ahead, somewhere among the handful of trailers and storage containers that had been placed at the edge of a clearing ringed by high power floodlights; glancing to his sides, Ocelot realized his protective cover was running thin and began to slow, sizing up his options. There weren't many to choose from, and even fewer when he realized the semi was on the verge of turning onto the aisle where he was running. Skidding to a stop in the hard-packed gravel, he pressed his chest against the cold metal of the final stack of storage containers and held his breath just as the semi's headlights washed over him and hoped beyond hope that the dark hunter green of his outfit made him appear to be just another shadow among many. When there was no shout of alarm, nor stopping of the big rig, he let go of the breath he'd been holding then took a deep gulp of air in relief, ignoring the urge to cough at the heavy diesel fumes that had enveloped him.

That was a bit too close, he thought as he tried to still his pulse. *I probably should have used a shielding spell. Live and learn.*

Dropping into a crouch, Ocelot kept his back pressed to the corrugated metal of the container and crept to the edge, trailing a gloved hand along the ridges as he went. Pausing just inside what little shelter was left, he knelt once more and scanned the clearing, confirming it was, indeed, some sort of loading area; the semi in question was backing up to one of the flatbeds that had been parked along the edge, and a rather stout forklift was gently lowering a dull, gray-colored container onto it. Watching the container for a moment, he nodded slowly when he confirmed it was the source of the now-frantic *thumpa-thumpa-thumpa* heartbeats; it was clear panic had overtaken whoever was inside, and with good reason. Squinting his masked eyes slightly, he counted four men — no, *five* if he included the driver of the semi — each focused on some aspect of the loading process. Smiling wickedly, he tried to remember a time when the odds had been so much in his favor; toward the end of his training, he'd never had hand-to-hand with less than a full cadre of adepts.

Rolling his neck, he smiled wider. *Just a little warmup, Ocelot — especially since they won't be shooting counter spells at you.*

Seeking to make the odds even *more* in his favor, he brought his gloved hands together and rubbed them three times in one direction, then twice in the other; turning his attention to the first of the massive floodlights, he uttered a single word.

"*Apaga.*"

He watched the lights expectantly and frowned a few moments later when nothing happened. When repeating his process a second time — and then a third — resulted in no difference, he felt the first vestiges of his own panic just beneath his breastbone.

I've cast that a million times! he thought as he frantically went through the motions again and then again. *This should work! It's such a simple elemental spell; you just disrupt the —*

The sound of the gun being cocked just behind him stopped any further consideration of his spell casting woes and instead became an audible reminder that he'd failed to keep his attention on his surroundings. The flashlight beam came next, illuminating his screwup in washed-out white light. "Stand up," the harsh voice over his shoulder said. "And keep your hands where I can see them."

Slowly, Ocelot stood and turned, then raised his hands up slightly. As he'd suspected, it was one of the two rental security officers he'd known would be on duty, though he'd also made the cardinal sin of assuming both were in the SUV he'd seen earlier. *Another lesson there, that,* he sighed as he took in the somewhat fearful expression on the young woman's face. *Check and double check; never assume.*

"It's a bit early for Halloween," the security officer said, nodding at Ocelot's outfit. "What are you supposed to be, some sort of hero?"

Not tonight, Ocelot sighed inwardly. "This would be a good time to walk away," he said out loud with a slight smile. "Things are going to get kind of messy; you might not want to be a part of it."

The officer swallowed, but to her credit, stood her ground. "Last I checked, I was the one holding the gun," she replied. "Whoever you are, you're trespassing on private property. I'm going to have to call this in; turn around and place your hands on the back of your head."

"Last chance," Ocelot said before turning. "You really don't want to do this."

"We've got rules here," the officer said as she approached him warily. "They apply to—"

Ocelot swiveled on the heel of his boot and quickly brought his left hand toward her, palm facing outward; raising his right hand toward the sky, he let his training take over and simply felt the lightning as his gloved fingertips quite literally gathered it out of thin air. A heartbeat later, it sizzled from his open palm and struck the officer squarely in her chest. Stunned, she dropped her gun and sagged against him; gently, he lowered her to the ground all the while wondering if his version of a stun gun was slightly more potent than the device she'd had strapped to her hip.

His acute hearing told him his actions had attracted attention; turning, he easily parried the blow from some sort of heavy object with his forearm, and countered with a series of kidney punches that resulted in his assailant grunting, then crumbling to the ground. Spinning toward the sound of running footsteps, he leapt sideways a fraction of a second before the bullet pierced the space where he'd been standing; rolling out of his dive, he did a backflip into a crouch and narrowed his eyes at the burly man who was turning the gun back in his direction. Despite being relatively confident his costume had been bewitched enough to prevent most forms of injury, he wasn't entirely willing to test that particular magic — at least, not until he *had* to. Leaping upward, he twisted in mid air and landed just behind his prey, then swept his leg out in a semicircle to drop the man forward. Before his second assailant could push himself up, Ocelot deftly conjured up a petite tornado just large enough to relocate a small pile of dirt over his back, effectively pinning him to the ground.

Circling slowly and now bathed in the brilliant white light of the spots, Ocelot saw the remaining three as they warily watched him. Allowing a bit more of a breeze to develop around him, he smiled in the menacing way an apex predator might just before the kill. "Leave now," he said, raising his voice above the wind. "Leave now and no one else will get hurt."

For a long moment, he thought they might stick around; it was long *enough* that he dialed up the wind a bit more, causing his hair to pull free from the leather thong he'd used to tie it back and whip around his masked face almost painfully. In the end, they decided to cut their losses and bolted. He waited until he heard their footsteps fade in the distance before he let the breeze fade to nothing, then dashed to the flatbed trailer and the waiting storage container resting upon it. Knowing that the clock was now *truly* ticking, he quickly leapt up to the edge of the trailer, then bent slightly to examine the excessive padlock that had been threaded through the metal locking mechanism of the door. He'd expected something like that and had come prepared, though his confidence at casting a complicated spell had been badly shaken by his earlier misfire. Pressing his ear to the cold metal of the door, he thought he could hear sounds from within, and maybe even a slight whimpering.

"*¡Estoy aquí party ayudar! ¡Arevántate!*" he said loudly in Spanish, knowing his voice would carry through the metal.

Ocelot wasn't sure if he'd heard some sort of acknowledgment, but continued as if he *had* and grasped the lock between his gloved hands. Taking a deep breath, he silently called out to all of the named and unnamed gods in the pantheon for assistance before closing his eyes and focusing on a singular image of the brilliant sun. It started small but quickly grew into an angry ball of white-hot energy that whorled, twisted and contorted before him. He could feel that energy as it rolled through him and down onto the lock he held; the heat grew intense enough that Ocelot wondered if the skin beneath his protective costume might still sport a nasty sunburn. He continued right up until the pain was nearly unbearable; at the last possible moment, the metal beneath his hands gave way and dropped to the ground with a loud *clank*.

Opening his eyes, Ocelot could see that the metal of the handle had twisted beneath the heat from his touch and frowned; it required a little extra muscle for him to pull it back before he was able to throw the doors wide open. Behind those doors stood a bedraggled collection of women wearing little more than rags crammed into a space that smelled intensely putrid. Moving into the interior, he counted nearly thirty in total, and all appeared to be barely out of their teens. Thin mattresses had been stacked in one corner, and several crates of nonperishable food in the other; a handful of camping chemical toilets were about the only nod to civilization he could see, aside from the single battery-powered lamp they'd been allocated. The anger he'd felt earlier when he'd discovered human trafficking might have been taking place in that very intermodal yard threatened to overwhelm him, but he held it in check while he carefully helped each and every one out of the shipping container. It wasn't lost on him that none of them spoke English; even harder to ignore was that their accents placed them from southern Mexico or the northernmost portion of Central America. One woman in particular appeared to be the de facto leader, and had been watching him carefully as he checked over the women; despite knowing the timer in the back of his head was ticking dangerously close to zero, he moved over to where she had been standing and waited for her to speak.

Taking in his costumed form, she continued to look at him in wonder. "It's been *centuries* since the gods walked the Earth," she said in Spanish. "And even then, only in stories passed down through the generations." She paused again. "I didn't think you were real."

"Do I look like a myth?" he asked quietly. This close to her, he could see that at one point she'd had blonde streaks dyed into her jet black hair; their diminishing length told him a bit about how long they had been in captivity.

She shook her head. "No," she replied after a moment. Her eyes widened when they caught the circular piece of obsidian embedded in the fabric of his costume just below his neck. "*Tezcatlipoca*," she breathed before taking a protective step backwards.

It pained him to see the panic return to those lovely eyes, but he also understood where the fear was coming from, for even *uttering* the name of the deity he served often brought with it vestigial memories of how it had once been, especially for those who still retained knowledge of the old ways. Ocelot carefully moved toward her and placed a gloved hand on her shoulder, then gently smiled; he could feel her relax slightly beneath his touch.

"I am but his humble servant," he replied. "One of many seeing to the safety of our world."

"Then you're not...*him*?" she asked, faltering.

"The god incarnate? No," he laughed slightly before stepping back and bowing grandly. "Ocelot at your service, *señorita*."

A smile lit up her young face, a welcome change despite the

circumstances. "I feel like I've been through too much to be called that anymore."

"I can understand that," he replied before catching the sirens on the evening wind. "Nonetheless, someone as beautiful as yourself will always be a *señorita* in my book." Glancing in the direction the vehicles he knew were approaching, he turned back. "I've got to go, but good people are about to arrive. They will help you get back home."

She arched an eyebrow. "I've heard how the *gringos* help," she replied.

Ocelot shook his head. "These people are *my* people," he said. "If you trust me, trust them."

The woman looked at him again for a long moment before nodding slowly. As he turned to go, she reached out and stopped him. "The world could have used you some time ago," she said softly. "Where have you been all these years?"

"Hiding in the shadows," he replied honestly. "At least, until tonight."

The sound of rubber skidding across gravel was his final warning to escape the scene; breaking into a sprint, Ocelot made for the maze of stacked storage containers and dove back into the darkness just as three police sedans from the Santa Marcel Municipal Police Department screeched to a stop in the clearing behind him. Leaping upward, he caught the edge of the container he was beside and heaved himself higher; it took more effort than he thought to climb to the top of the stack — claws would have made the ascent easier, he noted — but once there, curiosity compelled him to crouch at the edge and look back down at the scene. He smiled slightly that the anonymous call he'd made earlier that evening had paid dividends, for the responding officers had clearly brought with them case workers from DHS. Ocelot smiled a bit wider when he recognized the petite blond woman sliding out of the unmarked SUV that had also appeared; a tiny part of his heart had hoped she'd be the lead on this particular case, and not just because the young detective had quite the track record of taking down criminals. As she strode purposefully toward the gathered group of immigrant women, he allowed himself a brief moment to mourn what might have been before carefully backing away from the edge once more.

Deciding he wanted to put some distance between himself and the activity behind him before opening another mirror portal, Ocelot leapt across to the next stack of containers to hunt for a good location. As he landed, though, the gentle breeze shifted again and brought with it the definitive odor of something cooking; pausing, he sniffed the air and realized that what he'd originally taken for someone's late night backyard barbecue was actually emanating from *within* the intermodal yard. While it wasn't all that unusual for the unhoused to have struck up a bonfire in such a location, warning alarms in the back of Ocelot's head made him turn around and begin to seek out the source of the scent.

Jumping across an alley between stacks of containers, he carefully scampered toward the fire, aware that his path was taking him uncomfortably close to the ongoing action in the clearing. The stacks weren't quite as high along the edge of the loading area, but with the floodlights pointing down and away from him, Ocelot felt like he had a good chance to keep from being observed. Still, caution remained the order of the evening, so he dropped into more of a crouch as he noiselessly made his way across the corrugated metal container. Sniffing the air again, his nose wrinkled in distaste, for whatever was being cooked had crossed the line into being extremely well done; it would be some time before he ordered a steak at his favorite restaurant.

Dropping to his knees at the edge of yet another container, his masked eyes caught the telltale plume from a bonfire; why he had missed it earlier was a mystery, for as he looked down into the conflagration, it appeared to be roaring away in good shape. Holding his gloved hand to his masked eyes against the brilliance of the flames, he found it odd there was no sign of anyone attending to the fire; nor could he immediately see what it was that had been the source of the smell — at least, not until those same sharp eyes of his spied the bright red sneakers sitting beside a carefully folded stack of clothing off to one side.

Glancing over his shoulder, he wasn't entirely certain if the fire had attracted the attention of the police officers who were just a few hundred meters away; given how it seemed to be raging, he guessed it wouldn't be long before it did. Again driven by curiosity, Ocelot flipped over the side of the container and easily dropped to the ground in a crouch, then warily approached the pile of clothing. Ignoring the flames and their intense heat against the back of his outfit, he knelt to examine the sneakers and confirmed they were ones he'd seen online for easily three hundred dollars; the cargo shorts and polo shirt stacked beside it were also from a high-end retailer, one where the customers availed themselves of services from a personal shopper in order to get *just* the right look. It was quintessential Southern California, but also completely at odds with where he had found it.

Something about the way the clothing had been left struck him as both unusual and yet strangely familiar; frowning, he tried to recall why but set it aside when a spark from the fire whistled by him and landed beside the pile. It flamed brightly for a moment before fading to a whisper of smoke. Turning, he had to put his gloved hand up once more against a glare that felt as though it could burn out his retinas if he stared at it too long.

I've got to put this out, he thought as he quickly scanned the containers that were surrounding him. *There's no way to know what's inside these things and how they might react even to just this intense heat — and by the time the fire department gets here it might be too late.*

Glancing over his shoulder, he felt himself committing to the path. *They still seem occupied back there. This won't take long... I hope...*

Standing slowly, Ocelot felt that wave of uncertainty again as he held his hands up and then whispered softly: "*Lluvia...*"

Ocelot held his breath as he willed a small cloud into being just above the fire; his heart leapt when the cloud grew larger, darkened and then began a targeted downpour over the bonfire. He started to breathe easier when the dancing flames were quickly reduced to bright orange embers sizzling beneath the onslaught of the deluge. Dropping his arms, he smiled as the small cloud thinned out into nothingness; all that remained was the small plume of steam rising into the night, a last gasp of what had once been. As the steam began to clear, Ocelot knelt once more to peer beneath the haze at whatever it was that had been burning. It took less than a heartbeat for his skilled eyes to take in what was left of a human body; while the fire had burned through much of the organic material (save for bile-inducing still-bubbling blob here or there), the underlying skeleton was more or less intact, if not seriously singed. Waving away the last vestiges of smoke and steam, he dared to move slightly closer; while he was no expert in human anatomy, the overall size of the body was close to six feet, matching the large sneaker size on the ground behind him. Odds were that this had been a male, given the cut of the clothing he'd looked at earlier; sneaking a peak at the tags might help in that regard, though now that he thought about it, maybe not, given how most brands tended to cater to all these days. Regardless, Ocelot knew without entirely understanding *why* that whomever it was he was looking at had met an untimely demise; frowning, he realized it wasn't much of a stretch to assume it had been at the hands of another. Save for one particular religious sect he'd read about during his training, very few people willingly set themselves on fire.

With a start, he suddenly realized *why* the clothing had struck him as so familiar.

I've seen it in a text, he thought, his eyes going unfocused for a moment. *Hadn't there been an illustration of ancient rituals performed during the pre-conquest era—*

"Hands where I can see them!"

Startled by the command, Ocelot jumped to his feet and whirled in a single movement, then paid for it with a massive wave of vertigo. It was the initial warning that he was close to exceeding the limit of his powers, at least until his body had a chance to recover. Blinking hard against the way the world was spinning — and attempting not to vomit all over himself in the process — he cursed inwardly for pushing himself too hard, too fast. That he had been caught unawares *twice* in the same evening was something else entirely.

"Hands on your head! *Now!*"

As he slowly placed his hands against his long hair, his vision finally cleared, allowing him to see that the blond-headed detective was the one training the latest gun on him. It took all the energy he had left not to burst into laughter at the insanity of the situation, especially when he watched her carefully take in every inch of his outfit. When her bright hazel eyes finally locked on his masked brown ones, his heart sank when he read an unspoken accusation behind them.

"Who are you?" she asked.

His heart did that familiar tango two-step at the sound of her voice; it was just the same as he remembered it, and yet had something more to it that hadn't been there before. "A friend," he replied, which in many ways was the truth.

She nodded at the body behind him. "That seems unlikely."

Ocelot shook his head. "This isn't me," he said. "I mean, I put out the fire, but the body was already here."

The detective looked at him. "You? Put out the fire?" she said with a tone that spoke to how she thought he had lost his grip on reality. "How?"

Seeing where the conversation was headed, he shrugged. "I imagine my explanation would strain credulity."

A slight twitch of a smile appeared. "Considering you're dressed in skintight latex, yeah," she agreed.

Ocelot looked down at his hunter green costume. *Latex?* he thought. *I never really thought about the material when I conjured it, but I suppose it might look like that. Or that funny Spandex that looks shiny...*

"Is that supposed to be some sort of costume?" she continued, interrupting his thoughts.

"Of a sort," he nodded.

"Whatever," she said. Ocelot noted that her gun hadn't wavered in the least. "I'm going to have to take you down to the station. Take off that mask so I can get a good look at your face, please."

"That will be kind of hard to do," he smiled slightly. "And not just because I need to protect my identity."

"Look," she sighed. "It's late and I *already* have a ton of paper-work ahead of me. Keep up this tough guy act and you run the risk of *seriously* pissing me off."

Ocelot knew there was no universe in which he willingly accom-panied her to the police station; a second wave of vertigo had already begun to wash over him, the final warning he had but a few moments at best before he'd be a mere mortal once more. Given who was hiding behind the mask, the last thing he needed was to blow the one secret he was supposed to protect at any cost — *especially* on his very first night in the field. The bile was at the back of his throat as he cast about for options; the small puddle that had formed just to the left of his boot brought a coy smile to his face.

"It was a pleasure meeting you, Kate," he said with a slow bow before winking. "Until we meet again."

"Meet? What do you—"

Pulling together everything he had left, he let the toe of his boot tap the puddle, then pushed himself into the mirror portal that immediately opened. The world around him swirled and then rushed past him as he focused on where he needed to be; it was only after he felt the portal tug his soul through to the other side that he realized the detective had never introduced herself to him...

TWO

Detective Kathryn Oliver wasn't one to party.

All through college, she had avoided the social scene like it was the plague, intent on sopping up the knowledge on offer as quickly as possible so she could move on to the next stage of her life. It wasn't that she didn't enjoy the occasional drink or two; on the contrary, most evenings were spent curled up with a good novel and a glass of the finest wine on sale that week at the warehouse store. Going out with friends with the intent of getting smashed had never really appealed to her, even back in high school when it had been their preferred method for protesting against the strictures of their parents. Perhaps that was why as a twenty-something she'd suddenly discovered there were hardly any contacts in her phone that she could reach out to for even casual conversation; maybe it was also the reason she felt so gutted that her mentor was leaving her behind for a quiet retirement in Florida, fishing along the shores of the Gulf of Mexico.

Raising her Cosmopolitan to her lips, she barely tasted the cocktail as she drained what had to have been her second — or maybe it was her third? — round. Waving to the bartender, she had but a moment to wait before a fresh glass appeared to replace the empty one. Tapping at the stem with her manicured nail, she turned back toward the gaggle of department personnel who were crowding around Francine Huerta, listening intently to whatever old war story she was telling for the hundredth time. Sipping at her Cosmo, Kate watched as Francine's eyes danced in the telling and sighed again. Coming out of the police academy, she'd had both a mission and a sense of purpose; Francine had been the one to ease her back on the first and underscore the importance of the second. Kate had learned more from her mentor in the two years they had worked together than in all the endless hours she had put in prior to becoming her partner; while Francine's retirement was well earned, Kate couldn't help but mourn the loss of talent. Tapping at the badge clipped to her belt, she knew she had big shoes to fill, but also understood there was no way she could ever replace her.

The chuckles issuing forth from the corner of the bar where Francine was holding court told Kate that the latest story had ended; sipping again at her drink, she saw Francine look up and then excuse herself from the group. Working her way through the crowded bar, the older detective sidled up to Kate at the counter, then brushed a lock of her gray hair behind an ear. Smiling at her protege, she nodded toward the drink.

"Is that what they serve in college these days?" she asked.

"I wouldn't know," Kate smiled. "I've not been undercover there in a while."

"That you haven't," Francine laughed before reaching over to put a hand on Kate's arm. "I know it's my retirement party, but you look like you're at a funeral. What's wrong?"

Trying — and failing — for a wry smile, Kate looked away. "I don't mean to dampen the mood. I'm just not looking forward to your departure."

"Honey," Francine said quietly, "I've already left."

Kate looked back at her. "I suppose you have," she sighed.

Francine eyed her for a moment. "This isn't about me leaving," she correctly intuited, showcasing again what had made her one of the top investigators in California. "Is it?"

Kate looked away again. "If I'm being honest? Not really, no."

"Kate," Francine said in that way that made the younger woman turn toward her. "You *are* ready for this. I'm leaving the department in solid, capable hands; there isn't anyone I would trust more with this role than you."

"That is kind of you to say," she replied. Picking up her Cosmo, she looked away again. "I can only hope to succeed you."

Francine considered Kate for moment. "I'll be around for a while yet," she said softly before pulling her phone from a pocket in her jeans and waving it. "And they make these cool devices now that allow you to talk to someone, even if they are hundreds of miles away."

Kate rolled her eyes. "Seriously. This coming from a woman who still can't figure out the difference between a text message and an email."

"Maybe that's why I retired," Francine chuckled. "I don't want to keep up with the technology any longer."

"I worry you're going to become one of those reclusive retirees who spend all of their time out on the water, muttering curses at their fishing pole without realizing they've forgotten to bait it," Kate said, feeling her mood lifting slightly.

"Why would you bait a hook?" her mentor asked. "That would only mean having to actually *catch* something."

"I thought that was the entire point of the endeavor," Kate said, frowning. "Isn't it?"

Francine leaned closer and whispered conspiratorially. "Come down to St. Augustine and I'll show you what it's all about."

"All right," Kate smiled. "Once you get settled, I'll take some time off and visit. I have to admit you've piqued my curiosity."

"Always a good thing for a detective," Francine chuckled. Glancing over her shoulder at the crowd she had left, she sighed. "Once more unto the breach. Are you going to join us?"

"In a minute," Kate lied.

"Liar," Francine laughed before pushing away from the bar and making her way back to her corner.

Feeling the uplift in her spirits immediately starting to fade, Kate sighed and drained the last of her drink; setting it down on the bar with a *clink*, she wondered briefly if she would actually follow through on her quasi-promise to head to Florida. She'd not taken any time off since starting with the department; vacations weren't really her thing, and besides, without someone to share the experience with, what was the point? A wave of depression washed over her when she realized her last meaningful relationship had been back in high school; save for a few casual encounters since that had helped knock the edge off, Kate had more-or-less become married to her career. Turning back to look at Francine's corner of the room, she knew that dedication had been *why* she'd been fast-tracked to the Detective, Senior Grade position, but now wondered how much it might have cost her personally.

Fuck this, she thought as she waved to the bartender. Ignoring his frown before beginning to make her a fresh drink, she turned and scanned the room. *I'm going to get drunk, and then I'm going to find the most gorgeous man in the room—*

Her iPhone took that opportunity to buzz repeatedly in her pocket; frowning, she recognized it as the vibration pattern she had set specifically for Dispatch and groaned inwardly when she yanked it out and confirmed the number on the screen. Pressing the phone to an ear and covering the other with her hand so she could hear something over the hubbub in the bar, she answered. "Detective Oliver."

"Detective, it's Sam," the officer of the watch said. "I hate to interrupt the festivities, but an unusual call just came in."

"No worries," she said. "What do you have?"

"An anonymous caller is claiming there was a container at the Santa Marcel Railyard full of women," he answered. "Part of some sort of human trafficking ring. The container arrived this evening and was scheduled to be loaded onto a truck and shipped elsewhere."

Kate's eyes widened. "How credible is this tip?"

"The caller provided both the container number and the GPS tracking for it." Sam paused for a moment. "Kate, the container came in via rail from Mexico."

A surge of adrenaline temporarily washed away the worst effects of the alcohol. "Who do we have available?" Kate asked as she fished through her purse to grab a credit card for her tab. Waving it at the flummoxed bartender as he plopped down her latest Cosmopolitan, she continued. "Screw that. Roll everyone we've got on duty at the moment."

"Already did," Sam replied.

"Good man," Kate laughed. "I'm less than ten minutes out myself."

"I'll let Officer Ryder know. Do you want DHS there?"

Kate frowned. "No, but you'd better call them anyway. Make sure you get Dianne, though? She's the most reasonable of the bunch."

"That's saying something," Sam chuckled. "On it. Good hunting."

Sliding her iPhone back into her jeans, Kate considered downing the Cosmo that had arrived along with her eye-popping tab — so much for the police discount that evening — and decided it might be wise not to push her luck. Grabbing her purse, she headed off to the bar's exit without so much as a backwards glance at the party that continued on without her. She wondered if anyone other than Francine would realize she was missing, then decided that she pretty much didn't care either way.

In what was likely just the first of her departmental policy violations since becoming the lead investigator, Kate had driven her unmarked SUV to the party; the second had been cramming her road cycle into the trunk between the standard crime scene kit and her hazmat suit. The late model Honda Civic she'd had since high school had rather conveniently decided it needed a new powertrain a week earlier, an expensive repair that wasn't easy to stomach even after the nice bump in pay she'd received as part of her promotion. So she'd simply begun ending her morning workout at the station, though it had meant adding a *second* workout for her commute home each evening. The timing on the party had been such that she'd not wanted to arrive at the bar sweaty and dressed in her cycling Spandex, so in deference to the importance of the moment to her mentor, she'd opted for being professional instead. As she unlocked the driver's side, she snorted at how she'd thought it would matter; half the attendees had arrived in casual clothing that would have shocked her prim grandmother. The other half had quickly gotten inebriated enough not to have noticed her diligence in the first place.

You're in a bad place tonight, she thought as she tossed her purse into the passenger wheel well and slammed the door closed. *Probably why you don't drink more than that one glass of wine each night.*

Starting the SUV up, she backed out of her spot and then turned toward the exit of the parking lot, surprised to see from the clock on her dashboard just how late it had become. She snorted again at how time could fly when one was drinking. Pulling out onto the main four-lane road that bisected Santa Marcel, Kate ignored the gaudy lights for the various fast-food joints and twenty-four hour pharmacies that were still hawking their wares at that hour and focused on ensuring she kept the SUV between the lines on the pavement. Traffic was blessedly light, a rarity in any part of Southern California; Kate had no trouble crossing the city to get to the more industrial section where the rail yard was located. Santa Marcel had been little more than a Spanish missionary outpost before the railroad arrived during the boom of the late 1800s; the city had essentially grown outward from it, benefitting from the various support industries that fed the insatiable appetite of what had once been known as the iron horses.

The ornate structure of the passenger station that Amtrak still used appeared off to her right, and Kate slowed to turn onto the main access road that led to the yard proper. She was vaguely aware that passenger traffic had increased in recent years, a result of travelers seeking cheaper alternatives to airfare; it also didn't hurt that the accommodations were far more comfortable, something she had discovered a few months earlier when she'd had to go to San Antonio for a case. While the trip had taken far longer, she'd arrived relaxed and ready to work, a marked improvement from the anxiety she always experienced when traveling by air. Slowing to turn into the security gate for the yard, Kate wondered if she could take it all the way to Saint Augustine to see Francine; she made a mental note to look it up as she pulled to a stop at the guard shack and rolled down her window.

Flashing her badge at the rumpled overnight centurion, she smiled. "Detective Oliver."

"Joining the party?" he asked with a note of sarcasm.

"Might as well," she replied as she tucked her badge back into her waistband. "I take it other units are already here?"

"Yes," he nodded. "It shouldn't be hard to find them; they are over on the southwest side of the yard where the shipping containers are transferred. Just follow the flashing lights."

"Thanks," Kate said as she rolled her window back up. *For nothing*, she added as she pulled through.

What passed for directional signage in the yard prevented her from getting lost in the amazingly complicated layout of track; the number of boxcars and other rolling stock all around her was somewhat staggering, making her wonder what the current value of product sitting in the yard at that moment might be. Even accounting for some of the boxcars being empty, it still had to be a rather significant number. Slowing, she carefully crossed in front of three massive locomotives that were idling on a siding; their rumbling engines vibrated through the frame of the SUV, almost as though she were going through a low-end earthquake. Turning again, she finally saw a wider clearing filled with cranes, semi-trucks and the half-dozen patrol vehicles Dispatch had managed to send; pulling to a stop behind one of them, she put the SUV into park and took in the scene outside of her windshield.

Beneath the harsh glare of the floodlights, she counted nearly two dozen women in the space wearing little more than rags; most were in gaggles of two or three, and all looked shell shocked. The horror of what they had to have gone through suddenly shot through Kate's soul and caused her blood to run cold; for a moment, she could almost feel the panic that they had to have experienced when the doors to the shipping container had been closed and locked. While she had already dealt with her share of human trafficking victims during her short career in Santa Marcel — Southern California was one of several hotbeds of activity, given its varied transportation networks — working such cases invariably left her with a significant amount of fatalism at ever successfully addressing the root cause of *why* it was so profitable for so many. Shutting off the SUV, she grabbed her Glock from the safe in the glovebox and opened her door, holding on with grim determination to the notion that she could at least do *something* for these women, however little it might be. The twin scents of body odor and, paradoxically, someone barbecuing meat filled the air as she approached, causing her to wrinkle her nose; it wasn't the worst mix of odors she'd ever encountered, but it was close.

The slightly rotund figure of Officer Bruce Ryker was standing at the edge of a black-and-white, tapping away at a tablet. Kate moved over to him and nodded when he looked up at her. "What do we have?" she asked.

He grinned slightly. "And good evening to you, too, Detective," he chuckled, eyes dancing merrily. She never understood why the twenty-year veteran was always in such good humor no matter the circumstances. "How was the party?"

"About what you would expect," she replied curtly, then meaningfully glanced at the scene in front of them.

Ryker got the hint. "Twenty-six women between the ages of 16 and 24," he said. "As you know, my Spanish is not that great, so I've got Sylvia and Ted taking their statements."

"Didn't the department buy you one of those self-learning language training packages?" she asked, smiling slightly as she already knew the answer to their old joke.

"I'm in the twilight of my career, Detective," he chuckled. "This old dog is having trouble learning new tricks."

Kate reached over and tapped at the tablet in his hands. "Indeed," she said, her tone telling him exactly what she thought of his excuse.

Chuckling again, Ryker continued. "We believe they were loaded into the container ten days ago somewhere in southern Mexico — Oaxaca possibly, based on the timing — but they actually are all from Guatemala."

"Ten days. Shit." Kate shook her head. "How did they get to the Oaxaca? Did they walk?"

"That might have been a safer option," he sighed. "They were in the back of a shipping van."

Kate's eyes widened. "*All* of them?"

Ryker paused for a moment. "They started with thirty," he said.

She felt her stomach churn. "Holy shit."

"Dianne Bennimaker," Ryker said as he pointed to where a tall woman in a pantsuit was speaking with three of the women. "She got here a few minutes after we did; DHS has already agreed to expedite their asylum claims and will be putting them up at the Marriott tonight until more permanent accommodations can be arranged."

"That makes me feel a bit better," Kate replied. "Dianne is one of the good ones."

"She is," Ryker nodded. "Other than that, we've got bupkis. They saw who put them in the container, of course, but that's just a tad out of our jurisdiction."

"Great. I can turn that over to my contact at the Feds, but it won't go anywhere. Again." Kate's eyes flicked to container on the back of the flatbed they were milling about. "Who owns the box?"

"That's where things begin to get interesting," Ryker replied. "A local firm. Vasquez Industries."

Kate started, then struggled to keep her expression neutral. "Are you sure?"

"Yes," Ryker replied. It wasn't lost on her that he'd seen a flicker of something in her face, but opted not to follow up on it. "Dispatch probably told you how we got this tip—"

"Sam did, yes."

"So then you know that we had the GPS tracker for the container." He paused. "We also got a set of login credentials for the global system shipping companies use to share their manifests with each other." Ryder turned up the screen of the tablet and showed her a screen. "Our mysterious tipster seems to have done their homework."

Kate took the tablet and quickly scanned the data; her eyebrows went up as she reached the section showing ownership, then even *higher* when she saw the ultimate destination. "Prague?"

Ryker nodded. "There are still many places in the former Eastern Block that have uses for such cargo," he replied softly as he took the tablet back.

Looking at the container, Kate shook her head. "It can't be a quick trip, can it? How on Earth would any of them have survived in that thing?"

"I imagine that was baked into how many women they collected," Ryder replied.

"Shit," Kate swore. "Treating people as cattle... just, shit."

"At least they had toilets."

She swung around to look at him. "Seriously?"

"Yeah," he nodded before pointing at the back of the container. "Come on, I'll show you."

Kate followed Ryder to the trailer, and then climbed the short ladder someone had retrieved in order to get into the back of the container; her eyes immediately started to water at the stench that greeted her when she entered. Two portable floodlights had already been installed at either end, fully illuminating the miserable existence the trapped women had been enduring. Thin mattresses stained by fluids she didn't want to identify were everywhere, and more were stacked up at one end beside what appeared to be the small, squat chemical toilets campers might use; based on how the stench increased as she neared them, it was a good bet they had been pushed beyond their manufacturer's recommended limits. Beside them were stacks of cardboard boxes containing pouches of dehydrated meal packages favored by survivalists with shelters in their backyards; a pallet of bottled water sat in the other corner. Neither supply looked to be enough to support so many people for the trip Kate knew they'd been sent on.

Turning around in the space, she had a pretty clear impression of what it must have been like after the doors had closed and the group had been plunged into darkness; she doubted the one battery lamp she'd seen would have done much to make their situation less depressing. Shaking her head, she started back toward the relatively fresh air outside of the container, then paused when she saw the pieces of a lock piled up on the bumper of the trailer. Hopping down to the ground, she found she was closer to eye-level and able to confirm what her first glance had caught.

Turning to look up at Ryder, she arched an eyebrow. "This looks melted."

"And now we get to the even *stranger* portion of the program," he said before slowly pulling one of the doors closed. "Check this out."

Both eyebrows went up when Kate saw the locking mechanism for the door; it almost looked as though it had been exposed to something burning at a high enough temperature to bend solid metal. "Blowtorch?"

"I don't think so," he replied as he gingerly came back down the ladder. "You'd see scorching if that's what had been used."

Kate's head snapped back to the door. "You're right," she nodded. Pulling a pair of gloves from her back pocket, she snapped them on before picking up a part of the melted padlock. "What can get hot enough to do this *and* be portable?"

"Nothing in the immediate area," Ryder replied, though there was something in the way he answered that had Kate flick her eyes at him. "We'll do a complete search of the rail yard if you like, but I don't think we'll find anything."

"What makes you say that?"

Ryder looked uncomfortable. "Our witnesses said it was a... god... that let them out."

Kate rolled her eyes as she put the padlock back down. "Seriously?"

"Yes."

Peering back into the container, she frowned. "They must be dehydrated and hallucinating," she said.

"Dehydrated, yes," Ryder said. "But I think they did see something."

Kate eyed the officer. "You don't actually believe them? That they saw the Almighty releasing them?"

Ryder looked even more uncomfortable. "Not *God*," he corrected. "*A* god. Something from a Mesoamerican myth, if I understood how Sylvia translated it."

"You've got to be kidding me."

"I wish I were."

Kate sighed. "And here I was worried that drinking *before* I got here would make things weird."

"Sorry," Ryder said.

Looking at the crowd of women, Kate saw one of them was watching her intently. "Which one told you this fish tale?"

"That one," Ryder said, pointing to the woman she'd already spotted. "Do you want Sylvia?" he asked as they started in that direction.

"I'm fluent," Kate said, before looking sidelong at Ryder. "Unlike some people I know."

Chuckling, Ryder held up his hands in defeat. "All right, *all right*. I'll finish the damn course."

"Good boy," she smiled slightly.

The woman saw Kate's approach and detached herself from the group of women she'd been speaking with; she stood patiently, hands clasped in front of her, though her eyes did a thorough job of sizing up the detective. Once she was within polite speaking distance, Kate noted that the woman had blonde streaks in her hair of the kind applied at a high-end salon. As with most Americans, Kate had a hard time not falling into the trap of assuming women who found themselves in such situations were from the lower echelons of society; based on the woman's demeanor, it was clear she'd been schooled in social graces. Kate chastised herself for once again making assumptions.

"Hello," Kate said in Spanish as she held out her hand. "I'm Detective Kathryn Oliver, Santa Marcel Municipal Police."

"Consuelo Muñoz," she replied as she shook her hand. "A pleasure to meet you, despite the circumstances."

Kate cocked her head at the accent and the more formal language. "Where are you from?"

"A suburb of Guatemala City," she replied before glancing over at Dianne. "She says we may be able to return home."

"If that's what you wish," Kate nodded before arching an eyebrow. "Usually people want to stay."

Muñoz shook her head. "I am a schoolteacher and have a two-year-old," she said. "I very much need to get home."

"Then we will make sure that happens," Kate replied. "Is there anyone we should contact to let know you're safe and sound?"

"Your colleagues were nice enough to allow me to call my husband earlier."

"Good," she nodded. "My officer says you were rescued by a god," Kate continued, unable to keep a note of skepticism out of her voice.

The woman picked up on the tone in Kate's voice and smiled slightly. "That's right. We heard him remove the padlock from the container, then saw how he'd incapacitated those that had imprisoned us."

Kate followed her eyes and looked to where two men were being questioned by other officers; based on their attire, they looked like the typical sort of employee for the rail yard. "Incapacitated?" She asked before translating what Muñoz had said to Ryder.

"According to their statements, one was stunned by lightning, and the other buried beneath a pile of dirt dumped on them by a tornado," Ryder helpfully answered. At the glare he received from Kate, he simply shrugged. "I can only report what they told us. I offer no commentary."

"Right," she sighed. "So what was the name of this god, then?" she asked Muñoz.

"He called himself Ocelot," she replied.

Kate frowned. "Honestly, I thought you were going to give me something out of a comic book. I don't think I've heard of that particular deity."

"That's because, technically, he's not *actually* a god," Muñoz said. "Ocelot is working on behalf of Tezcatlipoca."

"I've not heard of them, either," Kate replied. "Are you sure you actually saw someone? You've been through quite a bit to get here —"

"I spoke with him myself," Muñoz answered easily. "He told me that you would be coming to help us, then he leapt away."

"Describe him."

Muñoz cocked her head. "He *saved* us, Señora. I would not want him punished for that."

"I only want to clarify a few points of this situation," Kate replied. "And it would be helpful to get his explanation on how he uncovered your predicament."

The woman hesitated before nodding slowly. "He was about two meters tall, with long black hair tied back with a leather thong."

"Caucasian?"

"Latino," Muñoz replied instantly. "At least, from the way he spoke and what I could see around his mask."

"He wore a *mask*?" Kate asked incredulously. "Next, you'll tell me he was wearing a Spandex onesie."

Muñoz simply shrugged. "Whatever it was made from, the outfit was a deep, deep green color and covered him from neck to toe."

Kate felt her jaw drop. "You've got to be kidding me," she

31

breathed before realizing Muñoz was deadly serious. "Well, *fuck*," she continued in English. "Now I've got to deal with some *fucking* Good Samaritan running around Santa Marcel in his pajamas."

Ryder looked taken aback by her language. "Detective—"

Kate waved at him. "I think I've about had it for this evening," she said, cutting him off. "Make sure everyone gets settled into their new accommodations, would you?"

"Detective—"

"I'll read your report in the morning," she continued as she turned and began to walk away.

Muñoz grabbed her arm. "Ocelot is *real*," she whispered. "Whatever you think of me or these other women, know this: we'd be halfway to our doom if he'd not intercepted this container when he had... and called you."

Kate started to protest before hearing something in what the woman had said. "You're right," she nodded slowly as a strange tingling crawled down the back of her neck. "He did call us. And if he is as real as you say he is, this clown's probably watching us to see what we're going to do." Kate turned to Ryder. "Pull whoever is done questioning the victims and start a standard search pattern; unless he has a jetpack, he can't have gotten too far."

"Yes, ma'am," Ryder replied before hustling off.

"You won't find him," Muñoz said with a certainty that grated on Kate's last nerve.

"Watch me," she replied as she turned away from her.

Kate knew she should have waited for Ryker to return with the search plan in hand, but something about Muñoz's unwavering belief in the identity of the masked vigilante had truly begun to irritate her. Feeling the woman's eyes on her back, the detective randomly picked one of the many aisles that opened into the clearing and strode away, intent more on putting distance between them than actually looking for the man in question. Her steps along the packed gravel of the roadway began to echo as she entered the artificial canyon; looking around her, she had a small sense of claustrophobia based in no small part on how high up the containers were stacked. Slowing slightly, she tried to read what had been stenciled on the sides of each one but quickly realized the names and numbers meant very little to her. She slowed even more when the wind shifted slightly and brought with it the overwhelming stench of something organic burning.

Realizing that what she had earlier thought was some sort of barbecue might be something far, far worse, Kate pulled her Glock from the holster and held it at her side as she started to walk faster in the direction of the smell. Approaching an intersection of sorts, she paused to gauge the direction from which the smell was coming and turned; within moments, she saw the telltale flickering of orange light as it danced along the sides of the shipping containers closest to the blaze. Shifting her gun slightly, she yanked her iPhone from her jeans and hit the speed dial for Dispatch.

"Dispatch, Officer Watson."

"Sam, it's Kate. I need a fire crew at the rail yard *now*. Fire in progress at my coordinates."

"On it," he said before disconnecting.

Stuffing her phone back into her pocket, she slowed down and pressed herself to the side of the container; she was close enough now that the brilliant glare coming from what looked like a roaring bonfire was forcing her to squint. *What* had caught on fire didn't seem to be easily evident, which made her frown; given how she could feel the heat fifteen yards or so away made her think it might have been a pile of tires, or something else that could easily catch—

Her heart skipped a beat when someone dropped out of the sky and landed with a slight flourish just in front of the fire. Whoever it was didn't seem phased in the least by the intensity of the conflagration, and instead deliberately inspected a small pile of debris that she'd not noticed earlier. Given how they were backlit by the flames, it was hard for her to make out much more than the fact they were tall, and quite solidly built. Kate's heart skipped another beat when she realized she might have inadvertently cornered the vigilante; bringing her gun up, she started to move forward to confront the figure — and then came to a dead stop when they suddenly stood and held their hands toward the flames.

What happened next she decided later to *not* include in her after action report. Besides, who would have ever believed she'd actually witnessed someone conjuring a thundercloud out of nothing to extinguish the flames? Still, she found herself in something of a state of shock when the bonfire was quickly reduced to a billowing cloud of steam; the only thing that pulled her out of it was seeing the body that had been masked by the flames. Mustering what little sanity she had left, Kate lifted her gun back up and took a determined step toward the back of the figure.

"*Hands where I can see them!*" she shouted.

The figure had been crouching beside the singed bones and started at her yell; they jumped to their feet and whirled on her — and then appeared to have regretted the sudden movement, almost as though they were fighting a wave of vertigo for having stood up so quickly.

"Hands on your head! *Now!*"

Slowly, arms were raised in front of her, flexing some very well-defined biceps in the process. As hands went behind a head covered in long, black hair, Kate began to examine what she had in front of her; the vigilante was attired in some sort of form-fitting outfit that left very little of their chiseled body to the imagination, including his gender. A small circular amulet of some sort was embedded in the suit just below his neck, and rather oddly seemed to reflect what little light there was. And while Muñoz had been accurate about the mask, she had undersold just how handsome the Latino face beneath it appeared to be. In fact, taking in the entire package — and ignoring the bonkers getup he was wearing — the mysterious figure before her was *insanely* attractive in a way she'd never experienced before.

Except, maybe, for one other time.

Forcing her attention back to the man in front of her and the smoldering body behind him, she realized those light brown eyes framed by the domino mask appeared to have been similarly appraising Kate; based on the slight frown that creased his features, she somehow knew he understood exactly where he stood with her. For a brief instant, she felt like a weird connection had been made between them, though for the life of her she couldn't understand why; whatever it was quickly flickered out.

"Who are you?" she asked.

A slight smile appeared. "A friend."

She nodded at the body. "That seems unlikely."

He shook his head. "This isn't me. I mean, I put out the fire, but the body was already here."

Realizing he was being literal and fearing that maybe she *had* seen what she had seen, Kate blurted out her response. "You? Put out the fire? How?"

The vigilante seemed to read the incredulousness in her expression and shrugged. "I imagine my explanation would strain credulity."

Something in the elocution seemed familiar, not to mention the dry wit, but Kate shoved it aside — though not fast enough to prevent a slight twitch at the corner of her mouth. "Considering you're dressed in skintight latex, yeah."

Those masked eyes widened before looking down at his outfit; for a moment, she got the strange sense he was seeing it for the first time. Which would be odd... unless this *was* his first outing as some kind of cartoonish supervillain/superhero persona. Kate felt herself suddenly wondering if maybe she had interrupted his inaugural spree of mayhem.

"Is that supposed to be some sort of costume?" she asked.

"Of a sort," he nodded, confirming her suspicions.

"Whatever. I'm going to have to take you down to the station. Take off that mask so I can get a good look at your face, please."

"That," he said, "will be kind of hard to do, and not just because I need to protect my identity."

The headache that had been threatening behind her eyes suddenly began to pound. "Look. It's late, and I *already* have a ton of paperwork to do. Keep up this tough guy act and you run the risk of *seriously* pissing me off."

Something washed across that masked face, and for a moment, she though he might actually comply and remove his mask; when he instead began to bow at her, Kate tightened the grip on her gun. "It was a pleasure meeting you, Kate," he said with formality before he straightened. Winking, he added with a smile: "Until we meet again."

"Meet? What do you—"

Kate wasn't easily shocked.

And yet, the tall man she'd just been speaking to, the guy who'd been standing just a few feet from her a fraction of a second earlier *appeared* to have suddenly been sucked into the small puddle that had collected in a depression beside his boot. Blinking to ensure she wasn't seeing things, she realized she was still pointing her Glock at the now empty space; sliding the gun back into her holster, she knelt to consider her reflection in the water and wondered if maybe she *had* drunk one too many Cosmopolitans. Glancing to the still-smoking bones, she thought that if she *was* having some sort of alcohol-induced hallucination, it figured that it would be a murder.

Still, she was certain she had seen — and had been talking too — that mysterious figure. Examining the ground around the fire, she began to feel slightly vindicated when she located his trail of boot prints in the loose soil, right where he had dropped down from the stack of containers. Putting a hand on her hip, she estimated the stack to be nearly thirty feet high (assuming each container was around ten feet tall); as there didn't seem to be any climbing gear about, she wondered if he had actually scaled the damn thing. *Why* he would have been up there seemed obvious, considering how easily he could have moved around undetected high above the yard. But getting *up* there seemed equally as problematic. Returning to the remnants of the fire, she wondered how she'd tell the Chief that her prime suspect had simply vanished. It felt like it might be something close to career suicide to commit any of what had happened to the official record, so for the moment she decided it might be wise to keep her chance meeting to herself; that *didn't* mean Kate's professional curiosity hadn't been piqued.

No, she thought to herself, *I'm not finished with you yet — whoever you are.*

Kate turned at the approach of footsteps behind her and smiled when the patrol officer she had left in charge of the scene back in the loading area appeared. "Search underway?"

"Yes," Ryker replied. "Do you still think we'll find someone?"

"No," Kate said after a thoughtful moment. "But it doesn't hurt to be thorough, right?"

"Never," Ryker chuckled. "There was also bit of a squabble between DHS and DCS over one of the victims as she is underage, but I think it's been worked out."

The detective looked over his shoulder. "Thank *God* a warm meal, hot shower and comfortable bed are in their collective future. What a mess."

"I still can't fathom the depth of darkness in a soul that would willingly sell one human being to another," Ryker said.

"Me either."

Ryker eyed the embers. "Looks like you found the source of the fire we've been smelling. Was it out when you got here?"

"Yeah," Kate lied.

The officer squinted into the embers. "Is that a *body* in there?"

"Yes," Kate nodded.

Ryker rolled his eyes. "A long night just got longer."

"That it did," she frowned. "That it did."

THREE

Everything ached. *Everything.*

Groaning slightly, Tenoch gingerly rolled over onto his side and slowly blinked the sleep out of his eyes; to his surprise, the sliding door to his patio appeared to be open, which helpfully explained the slight chill to the bedroom. Pulling the satin sheet closer to his chin, Tenoch took a deep lungful of the ocean air and smiled. While it had cost him a small fortune to purchase the corner condo, he'd never grown tired of the unique view his wrap-around balcony afforded. Many an evening had been spent sitting out there on the cozy chaise lounge, drinking a Corona while watching the sun slowly settle beneath the horizon. He'd never found a better way to decompress from the demands of his day — at least, nothing that didn't involve someone sharing the bed beside him. Glancing to the empty pillow beside him, Tenoch frowned slightly, for now that he thought about it, he couldn't remember the last time he'd scored. Running a hand through his unruly black curls, he wondered if he was disappointing any of his forbears by not doing his part to uphold the Latin lover stereotype; smiling slightly, he figured it didn't matter. He'd never been one for labels anyway.

Sitting up, he let the sheet slip to his waist and immediately regretted the move; not only did the room spin for a moment, but goosebumps also immediately erupted across his naked torso, a leading indicator it was far cooler in the room than he realized. Waiting for a moment to steady his vision and being rewarded with a pounding headache as a result, Tenoch threw off the sheet entirely before padding across the carpet in his briefs to the open balcony door. There he paused, for his fuzzy brain began to warn him that he *shouldn't* be seeing a sunset so early in the day. Blinking, he looked over his shoulder to the nightstand beside his bed and the time being displayed on the Bose radio sitting there; blinking again, it took a moment for the cobwebs part *just* enough for him to realize something was off.

The bolt of adrenaline that subsequently shot through him chased away the last of his somnambulant lethargy, though did little to assuage the full body ache that didn't seem to want to quit. Pulling the glass door shut with a metallic *clunk*, he hurried back across the carpet to the pile of clothing at the foot of his bed, then knelt down rather unsteadily to dig through his pants to find his phone. He groaned when he saw the seventeen missed calls and text messages displaying on the lock screen, and groaned even further when the phone decided at that very moment to begin ringing. Sitting down with his back against the bed, he took a deep breath and then answered the phone.

"*Madre,*" he said perfunctorily.

"*Mijo,* where the *fuck* have you been all day?" came the vibrating voice of the matriarch of his family. "I've been calling you since five this morning."

Tenoch pulled the phone away long enough to confirm that was the case and groaned a third time. "I... went out last night," he replied. "I'm just getting up now."

"Just *now*? What the *fuck* kind of party did you go to?"

"I—"

"You know what? I don't give a crap," she cut him off. "And I don't have the fucking time to yell at you for even *thinking* about carousing in your current condition."

"I'm fine, *madre*."

"The hell you are," she replied. "You've two more months—"

"Six weeks," he corrected. "Maybe four, depending on how you count."

"*Eight weeks*," she thundered, "but the hell with that. Get your ass over to the rail yard *now*, and then report to me at the office afterward."

Tenoch felt a slight shiver of fear roll down his spine. "The rail yard?" he asked carefully. "Why?"

"*Dios mío*," she sighed. "You really *did* just get up, didn't you?"

"Yes," he answered.

"Then get a copy of the *Register* before you go over."

The click from the other end was the only indicator that the call was over.

Tenoch dropped his iPhone to the carpet and wondered if he were really cut out to play the game he seemed to have been thrust into. His mother had become a formidable businesswoman, deftly steering Vasquez Industries in the ten years since she'd been unexpectedly forced to take the reins after her husband's sudden passing. She'd run her personal life with the same militaristic precision, demanding nothing but the best from her only offspring. He'd learned from a very early age that failure was not a viable option, sometimes in the most painful way possible. Pulling his knees up to his chin, Tenoch could still feel the sting of her anger from the evening years earlier when he'd been bold enough to challenge her plans for his future; he'd lost that battle, of course, along with countless others, but somehow, he'd still managed to wrangle a tiny sliver of his life away from her domineering control. Glancing to the wall of glass that led to the balcony, he smiled slightly when he saw his faint reflection. He'd done as she'd asked, but maybe had done a bit *more* than she realized; flexing a bicep, he smiled wider to think that his mother had proven to be far more effective motivator than any personal trainer he'd ever used.

Pulling his phone from the carpet, he accessed the mobile version of the *Orange County Register* and quickly scanned the headlines; he frowned slightly when he saw the article about a possible human trafficking ring being interrupted at the Santa Marcel Rail Yard. Tapping into the story, he sped through the reporting and frowned further when the journalist name checked Vasquez Industries as owning the storage container in question. He wasn't surprised to see that when asked for a comment, the company had declined to say anything. Shaking his head as he stood up, Tenoch wondered if the negative press might *finally* prompt some sort of internal investigation; he'd long been suspicious their broad shipping network could be misused, but any official attempt on his part to dig into the potential problem had been rebuffed by his mother.

The aches and pains continued to plague him as he wandered into the master bathroom and took a shorter-than-he-wanted shower; he felt somewhat revived by the hot water when he stepped out to shave and then work on taming the mass of curls that always seemed to resist his best efforts. As he washed the last of the hair product from his hands, he twisted in the mirror to make sure he'd not overlooked an inadvertent nick; he'd once missed a spot and spent the subsequent evening soaking his shirt to try and remove the bloodstain from the collar. Those green eyes in the reflection drifted from his face down to the small circular obsidian disk hanging around his neck on a leather thong. Drying his hands, he reached up and tapped the cool surface with a finger and thought of his father for the second time that morning. Tenoch had been forced to deal with death as a teenager when his *padre* had disappeared from his life; much was jumbled from that period save for a fond memory of the three of them at the beach, and how the sun had glinted off of the medallion his father had been wearing. His mother had presented the medallion to Tenoch when he turned fifteen; running his finger around the smooth edge of the metal, he now understood his life had changed forever the night he'd tied that leather thong around his neck.

Letting his hand drop, he took another long look at himself in the mirror and saw where all the hard work had gone. Twisting again, he smiled slightly at how nicely defined his muscles had become; lifting an arm to flex, he watched his bicep ripple beneath the dark bronze of his skin and then grimaced once more at the deep ache that persisted. If he'd needed any further evidence that he'd overdone it, the fact that he suddenly felt like an old man instead of a twenty-something spoke volumes. Shaking his head at the reflection, he moved into the walk-in closet to don armor appropriate for the day.

Less than twenty minutes after receiving the worst wake-up call ever, Tenoch pulled out of the underground parking garage for his building and eased his Dodge Charger onto the small two-lane avenue. While his building was fairly new, the rest of the surrounding neighborhood remained comprised of bungalows built thirty or forty years earlier, and the access roads reflected that some-what more sedate era. The real estate agent that had sold him the unit had told him about the lawsuits that had tied the construction up in court for years; while it seemed the more established residents were more than a little pissed to have a ten-story high rise now blocking their view of the Pacific, in the end, there was very little they could do to stop the project. Tenoch had initially felt guilty over his apparent privilege, but that had lasted until he'd seen that those who were the *most* upset about his building had been uniformly monochromatic — and more concerned over how the neighborhood might "diversify" instead of how it was addressing real inequities in housing. He'd worked hard ever since on the sister projects to his building, helping to secure enough plots on either side to quadruple the number of units.

As late in the afternoon as it was, Tenoch found himself mired in the early vestiges of rush hour when he finally turned onto the Five. Punching the injected engine at key moments allowed him to easily weave around the stalled-out traffic, though it ultimately took him far longer than he'd hoped to reach the rail yard security gate in Santa Marcel. Rolling down the tinted window, he smiled his Fortune 500 smile as he flashed his company identification at the guard.

"I hear it was a busy night," Tenoch said as the woman examined his ID and then eyed his expensively cut suit.

"It was," she replied as she handed the card back to him. "Are you here to look over the damage to your inventory? Because if you are, you just missed the insurance adjuster."

"In a way," he nodded. "How close am I to shift change?"

The woman glanced at a clock he couldn't see. "Evening shift starts at six, so about three hours," she replied before hitting a button on her counter. "Watch where you drive," she admonished as the gate rose in front of him.

"Thank you," he nodded as he smoothly pulled through.

Tenoch had been in the yard enough times over the years checking on shipments for his mother that he knew the layout by heart; within a few minutes, he'd pulled the Charger to a stop in the small clearing where containers where transferred to trailers and killed the engine. Grabbing his sunglasses from the console, he exited his car and then paused beside the door, uncertain where to start. Crime scene tape had been strung around the entire truck and trailer, but since there didn't appear to be any uniformed officers guarding the perimeter, he decided it was more of an invitation than anything else and strode across the hard packed gravel to the rear of the trailer. Ducking beneath the fluttering tape, he found a small ladder had been placed against the bumper, which he quickly availed himself of; the doors to the shipping container had been closed, but when he leaned down to examine the lock, it appeared to be unlatched. Glancing back toward the clearing to ensure he was essentially alone, he retrieved a pair of latex gloves from his jacket pocket and pulled them on; while the equipment was, by rights, the property of Vasquez Industries, he was also cognizant that it was a currently a crime scene. Leaving behind evidence he'd made an unauthorized visit wouldn't do. Checking one last time that the coast was clear, he carefully twisted the handle down, then pulled the door open, unleashing the stench from inside.

Retrieving his iPhone from another pocket, he turned on the flashlight and then pulled off his sunglasses as he stepped inside. Unsurprisingly, aside from the stench, nothing was left inside save for a bit of plastic wrap that might have been around a water bottle or food packet. Still, he spent a few minutes exploring every nook and cranny of the space, unsure of what he was looking for until he nearly kicked it with his patent leather Oxford. Getting down into a crouch — and stifling an audible groan at the effort to move in that manner — Tenoch picked up the small piece of flint and held it to the light; to anyone else, it looked for all the world like a strangely misshapen rock. To him, though, the rough edges hinted at something else entirely, one that was confirmed when he saw the quartzite shimmer beneath the light.

Well, shit, he thought as he pulled his pocket square out and carefully folded the stone into it. *This complicates things a bit, now doesn't it?*

Standing — and this time, groaning audibly at the pain — he

took one final sweep through the container before exiting and then closing the door; there wasn't anything left to see that he'd not seen the first time. Sucking in lungfuls of fresh air did little to erase the lingering scent from the interior, though. Sniffing at the fabric of his suit jacket made him frown, for it appeared he had another dry-cleaning bill in his future. Jumping down from the bumper of the trailer, he yanked off the gloves as he ducked back under the crime scene tape and then paused again; a strange flapping noise floated across the breeze, and his eyes went to one of the many canyons formed by the stacks of containers. Cocking his head slightly, he started toward the aisle closest to the clearing, listening intently for what had attracted his curiosity. The metal of the containers acted as a sort of echo chamber, enhancing and yet simultaneously obscuring the source of the flapping, but at length, he turned a corner and suddenly found himself staring at a second crime scene. His eyes darted to the sound of the flapping, which turned out to be an end of crime scene tape that had pulled loose from where it had originally been fastened to a container; the idle breeze blowing through the manmade canyons had clearly done their work. It also meant nothing was *technically* preventing access to what looked like the remnants of a bonfire, though it was hard to see what exactly had been set aflame. Sniffing at the air, though, Tenoch *thought* he could pick up the faintest whiff of something familiar, but as tired as he remained, he wasn't able to place it.

Circling the burned-out area, he nodded at how thorough the authorities had clearly been; nothing was left to find, though he did make an effort to uncover *something*. Dusting off his hands, the best he came up with were signs someone had taken an impression of what he assumed had been shoe prints in the soft soil; that in itself was interesting, for it made clear that whoever was investigating *this* scene clearly thought it might be evidence of who had been there. As he walked back to his Charger, he wondered if he had made enough connections at the Santa Marcel Municipal Police to get a peek at the file that had been created; if nothing else, it might give him insights into how decent this particular investigator might be.

Smirking slightly as he got back behind the wheel, he knew he probably didn't need to ask.

Rush hour was in full swing when he exited the rail yard and charted a course for the World Headquarters of Vasquez Industries. Despite having grown up driving in Southern California traffic, there was only so much even he could do on the clogged surface streets; it wasn't hard to imagine how his hunter green sports car was chafing at the sluggish speeds it was being subjected to. Each time he gently touched the accelerator, the Charger instead tried to jump to warp speed; gently brushing the dashboard, he whispered a few words in Spanish to try and get the wily spirit within his engine to relax, unsure if the calming phrases would work as well on a car as the horse they were truly intended for.

It was close to five by the time he turned into the magnificent sweeping driveway that led to a three-story structure built along traditional Spanish Colonial lines. He'd always thought that his grandfather had envisioned a mid-century modern take on the traditional hacienda when he'd built it, and for the most part had pulled it off. Tenoch continued around the massive fountain at the base of the wide steps leading up to the main entrance before turning into a small access way protected by a petite guard shack that looked like a miniature version of the building proper. Rolling down the tinted window once more, he smiled at the familiar face inside the shack.

"Jack, I thought you were off today?"

The elder statesman chuckled as he stood from the stool he'd been on. "So did I. That was before my wife decided to host a candle party."

"That is an effective use of overtime," Tenoch laughed as the arm went up.

"Indeed." Jack paused and then leaned in. "Your mother is in quite a state."

"I know," Tenoch sighed. "But thanks for the warning."

"Good luck," Jack said as Tenoch pulled away.

The small executive lot was empty save for the Lexus SUV his mother drove; his eyebrows went up when he realized she had likely allowed all of the senior managers to depart for the day to ensure the two of them would have the place to themselves. Sliding into his usual spot beside her, he killed the engine and tried to game out how the conversation was likely to go. For whatever reason, he found himself reaching to the medallion that he was wearing beneath his button down; tapping at it always gave him a sense of self-confidence, though he was loath to embrace fully the reason why. Exiting the Charger, he dug his ID out of his wallet and tapped it at the reader for the executive entrance; the device chirped before flashing green, and a moment later, the elevator doors parted. Tenoch stepped into the wood-paneled interior and tapped his card a second time against the reader inside; there were no buttons to press when the doors closed, for it was controlled entirely by the computer running security for the building. If he hadn't passed muster, the elevator would have simply locked him inside the carriage and then called 9-1-1 while he cooled his heels. Fortunately, he once again was judged worthy; he felt the elevator smoothly accelerate toward the executive suite on the third floor of the building, which appeared just a few moments later when the doors opened again.

He stepped out into an ornate hallway that he knew ran behind the main reception area, and quickly made his way past the thirteen tall windows that looked out onto the driveway below. The office of the CEO was about where everyone expected it to be: housed directly beneath the massive dome over the exact center of the structure. Tenoch found the door to the outer office was open, though when he stepped inside no one was waiting behind the semi-circular desk that served as the final line of defense for his mother. Two doors were on either side of the desk, both leading to the *actual* inner sanctum; unusually, the one to the left was open, and he headed for that, unsure of whether he should read into the anomaly at all.

Two steps into the space, he was brought up short. "Close the door."

Turning, he retraced his steps and closed the door behind him; as he turned back toward his mother, he knew it was all part of her theater, especially since there was clearly no reason to fear anyone would overhear them. Still, as he approached the massive desk that had been placed in the back third of the room, he decided to let her play the hand she was holding for it was the only way to find out what she really knew.

Or, more importantly, what she *didn't*.

Tenoch paused just behind one of the two visitor chairs and waited. He'd been in the space so many times he knew every inch of it by heart, from the built-in bookcases that showcased items his parents had collected during their travels to the hidden cocktail bar in the wall on the far side that could be accessed by pressing a button beneath the desk. Then there were the two doors on opposite walls, one leading to an executive restroom that featured a telephone beside the toilet; the other hid a closely guarded secret that had yet to be revealed to him.

He had vague memories of what the office had been like when his father had been in that space; he was certain that the widescreen monitor on the wall between the two doors to the reception area wouldn't have been present back then, a nod to the increase in video conferencing the current era had ushered in. The potted date palm a few meters from the desk was also unique to his mother, a visual reminder of the trip the two of them had taken ten years prior — a trip that he had fervently wanted to avoid but had been unable to prevent.

He continued to watch his mother, who was standing with her back to him as she looked out one of the tall windows behind the desk; from that angle, she had an excellent view of the hills that rose up behind Santa Marcel, not to mention the wide, manicured lawn where they typically held company events. The slice of green in the desert was a bit of a statement, given the current water crisis, one that was typical of his mother. She was wearing her standard pink pantsuit, and had twisted her long, silvery hair up into a bit of a bun that was resting at the nape of her neck. Per usual, the orchid that was her *de facto* symbol of power had been pressed into service above the knot of hair, completing the picture of a put-together corporate CEO. After what felt like an eternity, she finally turned from the window and fastened her hazel eyes on his; they were bright with intelligence, and he knew from experience, seldom brooked deception of any kind. Her lips were pressed into a grim slash of red lipstick, underscoring her displeasure — though he wasn't sure if it was directed at him, or the situation she found herself in.

Moving to her desk, she tapped a long, manicured nail against what appeared to be that day's edition of the *Register*. It was so typical of her to read the physical version, as if it could somehow freeze events in amber. "What did you find?" she asked without preamble. "And what do they know?"

"There's no question it's our storage container," he replied easily. "And the trailer/semi that would have continued its journey was also ours. We have quite a bit of exposure here, *madre*."

"I already knew *that*," she said slamming her hands down on the desk. "But thank you for reminding me of my earlier conversation with our lawyers."

"If you recall, I brought you my concerns that one of our partners was using our network in this way," Tenoch continued, trying to keep his voice steady. Dealing with his mother always provoked strong emotions within him. "You didn't seem all that keen on allowing me to dig into at the time."

She waved at him. "There have *always* been unfounded rumors," she said. "Your father constantly went down one rabbit hole after another. I won't do the same."

"This seems less academic now," he pointed out. "One of our partners — or worse, one of our *subsidiaries* — is using our shipping network to transport human beings. We need to stop it."

His mother turned her eyes toward him again, and pierced him with a glare. "Someone seems to have tipped off the police about this *specific* shipment," she said.

"You're worried we might have a whistleblower in our ranks?" he asked, a bit amazed that this appeared to be the issue of most concern to his mother.

"I do."

"And you want me to find them?"

"Yes," she replied.

Tenoch tilted his head. "That's not normally the role for a corporate vice president," he pointed out. "We do have a whole security team for this sort of thing."

"I am aware of that. I also know that the staff are more likely to talk to you than them."

He frowned. "I'm not sure that's the case. And I'm not comfortable—"

"Handle it."

Tenoch nodded reluctantly, but couldn't resist needling her slightly. "Just so I'm clear, you're more concerned about someone leaking secrets than what our container was actually being used for?"

"I am capable of multitasking," she admonished, "as are you. Bring me anything you find on either."

"All right."

"Did you see anything at the scene that they had missed?"

The piece of flint in his pocket suddenly felt like a ton of lead. "No," he lied. "They'd removed anything that could be carried off. We'd need to talk to the investigators if you wanted to know more."

That dangerous smile she often wore when a business rival unwittingly stepped into one of her more devious designs appeared. "Funny you should say that — the lead detective is currently in your office, waiting. See what you can get out of them."

Tenoch groaned inwardly before arching an eyebrow. "That's not generally how these things work, *madre*. I imagine they are looking for information from *us*, not the other way around."

"Then you'll have to work hard to turn the tables, *mijo*." She turned away from him. "Call me later tonight with whatever you get."

"As you wish," he sighed. "Good evening, *madre*."

Her lack of response was the only clue he'd been dismissed; taking his cue, he nodded once at her before turning around and exiting through the door he'd used, then paused in the reception area for a moment to gather his thoughts. Tenoch expected he knew who *exactly* was waiting for him in his office and wasn't entirely sure he was ready for the challenge. Still, an order was an order; pulling his jacket taught against his frame, he plastered his best retail smile on his face before moving down the hall to his office and the fate that waited him within.

FOUR

K ate wasn't one to wait patiently for *anyone*, but most
especially the corporate types who tended to treat law
enforcement as an irritant to avoid at all costs. While it
wasn't her first time visiting the headquarters for Vasquez Industries, she'd generally been there in the past for social reasons;
appearing in her official capacity had made things rather tense with
security down in the lobby. Still, even after leaning on her badge to
get through the door in the first place, she'd expected to be palmed
off onto someone from Legal, or worse, Public Relations; that she had
wound up in what her guide had told her was the office for the Vice
President of Operations had given her pause. Was it possible they
knew more about what had gone down in the rail yard than she'd
initially suspected? If they *did*, it certainly framed the case entirely
differently.

Getting up from the pleasantly overstuffed guest chair for the
fourth time, she roamed the modestly sized office once more, taking
in the somewhat sterile nature of the space. It was hard to say it had
been personalized in any way, save for a small, framed photo of some

forest-laden mountain that didn't seem noteworthy. Several shelves of what appeared to be Disney collectibles were on one wall, but had been arranged with a museum-like efficiency that made them seem more for show than anything else; the desk was typical industrial chic, with a clear top and matching clear legs that sort of made it appear as though it were floating in space. An iMac sat to one side, and a corporate extension to the other; about the only oddball thing she had found was an ancient-looking coffee mug sitting beside the keyboard bearing the logo for Universal Studios Hollywood. Given the dearth of items, it had been hard to get a sense of the person she was about to face, so she felt monumentally unprepared when the knock finally came at the door behind her.

"At last," she said as she turned. "I was beginning to think I'd been—" she continued before abruptly choking.

"Forgotten?" The handsome man standing just inside the door was wearing a bemused look as Kate struggled to make sense of what she was seeing in front of her. She might have even been huffing and puffing like a fish out of water. "I could never forget you," he said softly as he closed the door and moved toward her. "Not then, and certainly not now."

"Tenoch...?" Kate found herself whispering. "You're... you're *here*," she managed to add as he gently guided her to one of the guest chairs; after ensuring she managed to actually *sit down*, he took the seat beside her after first unbuttoning his jacket.

"I am," he nodded.

Kate felt like the world had gone into a tailspin and gripped the arms of her chair accordingly. "You disappeared, Tenoch. Completely."

"Yeah," he nodded. "It wasn't by choice, I assure you."

Something in the way he'd replied made her look up at him, and for a moment, she thought she could see a slight shading of embarrassment against his already dark cheeks. She couldn't help the slight smile that came to her lips, for the ease at which he could be flustered had been one of Tenoch's most endearing qualities. Kate had to admit that there were still traces of the teenager she'd once been madly in love with: the long, curly black hair that she'd often run her hands through when they'd been lying side-by-side on the beach telling each other their dreams for the future was the most obvious, of course, though it appeared to have been gelled into submission. Those green eyes, brimming with a strange mix of mystery and intelligence hadn't changed, either; despite all of the time that had passed, she still found it hard not to get lost in that intense gaze that was even now being directed at her. The face had lost its boyish charm and instead taken on the strong lines of an adult male just coming into his prime; in a similar fashion, his expertly tailored suit seemed intended to showcase his impressive physical assets. Blinking, she wondered if she were looking at one of those cover models for *GQ* instead of the once-gawky teenager who had spent endless hours playing video games with her.

"I'm sure you have questions," Tenoch was saying, drawing her out of her reverie.

"Questions?" she repeated blankly. The scent of his cologne, while subtle, seemed to be hitting her viscerally, almost as if he'd embedded his very essence into it.

"About the shipping container?" he prompted, then paused. "About me?"

A tiny voice in the back of her head reminded her that she was *actually* supposed to be working a case, but the sheer physicality of Tenoch's presence was making it hard for her to focus; it didn't help matters that up until about thirty seconds ago, she had all but assumed he'd walked out of her life a decade earlier never to return. "Uh, right," she finally heard herself say, aware that all of her abilities as a confident investigator had suddenly fled.

55

Tenoch's expression twisted into one of concern. "Kate? Are you all right?" he asked.

The temperature in the room felt like it had gone up a bazillion degrees, that and the musky sandalwood cologne had begun to make her lightheaded in a way she'd not felt in, well, a decade. Squeezing her eyes shut, she managed to steady herself enough to string together a coherent sentence. "Would you mind if we went outside? I think I'm feeling a little woozy for some reason..."

Before she truly understood what was happening, she felt herself lifted from the chair; Kate wasn't completely surprised at how easily he was able to carry her from the room, backhandedly confirming for her that those were rather substantial muscles threatening to tear through the fabric of Tenoch's suit. Closing her eyes again, she simply pressed her head against his chest and tried not to pass out completely.

Clearly skipping lunch was a bad idea, she thought morosely. *Some first impression I'm making.*

In mere moments, she felt a change in temperature and the welcome burst of fresh air; gently, she was set down into something comfortable that appeared to be facing the setting sun. Taking a deep breath, she let the warmth of the last rays of the day bring some calm to her soul, then cracked open an eye to see a *very* concerned Tenoch examining her closely. Somewhere along the line, his jacket had been discarded, exposing fully a perfectly pressed button down that complimented his complexion; idly, she noted that there was some sort of odd Native American design in the pattern of his matching tie. This close, she could also see that his eyebrows were just as perfect as ever, little arcs of emotion that were starting to drop down into a furrow the longer she went without saying something.

"Kate? I've got water," he said as he reached under the chaise she had apparently been placed upon. Unscrewing the top, he gently held it to her, and then quietly — but forcefully — commanded her to drink.

She took the bottle from him and downed half of it faster than she thought possible; when she went to hand it back, he frowned again and shook his head. Getting the hint, she slowly drank the remainder while taking in her surroundings. Tenoch had brought her out to the wide, grassy back area behind the building where the organization had hosted various community charity events over the years; she had fond memories of playing pickup soccer in the deep turf with Tenoch and the other kids who had parents that worked for his family. Kate frowned slightly when she realized she'd not felt him go down a staircase to get there, though, and wondered just how out of it she had been.

"I think I was down a few quarts," she said with a slight smile as she handed him the now-empty bottle.

Those green eyes looked at her in a funny way. "You're definitely dehydrated," he murmured before reaching below the chair again. "Here, take this and sip from it, but slowly."

"You are worse than my mother," she sighed as she took the bottle from him; strangely, the cap was already loose. "My apologies. I skipped lunch today and I think between that and the shock of seeing someone I thought was dead..."

"All evidence to the contrary," he smiled.

Kate arched an eyebrow. "You can't blame me for thinking the worst and then expect me to just *accept* that it was no big deal." She took a sip from the bottle. "Not the way you left me."

Tenoch's smile faded into something a bit more sheepish. "Like I said, it wasn't exactly my fault. Or my decision."

"You dumped me on our prom night," she reminded him. "And then were nowhere to be found the next day." Kate looked at him and the well-defined torso the dress shirt wasn't exactly hiding. "You were supposed to be playing professional soccer, weren't you?"

He shook his head. "That was what I wanted," Tenoch replied softly, "but after my father died, my plans changed."

Kate glanced at the building hulking behind them. "I never pegged you as a company man," she said before connecting her eyes to his again. "You *seriously* gave up soccer to be Vice President of Operations?"

"Something like that." Tenoch looked away for a moment; had he been a suspect, she would have thought he was trying to hide something from her. He turned those green eyes back on her again. "So you're a detective now?"

"Yes," she nodded, not missing the clear shift in the conversation. Her investigator radar started to ping, but she decided to hold off on following up — for now. "I went into the Academy after college and then managed to finagle my way into the Santa Marcel force."

"I bet you're pretty good, too," he said. "If I remember correctly, looking under rocks was something of a specialty for you when we were playing *Zelda*."

She started. "I'd forgotten about that, actually," she replied.

"I hadn't," he chuckled. "Since I always seemed to be the one who died when something rather nefarious was hiding under said rock."

"That's just because you insisted on always playing the chivalrous knight," she smiled. "A very old-fashioned notion that tended to get you killed."

That strange look crossed his face again. "It kept you safe, though."

"I suppose it did," she replied, wondering a bit at what it was she was seeing. Was that a trace of sadness? Or loneliness?

What the fuck were you doing for ten years? she found herself asking. *Soccer was your dream; how did you wind up wearing thousand-dollar suits and doing the bidding of your mother?*

Somewhat insanely, Kate decided she needed to know the answers to those questions; she'd get them, too, given enough time. Putting them aside for a moment, she drained the last of the second bottle Tenoch had provided and shifted gears again. "You're not wrong," she began. "As much as I would love to catch up, I am actually here about the situation at the rail yard."

Tenoch nodded and smiled shyly. "How about dinner, then?"

She stared at him for a moment. "You are seriously asking me out? After being MIA for ten years?"

"Yes," he replied simply.

Kate wasn't sure if she was more appalled at the idea that he seemed to want to pick up right where they left off as though nothing had happened, or the fact that a significant part of her had already leapt at the chance to do just that. "That's pretty bold," she replied. "You seemed to have learned quite a bit at business school."

A strange smile appeared. "It was in our 100-level class," he said. "A good predator knows when to pursue their prey."

Kate frowned. "What the hell are they teaching? *Prey*? Seriously?"

"Business is the epitome of the dog-eat-dog metaphors," he smiled wider. "So, what do you say? I can get us a table at Giovannis tonight, if you're free?"

"No," she shook her head.

"Tomorrow, then?"

"Tenoch," she said firmly, "it wouldn't be appropriate. Not while I am investigating this case and your company's possible connections to it."

"Oh," he replied after a moment. "I could see where that might look bad."

"You think?" She couldn't help the snark.

"I wasn't," he replied, his face shading darker again.

Even in the fading light, Kate could tell that he'd actually been genuine about wanting to talk; despite it melting her heart, she held firm — slightly. "When it's over, let's circle back to us."

"Okay," he nodded. "What do you want to know about our container?"

"It was yours, then?"

"Yes," he nodded. "Shipped up from Oaxaca, Mexico, via rail; transferred in Tucson to Union Pacific three days ago. Arrived in Santa Marcel early yesterday."

Kate blinked. "You seem well informed."

"I... made a guess as to what you wanted to know," he explained sheepishly. "And did some research."

"I see," she replied. "Who was doing the shipping?"

"I don't know," he answered. "I was in a... meeting... just ahead of this where I was trying to get those details. For the moment, it appears the main contract was handled by our shipping subsidiary, but I suspect someone subcontracted to us."

"Is that typical?"

"Yes," he nodded. "Aside from what business we do with our various manufacturing subsidiaries — and that is quite a bit, mind you — we generally provide logistics for others that are moving materials around the globe. Rail, ship, even air; it's a rather extensive operation."

"Do you have people on the ground in Oaxaca?"

Tenoch paused tellingly. "Not always," he ultimately replied. "While we do have Vasquez Industries employees in other countries, they are only in our busiest hubs where having a direct interface to our organization can smooth operations. Oaxaca isn't one of them, however."

Kate frowned. "I suppose it was a bit of a pipe dream that we might know who loaded those women into the container."

"All hope is not lost," Tenoch smiled. "I was planning on going down there myself in the coming days to see what I could uncover."

"Really?"

"Yes," he nodded. "I'm happy to share whatever I turn up."

"I want to go with you," she suddenly said.

"I'm not sure that is possible," he shook his head. "Mexico doesn't tend to look favorably on foreign law enforcement encroaching on their domain."

"I suppose not," she replied. "We know the container was destined for Prague — do you have a hub there?"

"Yes," he nodded. "We serve most of Eastern Europe from that location."

Kate looked at him. "Just how large *is* Vasquez Industries?"

"Large," he smiled.

"*How* large?" she pressed.

Tenoch shrugged. "Have you ever heard of Berkshire Hathaway?"

"Maybe," she replied after a second of thought. "Isn't that some conglomerate run by some billionaire based in Omaha?"

"Yes," he nodded. "We could buy them out."

"You're kidding me, right?" she asked before she saw the answer on his face. "There's no way that's true! If you were that big, it would be all over the news!"

"We prefer to do our work in the background," he replied. "And we're not traded on any stock market, so that keeps us off most financial publications' radar."

Kate shook her head. "You're pulling my leg."

Tenoch shrugged again. "The truck that was going to take the trailer to the docks was also ours," he continued, deftly steering the conversation away from himself again. "I imagine when you questioned the driver you discovered he was one of our salaried employees and had no idea what was inside the container."

"He didn't," she confirmed. "The two gentlemen that were found at the scene worked for the rail yard proper, and similarly didn't have a clue as to the true nature of the container. I don't think they were involved in any meaningful way."

"Were they the ones that released the women?" Tenoch asked, his eyes widening.

"Hardly," Kate replied. "They actually tried to stop whoever it was that *did* and got rather bruised in the process."

"Oh," Tenoch looked confused. "I understood that the container had been opened, but it sounds like you don't know who it was that freed them?"

"No," Kate shook her head. "I mean, *yes*, we do, but... aw, hell, it's kind of complicated to explain."

Dusk had fallen over the space, allowing the landscape lighting to click on; their soft glow made it feel as though the two of them were sitting close to a campfire. "Now you've made me curious," he said.

Kate mulled over what to say and then carefully chose her words. "The women claimed that a masked man unlocked the container," she said.

Tenoch's eyes narrowed. "Now you're pulling *my* leg."

"I wish I were," she sighed. "He was even wearing some sort of superhero outfit, too. Damndest story I've ever heard," she quickly added when she saw his eyes narrow.

"You saw him," he said.

"No," she lied, but could easily tell that he wasn't buying it. "Okay, yes, I did. He turned up at the scene of another crime we uncovered at the rail yard."

"The fire," he nodded. "And the body."

Kate looked at him sharply. "How the *hell* do you know about that?"

"We do a lot of business with the rail yard," he replied smoothly. "That affords us levels of access that others might not have."

She felt the anger flaming her cheeks. "Are you playing me,

Tenoch?" she demanded. "What do you *actually* know, and what is it you're not telling me?"

He sat back suddenly as though she had slapped him — which she supposed she had, verbally. "I've been completely up front with you about everything I know at this point," Tenoch replied. "I could never mislead you, Kate," he added softly. "I think you know that."

"The man I knew ten years ago I could believe that of," she said tightly as she swung her legs off the chaise and stood. "Whoever *you* are hasn't gained back that level of trust. Not yet."

He stood with her. "Kate, I'm sorry—"

"I bet you are," she said as she tugged her purse over her shoulder. "I'll be in touch. Have a good evening."

With that, she turned on his shocked expression and deliberately left.

FIVE

What little they had gathered so far on the case sat spread across the floor of Kate's tiny living room; the rest was glowing on her department-issued laptop from where it was sitting on her coffee table. For her part, she was sitting with her back against the loveseat and admiring the quarter glass of red wine she was holding in her hand and wondering why she had acted like such an asshole with her former boyfriend just a few hours earlier. She'd replayed their conversation over and over in her head as she'd driven back to the station, and then a few more times on the way to her home; no matter how hard she looked, Kate couldn't find any signs that he'd not been frank with her. Tenoch had been right about one thing: in the time they had been together, he'd never once done anything to betray her trust. Except, of course, for that one pesky time when he'd decamped for parts unknown without so much as a farewell card; as she sat there, she wondered if the pain over that breakup had prevented her from truly *hearing* what he'd been saying earlier that evening.

Well, she thought, *he was being honest about what he knew regarding the container. I'm not sure he was totally up front about where he'd been all these years, but then again, it really wasn't the right time for that discussion, was it?*

Putting the wine down on the glass top of the coffee table, Kate shifted screens on the laptop and returned to the virtual yearbook for her senior year at Santa Marcel High School; the insanely cute image of eighteen-year-old Tenoch was smiling back at her, looking every bit like the future soccer player he had dreamed of becoming. She was never quite sure how he had talked his domineering mother into allowing him to wear the headband bearing the national colors of Mexico for his senior photo, but was glad he had; the way it had pulled his massive mane of curly black hair away from his face had made him seem even sexier, something she had mercilessly teased him about right up to the day he'd walked out on her.

"What the hell happened to you?" she asked the photo. "Where did you go?" Kate paused, then asked the *actual* question that had been deep inside her all those years. "And... and *why* did you leave me?"

The photo didn't appear disposed to answer her, so she sighed and swapped back to the case files.

Stretching her hands over her head, she rolled her neck a few times to try and relieve the kink that had developed from being hunched over her stationary cycle; Kate actually detested the device and its canned workouts, but given how late it had been after she'd gotten done with the postmortem on the fire victim, it had simply been too dark to do her normal evening cycling route without risking an errant driver running over her. There'd been no question that she'd needed an outlet for the turbulent events of the past twenty-four hours, though; only after she'd slipped off the machine and started to towel down the sweat she'd worked up did she *finally* feel centered enough to begin sorting through what she had.

Adjusting her compression bra to keep it from pinching again, she reached for her wine and considered the files around her. The contents of the shipping container had been hauled back to the Orange County Crime Lab for review, and the results had trickled in all day; she'd not been all that surprised that there wasn't anything unexpected there, but had held out hope that some strange DNA sample might appear (it hadn't) or that a wallet bearing the identity of the kingpin for the operation had been buried beneath the food packets (it wasn't). No, the food packets were ordinary enough to have been sourced at any big box retailer worldwide; the same went for the water. The chemical toilets were, oddly, from a camping goods supplier outside of Seattle, but that meant little since their website proudly proclaimed that they shipped globally. Sipping at her wine, Kate smiled at how helpful the person she reached in that corporate office had been but held out little hope that the lot numbers she'd provided would lead anywhere.

Flipping through the photos that had been taken at the site, and then the photos of each of the victims they'd interviewed, she saw again the squalor they had endured before being rescued. From the transcripts she had read, none of the women had been willing participants on the journey; to a person, they had recounted variations on a horror story that included being taken against their will. Kate had touched base with Dianne from DHS who had assured her that the group was being treated well — and that most had asked to be returned to their homes in Guatemala as soon as possible. She supposed that was something of a victory in itself and wondered if there was any point to poking around what seemed like one end of a human trafficking ring. Glancing at the photos of the women again, she nodded to herself as she decided it did, for if she could shut down even one *tiny* portion of the scheme, it would be a win.

Toggling screens again, she sipped at the wine as the photo of the container appeared; using the touchpad, she zoomed in on the logo for Vasquez Industries and mulled over what little she had gotten out of Tenoch. Granted, she'd not exactly been at her best — or on her best behavior, for that matter; still, as she replayed their conversation in her head one more time, she suddenly realized he had offered to keep her in the loop on whatever he found in Oaxaca. Sitting up, she found herself wondering if it had been Tenoch's way to telegraph that he was willing to work with her — at least, as much as he was *officially* allowed to do. Smiling, she decided to call him back in the morning and formalize the offer as best as she could.

Closing the files from the container, she re-opened the updated file on the fire victim. Kate had been unlucky enough to draw the Chief Medical Examiner herself for the postmortem; that had meant patiently watching as every inch of the body had been reviewed in painstaking detail. In the end, the actual cause of death wound up surprising both of them, especially since Kate had assumed the flames had destroyed whatever evidence there had been to find. As it turned out, her mysterious masked vigilante had done them a favor by putting out the fire when he did, for it had preserved the fact that the victim's heart had been rather messily removed from his chest. That it had not been found at the scene troubled her greatly; more so, perhaps, how the victim's clothing had been so carefully folded beside the body. Sitting back against the couch — and adjusting her damn compression bra *again* in the process — Kate couldn't help the sense that there was something ritualistic about the entire scene.

Unsure if she wanted to actually dig through the archives at that late hour to see if her suspicions were accurate, she drained the last of her wine and decided to finally call it a night. Pushing herself to her feet, she closed the lid to her laptop and then reached over to turn off the light on the table beside her loveseat; she'd lived in the house long enough that she could easily make her way through it in the filtered light coming through the windows facing the street out front. As she passed the glass slider to the patio on her way to the kitchen, she stopped long enough to pull it closed against the night breeze she'd been using to cool off after her workout. Halfway shut, Kate paused, for she *thought* she'd caught the soft whisper of movement from her back yard; straining her ears, she picked it up a second time and squinted out into the darkness to see what it might be.

Nothing seemed out of the ordinary in the tidy space — at least, nothing that would account for the sound she thought she had heard, anyway. Looking at the wineglass in her hands, she figured it was a combination of being bone-tired and in a *very* relaxed state of mind, and started to pull the door shut once more when she heard something again — or did she? Focusing a bit more, Kate couldn't hear anything beyond the gentle tinkle of the wind chimes her mother had gifted her as a housewarming gift and the subtle hiss of the traffic rushing by on the 57 a few blocks away.

Still, she had learned to trust her senses.

Kate swiftly moved though the darkness of her living room and put the wineglass on the counter beside the holster holding her Glock; quietly sliding the gun from the holster, she moved back to the patio door and then carefully pulled it open to step onto the covered patio. Holding the gun at her side, she let her eyes adjust to the shadows and then began to scrutinize the backyard. The sound came again, and this time she caught the simultaneous movement of a slightly darker shadow as it shifted position along the top of the brick wall at the edge of her lot. She was not at all surprised when her brain connected the dots, and even less surprised when it sunk in who the intruder was.

"You've got a lot of nerve coming here," she said as she raised the gun and took a step toward him.

"And good evening to you, too," chuckled the rich voice from the form still hiding in the shadows. "Do you always accost your male visitors with a gun?"

"Only the ones that arrive unannounced," she replied.

"That's on me," he said cheerfully as he hopped down from the wall and landed easily in a crouch a few yards from her. "You would not *believe* how many Olivers live in Santa Marcel. It took me *forever* to find your house."

Something in his manner told Kate that he was concerned about appearing overly aggressive; what little light there was in the backyard showed how his masked eyes were carefully watching her, and the gun that was still pointed in his direction. Those same senses that she relied on during life-and-death situations were telling her that he was no threat; then again, she'd never had a costumed man appear on her wall in the middle of the night, either. She kept the gun steady but also decided she had something of an opportunity as well.

"I'm flattered," she said. "I've never had a stalker before."

Those masked eyes went wide. "*Dios mío*. I never considered how this would look," he breathed. "That's not my intention at all — look, I'll go—"

Kate found herself unable to contain her amusement at how flustered the young man had become — and he did seem *young* to her, though she hadn't truly gotten a good look at him yet. As he stood and moved to leap up to the wall again, she lowered her gun and fought to keep the smile from appearing on her face. "You're not very good at this, are you?"

He twisted back to look at her, his ponytail flapping as he turned. Even in the dark, she could see the flash of teeth in a slight smile. "I'm not even sure what *this* is yet, honestly."

That gave her pause. "What do you mean?" she asked, genuinely curious. "Based on your outfit alone, I'd assumed you were trying to be some sort of hero." *Or a murderous supervillain,* she added to herself, though as soon as she said it, she knew in her heart it wasn't the case — *couldn't* be the case.

How she knew was another question entirely.

He turned toward her completely and waved his arms around his form fitting costume. "I suppose that was what I was going for," he said quietly. "I'm not sure I nailed it completely."

Something flashed in the light as he moved, and she frowned. "Speaking of nails — are those spikes in your gloves?"

"Claws, actually," he replied. "After scaling those containers last night, I thought they might come in handy. I'd rather not free climb like that again unless I have to."

"You're kidding me," she replied, but her curiosity got the better of her. "Come closer so I can take a look."

"Are you sure?" he asked. "I'm really not stalking you," he added in a rush. "I just wanted to talk."

"I figured as much," she finally chuckled before gesturing him closer to the door. "It goes against my better judgement, but come inside where I can get a better look at you. Behave," she added as she put a hand on her hip, "and I might be willing to serve you a beverage."

He stepped closer. "I am not a threat to you," he said softly and with such sincerity it nearly hurt. "Nor could I ever be. I only want to help."

"Whoa, cowboy," she smiled. "I'll be the judge of that. You can dial it back a bit, though."

"Okay," he replied. "Sorry."

"Quit apologizing," she sighed as she entered the living room and went over to turn the light back on beside the couch. "Take a seat."

Nodding, he carefully stepped around the coffee table and gently sat on the loveseat; as he moved, Kate was struck at how his costume seemed to shimmer in the soft glow from her lamp. Now that she had a proper view, not only could she see that the costume was nearly a second skin, it also didn't appear to have any seams to it. As the light continued to play off of whatever the strange fabric was, she could easily understand how it might allow him to go undetected in low light situations — perfect for skulking around in the shadows. Sliding her laptop to the side of the coffee table, she sat down across from him and then held out her hand; it took a moment for him to realize what she wanted, but when he did, he slowly lifted his gloved hand toward her, careful to keep what were definitely claws curled away from her skin.

Eyeing her visitor, she deliberately put her gun down on the surface of the coffee table, careful to emphasize that it was still in easy reach. His eyes were watching her closely, but also telegraphed that he was clearly going to follow her lead. Taking his gloved hand into hers, she slowly turned it one way, and then other, and found to her surprise it wasn't a glove at all but rather just another integrated part of his outfit. Running her finger at the base of his wrist and about where a seam *should* have been, she realized the fabric didn't feel like latex, but neither was it something stretchy, like Spandex. Frowning, it was also clear it also wasn't leather, either, nor any sort of synthetic material she'd ever encountered.

"What *is* this, exactly?" she asked as she held his hand up to the light and watched it shimmer again. What she thought had been a deep hunter green coloring was actually a far more complex layering of colors that seemed to appear or disappear based on how light hit it.

"My costume," he said simply.

"Did you make this? I can't see any stitches or seams."

"After a fashion," he replied oddly.

Her eyes went to his brown ones; the mask framing them was clearly made from the same material as the costume, and covered the balance of his face, from the tip of his nose to just over the eyebrows. Now that she was close enough to him, she could also see that it had to have been glued to his skin, for there were no visible straps holding it in place. And yet, unlike any domino mask she'd ever seen at Halloween, it appeared to be moving as he raised and lowered his eyebrows.

"What do you mean?"

Those eyes looked away for a moment, and she watched in amazement as the mask seemed to narrow the space around his eyes to help accentuate his expression. If he weren't sitting in front of her, Kate would have thought it a nice piece of CGI from a Marvel movie. "I'm not sure you'd believe my explanation."

"Try me."

He turned back. She wasn't sure, but thought he had subtly swallowed hard before continuing. "I... I conjured it."

She looked at him. "*Conjured*? As in magic?"

"Yeah," he said.

Considering she'd seen him summon a thundercloud out of nowhere, the explanation made a weird sort of sense. That she already seemed to be accepting the craziness of what had happened a night earlier didn't trouble her as much as it probably should; glancing over her shoulder at the empty wineglass on the kitchen counter, she wondered if she'd had just enough alcohol that *anything* he had told her would have seemed plausible. "Why?"

He looked at her for a moment and realized that she'd simply accepted his answer, and nodded slightly before a coy smile appeared. "Well, I can't very well run around saving the world naked, can I?"

Trying hard not to look at the solid six-pack of abs the guy had — and thinking she might not be the only one that would appreciate him sacrificing like that — she nodded. "I see your point. And, obviously, you're protecting your secret identity."

"Obviously," he smiled wider. The slight wariness he'd had earlier seemed to have subsided.

Releasing his hand, she stood. "Water? Soda?"

"Would coffee be too much to ask?"

"Not if you don't mind a wait," Kate said as she stood up. "I'll have to make a pot."

"You have an *actual* coffeemaker?"

The shock in his voice was enough for her smile as she headed to the kitchen. "That is the only *true* way to make coffee," she said solemnly. "I fear for your soul if you are a slave to those silly one-cup machines."

"My soul is already spoken for," he said in an odd way. "Come sit down," he said. "I'll take care of the coffee."

"You'll what—?" she started to ask as she turned toward him. To her surprise, he was now holding two mugs of steaming coffee.

"I can't do cream or sugar quite yet," he said apologetically as he held a mug out to her. "So if you want that, you'll have to fend for yourself."

Kate stared at the mugs. "Did you just *create* those out of thin air?"

He smiled. "The long answer is complicated," he said as she moved back to the coffee table and sat again. "The short answer is that, as long as all of the elements I need are present and in the right quantities, I can craft nearly anything I need."

Taking the mug from him, she sniffed at the rich aroma and then looked at him. "This is real."

"Of course it is," he smiled wider.

She took a sip and then looked up at him again. "This tastes like the bold blend in my cupboard," she said, then held the mug out. "And this is my mug!"

He shrugged. "Like I said, the elements all have to be present."

Kate took another sip from the extremely hot beverage. "That's a trick I would love to learn," she said. "Having an endless supply of hot coffee at my fingertips would come in handy first thing in the morning."

"There is a cost to these abilities," he replied enigmatically, "not to mention needing to spend a few years in the jungle mastering the spells involved."

"Costs?" she frowned. "Years? *Jungle*? That sounds suspiciously like some sort of trite superhero backstory."

"So it does," he smiled again before sipping from his own mug. "May I call you Kate?"

"Yes," she replied before cocking her head at him. "And you introduced yourself as Ocelot?"

"That's me."

"How did you know my name at the rail yard?" she asked, finally airing something that had been bothering her since the encounter.

Ocelot appeared to have expected that question, but even so, shifted uncomfortably on her loveseat. "I knew I would eventually run into someone from the Santa Marcel Municipal Police," he started. "So I made a point of memorizing the bios from the website. Just in case." He shrugged again. "It made sense to understand more about who I might be working with."

Kate's eyebrows went up. "Working? Like, as a consultant?"

That smile appeared again, and she had to admit, its boyish charm was growing on her. "Something like that," he answered before nodding his head toward the files still carefully splayed out on the living room floor. "I've been tracking this trafficking ring for a few months now, and pretty much have gotten as far as I can without... well," he smiled wryly, "without breaking the law myself."

"You're the one that called the tip in last night," she said, seeing a new piece to her puzzle appearing.

"Yes."

"The number was for a burner. Did you whip up that, too?"

"My powers aren't quite to that level — yet," he laughed. "I bought the phone a while back and tossed it after I called."

"So I won't be able to track down your alter ego, then," she smiled slightly. "Smart."

"I know who I am up against," he smiled before looking at her closely again. She had the strangest sense of *dejà vú* for a moment before he continued. "Look, I already knew I needed help closing down the human trafficking ring at this end — that's one of the reasons I'm here."

"One? There's more?"

Ocelot put his coffee down on the side table and stood, then went to the still open slider. "What forced my hand — and moved up my timeline — was that body I found in the rail yard last night," he said softly as he looked out into the darkness. Turning back toward her, he folded his arms against his chest, inadvertently flexing slightly as he did so. "We have a bigger problem on our hands, if my suspicion is correct."

"Murder does tend to trump everything," Kate nodded.

"It's not *just* that," he replied as he actually began to pace in front of the slider. Kate got the oddest impression of a caged predator, one who was feeling the constraints of his captivity; she had a hard time keeping her eyes off of his muscles as they rippled beneath the costume as he moved. "Have you already performed the postmortem on the victim from the fire?"

"That information wouldn't be made public anytime soon," Kate replied. "As much as I'm warming up to you, Ocelot, you're still a mysterious masked stranger wearing a skintight costume and one of my prime suspects."

He glanced meaningfully at her compression bra, then dropped his eyes to her workout tights. "I could argue you're wearing something similar," he countered with a sly smile. "And I don't think you truly consider me a suspect."

Kate felt a little uncomfortable beneath his earnest gaze. "I'm not exactly sure what this is supposed to be between the two of us," she said. "But whatever it is, I can't think we're to the point of sharing secrets with each other."

"I've had zero trouble confiding in you. I trust you — enough that I feel completely comfortable telling you my secrets."

She arched an eyebrow. "*All* of your secrets?"

He had the good sense to look abashed. "Maybe not all," he said before seeing her knowing smile and continuing. "At least, not yet."

"Then there we are," she replied. "You can understand where I'm coming from, then, for we both have things that need to be protected."

"Revealing my presence to anyone is a *huge* risk," Ocelot said, his brown eyes taking on a pleading look. He moved closer, but was careful not to crowd her, and then surprised her by getting down on his knees. "You *have* to trust me — I *am* here to help. You *need* my help. But in order to provide it, you've got to tell me everything you know."

She didn't doubt his sincerity at all, but rules were rules. "As much as I want to, I can't—"

"Was the heart removed from the chest?"

Kate tried to stay composed, but from the way Ocelot was slowly nodding, she could tell she'd not been successful. "If it had — and I'm not confirming or denying anything here — why would that be important?"

Ocelot countered with another question. "The other internal organs had been removed too, hadn't they?"

She raised her eyebrows, no longer able to contain her shock. "How the *hell* did you know that?"

"You interrupted me before I truly had a good look at what was left of that poor soul," Ocelot said as he started pacing again. Hugging his arms around his torso, she didn't need to be a trained investigator to detect the waves of anxiety now radiating from his tall form. "I did, however, catch the clothing that had been neatly stacked beside the bonfire."

"We assumed they were from the victim," she said, giving in and sharing — slightly. "Shirt was a men's medium; pants, thirty-four waist. The coroner confirmed they would fit the victim, who was just a hair under six feet tall. It seemed odd how the clothing was sitting there; it was almost like someone disrobing for the pool or hot tub."

"Without context, sure," he said, pausing halfway along his line. "The way they had been carefully presented struck a chord with me, so much so that I had to dig through my codex to see if it was what I feared it to be."

"Codex? Is that some sort of mystical volume?" she asked, unable to keep a slight trace of snark out of her voice.

Ocelot smiled at her dig. "Of a sort," he nodded. "I like to think of it as an illustrated guide to everything we have forgotten."

"I see," she replied, though she wasn't entirely sure she truly did. "From the angsty look on your face — even with a mask on it — I can tell you confirmed your fear and then some," Kate said. "Why does that worry me?"

"Because you are a brilliant woman," Ocelot said with sincerity. "What do you know about Mesoamerican mythology?"

"Not enough to live up to your admiration," she answered. "Maybe the odd thing here or there when I took Spanish in college, I guess."

He nodded. "I'll skip over the history lesson then and cut directly to the chase. The way my forbears kept track of time involved a very intriguing two-calendar system, one for measuring the solar year, and the other, what anthropologists have incorrectly assumed was a quaint way to observe our religious rituals."

Kate started to shake her head. "I'm going to need more coffee if you are about to dive into metaphysics," she groaned.

"Okay," Ocelot replied.

Maybe it was the wine, or just the late hour; whatever it was, Kate had a hard time peeling her eyes off of Ocelot's lithe form as he made his way back to the loveseat. It didn't help that the form-fitting outfit seemed to enhance every contour of his body in a way that seemed slightly more erotic to her than if he'd been sitting down in front of her naked. That she seemed to so focused on his insane physicality was an unfortunate reminder that she'd been flying solo for far longer than she'd cared to admit; apparently, ignoring her needs in that department had done little to make them go away. Trying to regroup thoughts that were going into dangerous territory — fantasizing about a possible suspect *had* to be listed in the manual as a top ten no-no — it took her a moment to register he was holding a fresh cup of coffee out to her. Gratefully accepting it, she sipped at the hot brew and hoped the slight flush she felt on her face wasn't visible; the way he was smiling at her, though, told her his senses were as keen as she was beginning to suspect, which caused her flush to deepen.

As only a true gentleman would, though, he tactfully ignored her reaction and continued. "I have to warn you, what you are writing off as metaphysics is, in fact, very, *very* real."

"I'm not sure I'm entirely writing them off anymore," she smiled, glancing meaningfully at her mug. "But if you tell me this is all magical mumbo-jumbo, I might begin to."

"There is a fine line between magic and science," he replied.

"I feel like I've heard that line somewhere before."

"Probably someone more famous than I," he smiled. "In the old tongue, the solar calendar was called *xiuhpohualli*, and the ritual calendar, *tonalphualli*. *Xiuhpohualli* had 360 days on it, while *tonalphualli*, 260. I don't want to get too far into the weeds on this, but suffice it to say that the two calendars are intertwined, with specific periods that represent various deities; one full cycle of going through this setup is fifty-two traditional years and is called *xiumolpilli*, or 'bundle of years' in English."

"You're talking about it in the present tense," Kate observed, finding herself enthralled by the conversation. "I thought such calendars died alongside the native peoples that had used them?"

Ocelot smiled. "We never died out, and neither did our time-keeping," he corrected. "We simply disappeared into the ranks of those of us who *thought* they had conquered us."

Kate looked at him. "I know I'm a bit rusty, but the Aztecs, Mayans and Incas vanished hundreds of years ago. Unless you're an immortal — or a time traveler of some sort — you don't look like you're much older than me."

"I'm only — that is, I'm not some sort of immortal," Ocelot replied, correcting himself before apparently revealing something about his alter-ego. "Nor am I a time traveler, though I *can* travel through time. I am, however, descended from those that *did* live during that time."

"You can? Then why are we having this conversation?" she asked honestly. "You could have gone back and stopped those women from being taken. Or prevented the murder."

That look of slight embarrassment graced his dark skin again. "If I could, I would," he sighed. "Not only is time a fickle mistress — or master, given your propensity — I'm not quite capable of moving more than a few hours in either direction. Yet."

"*Yet?* Did you leave magic school without your degree?" she teased, surprising herself as she did so.

The deepening flush across his exposed cheeks made her feel bad for doing so. "Something like that," he sighed before looking away.

"All right," she nodded, deciding it might be best to keep the topic moving. "I can buy that. So how do these calendars relate to our victim?"

His head snapped back at her use of *we*. "That wasn't so hard, now was it?" he smiled.

"We're *not* partners in this," she replied.

"Right," he smiled wider. "The end of each of *xiumolpilli* was celebrated by something known as the New Fire Ceremony — a massive festival full of rituals intended to satisfy the gods."

"Sounds like one hell of a New Year's Eve party."

"Yes," he replied, "if human sacrifices were allowed in Times Square."

Kate's mug froze halfway to her lips. "Our victim? Are you saying he was part of this... ritual?"

Ocelot looked uncomfortable. "It's never an exact science calculating the proper date on the *tonalphualli*," he said. "I wound up writing some software to make some guided estimates, and if my math is right — and I wish to *hell* it wasn't — we are just a few days from the start of a new *xiumolpilli*." Ocelot turned his brown eyes back on her, and she could easily read the pain behind them. "I think someone here in California is practicing the old ways; if we'd both not been in that rail yard last night, I'm not sure we would have known."

"The fire was burning hot enough that there would have been little left to sift through." She paused. "Don't think this gets you off the hook as a suspect."

Ocelot cocked his head. "Putting out the flames would be the *last* thing I would do if I wanted to escape notice."

"That's what a crazed murderer would say, too."

His smile told her that he knew she wasn't being serious. "The clothing — the way it was laid out — is part of the ritual. I found a page that described some of the last practices performed in what is now modern-day Mexico City, and there's no question whoever did *this* now working from the same source material."

"Why?" Kate asked, though something was stirring at the back of her mind. "You'd have to be pretty plugged into Mesoamerican history to even *know* about the ritual. And like you said, we weren't supposed to find the body."

"Until it had been burned completely," Ocelot replied meaningfully.

The thought crystalized for her. "You're right," she murmured as her mind raced. "We weren't supposed to find the body until it was *unrecognizable*."

"Exactly."

She looked at him. "You think you know who it is, don't you?"

"Suspect," he corrected, "but if I'm right, it ties to the trafficking ring."

"Shit," she breathed. "*Shit!* That's nuts! There wasn't anything there to connect it to those women."

Ocelot shook his head. "You're not seeing the whole picture. But that's okay, it's why I'm here. Have you identified the body yet?"

"How could we?" Kate replied testily. "There was nothing in the clothes that told us who it was, and the fire burned away all but trace DNA."

"Which you ran, of course."

"Yes," she nodded. "And it didn't match anything on file. All we know is that there is an unclaimed John Doe in the morgue."

The slight smile told her she'd accidentally given him something; it took a moment for her to groan inwardly. "What if I told you I could... expedite... your identification?"

"How?"

He smiled wider. "Tell me how we can break into the morgue, and I'll show you."

SIX

The flush of adrenaline at getting Kate to agree to his scheme had chased away the worst effects from opening the mirror portal, though like always, he still had a slight moment of vertigo as he stepped into a long, darkened hallway lined with industrial tile that had seen better days. The detective herself was in his arms, a wildcard that he'd not fully accounted for; the price of her acceptance had been to accompany Ocelot to the morgue so she could monitor what in all likelihood would be a massive policy violation. Swallowing hard against the bile, he gently lowered her to her feet and took stock of where they had landed; while he had pulled what plans he could for the Orange County Office of the Medical Examiner, he was aware that construction diagrams often differed from reality. Having Kate describe the building from her countless visits had provided him with a slightly better plan than he'd originally crafted, for if the signs on the wall were accurate, they were just outside of the exam room where the victim had been autopsied; that she had remembered the stainless-steel cabinet opposite had been huge stroke of luck.

"What was that?" she whispered.

"*El portal del espejo*," he replied quietly. "A mirror portal. It allows me to travel between two places nearly instantly."

"That's why you needed the mirror in the bedroom?" she asked.

"And a reflective surface here in the morgue," he nodded as he used a claw tip to tap at the steel behind them. He was still getting used to having them and was surprised he'd not accidentally drawn blood.

"How far can you travel?"

"As far as I want," he replied vaguely, unsure if he should reveal the limits of his powers quite yet.

Ocelot could already feel his strength flagging, a not-so-subtle reminder he had already pushed himself further that evening than he should have, especially since he'd not fully recovered from the events in the rail yard the prior night. He'd not lied to Kate earlier, for it had taken most of the night to find her home; as a police officer, she'd gone to great lengths to keep her personal information private, eliminating his ability to simply do a web search for her address. There were other systems available to his alter ego that might have made it faster, but they came with an even greater risk of discovery. Besides, he was in enough trouble already, for even telling Kate his name had breached one of the most inviolable rules they had. The obvious downside, of course, was that he'd been forced to make multiple transits as he crisscrossed Santa Marcel; that many trips through the portal were going to catch up to him sooner than later, despite how short they may have been.

"That sounds as handy as being able to pull coffee out of thin air," Kate said as they quietly moved over to the double-doors guarding the exam room. "I'd love to be able to bypass rush hour."

"It can come in handy," he smiled as they pushed through.

Kate put a hand against his. "You don't actually have a day job, do you?" she asked.

"Of course I do," he smiled. "I still have to pay the bills."

She rolled her eyes. "Why not just conjure the cash you need when you need it?"

"That would be illegal," he chuckled quietly.

"You sure have some strange rules around your magic," she sighed.

"It's what protects us," Ocelot said as they continued into the slightly colder exam room. "Rules, laws, codes of conduct: they create the line between harmony and chaos."

"There have to be bad actors in that utopia you're trying to sell me on," she pressed. "What keeps them from minting a billion dollars out of thin air?"

Ocelot turned toward her and took a leap of faith. "The gods are always watching," he replied. "At the end of the day, they make the final call on what is right, and what is wrong. We cross that line at our peril."

Kate looked at him askance. "You don't honestly believe there are omnipotent beings judging our actions floating around some sort of Mount Olympus?"

"I don't need to believe," he replied as he turned away and started to scan for the door that she'd told him would be there. Locating it, he moved toward it quickly. "I *know*. I've seen them — or at least, *one* of them."

His progress was arrested when she yanked at his arm, spinning him around to face her. In the half-light of the empty exam room, surrounded by the tools of science, he could understand the clear skepticism on her face. "Up to now, I was willing to keep an open mind; if you are trying to tell me you're just another run of the mill religious fanatic, I'm going to call 9-1-1 right now and have you carted off to the closest psychiatric ward."

Gently detaching his arm from her grasp, he sighed as he reached up to retie the leather thong holding his hair; he'd already decided the ponytail wasn't really working for him, but events had moved too fast for him to even think about how to replace it. "Look," he said as his eyes glanced at the clock on the wall. "You don't *have* to believe. All that's important right now is that I *do*, and that you have faith that I understand better what's going on right now." He put a hand on her shoulder. "When the dust settles, I will take you to the temple and give you a guided tour."

She rolled her eyes again. "Of *course* there is a temple. I bet it's in that jungle you spoke about."

He couldn't help the smile. "Wait until you see the sunset from the top."

Kate looked at him, and he saw that while the skepticism was still there in her beautiful eyes, she'd also decided to trust him, at least for a little while longer. He turned away from her and went to the door; pulling at it, he frowned when he realized it had one of those RFID panels beside it, with a glowing red LED across the top. Assuming that Kate herself didn't have access to the morgue freezer, he started to run his claws around the door, and frowned deeper at his inability to locate any sort of defect that would allow him to slip through the door.

So much for that spell, he sighed before turning to Kate. "I don't suppose you can unlock this?" he asked.

"Sorry," she shook her head. "Can't you just make the door go away?"

"That would defeat the purpose of sneaking in here," Ocelot reminded her as he started to hunt for another reflective surface. He hit pay dirt when his eyes alighted on the stainless steel surrounding the lamp over the exam table. "Let's try that," he said as he moved toward it.

Pulling the light down, he saw his reflection in the metal, and then gently tapped at it with a claw-tipped finger; it took a moment longer than it should've for the small clouds to form in the reflection, but once they drifted away, he found himself looking down at several gurneys holding body bags. *Must be the reflector behind the florescent,* he mused. *That means it will be a bit of a drop. Kate won't like that...*

Turning toward his companion, he held out a gloved hand. "Ready for another transit?"

"I'm not sure," she replied honestly. "That last one was rather intense."

"This one will be far shorter," he replied as she took his hand. "But there will be a drop."

"A drop?" Her eyes went wide. "What do you mean—?"

"Hang on!"

The strange tug on his soul happened again, and in mere seconds he felt himself falling; twisting in the air, he managed to somehow grab Kate *and* cushion her fall as they hit the cold tile of the freezer. He tried not to gasp as the wind was knocked out of him; as he fought to breathe, he found himself staring into her hazel eyes. Those same eyes widened a bit when she realized that she was literally on top of him; she quickly rolled off him, but not before his sensitive hearing picked up that same slight quickening of her pulse that he'd heard back at her home. Ocelot wasn't entirely sure why she was reacting that way, though he did suspect that his costume wasn't helping matters, either. When he'd been designing it, foremost in his mind was allowing full freedom of movement; that had resulted in an outfit that fit like a second skin, something that appeared to be having quite an effect on Kate. Twisting a bit himself, he flipped up to his feet and watched her carefully for a moment; as she'd not bothered to change into something more suitable for breaking and entering, the workout gear she had on was doing little against the severely cold temperature in the freezer. The slight shiver he saw ripple across her skin as her breath billowed in the cold told him it might be wise to hurry; one side benefit to his magical outfit was protection from such temperature extremes, but given the nausea he could already feel, even that had limitations.

"Let's split up to locate our victim," he suggested as he eyes went to the first bag and the small tag that was attached to it.

"All right," Kate replied, her teeth chattering. "Shit," she said after a moment. "I should have put on a sweater."

Ocelot couldn't help how his eyes went to her exposed — and finely toned — midriff. "The view wouldn't have been as good," he said under his breath.

Kate looked at him. "What did you say?"

Flushing slightly, he hastily replied: "That would've been good. I'm not sure why you didn't, knowing where we were going."

"I may have assumed you'd keep me warm," she replied, turning back to the body bag she was over.

Unsure if he was correctly picking up on the charged undercurrent, Ocelot wisely shifted his attention back to the body he'd started with. By the time they had located the victim — they were, of course, in the last bag checked — he could see that Kate was visibly turning blue; clapping her hands together for a moment, she then started to jog in place to keep warm. "Do you want to wait outside?" he asked. "I can take it from here. Just leave me your phone and I'll record what happens."

"Are you ki-ki-kidding?" she stuttered through her shivering. "I've come th-th-this far, I want to see th-th-the full show."

He nodded, then turned back to the bag. Taking a deep breath, he hooked a claw into the zipper, then slowly pulled it back, exposing the skull; his sensitive nose immediately wrinkled at the odor of decomposition that wafted out of the bag, but plowed on, unzipping the bag all the way to what remained of the chest cavity. Stopping there, he returned his attention to the skull; much of the organic material had been burned away in the fire, but some remained — including the eyes, which were staring blindly back at him in a most disquieting way. Squinting slightly, Ocelot thought there was a tiny patch of hair still present, just behind where the left ear might have once been. Turning to the torso for just a moment, his trained eyes quickly discerned where the ritual knife had been used to crack open the breastbone; leaning in a bit closer, the evidence of it also being used to scoop out the soft organs beneath it were clear. Ocelot hoped beyond hope that the victim had been dead when any of that had happened, but knew that the ritual, when performed properly, required otherwise.

Damn, he thought. *I wanted to be wrong about this. But I don't think I am.*

Returning to the skull, he held his hands just above it and then closed his eyes. Reaching down into his final reserves of strength, he focused everything into the phrase he uttered: "*Flor de muerto.*"

He felt rather than saw Kate start behind him, but ignored her as the sizzle of the magic rolled from his shoulders and out into his palms; slowly opening his eyes, he watched as a blooming Mexican Marigold appeared in the space between his hands. Catching it as it began to drop, he slowly rotated it, then plucked one of the vibrant orange-yellow petals from the flower; pressing it between his gloved fingers, he held it over the skull, then carefully let it fall. Halfway to the skeleton, it began to glow brightly, filling the room with a golden haze momentarily blinding even his enhanced eyesight. Blinking furiously, he waited until the air cleared, and smiled when he saw the skeleton had sat up from the body bag.

Despite not having any skin on its face, the skull still seemed to look surprised; glancing over his shoulder, he thought Kate had nearly mimicked the expression, though her white pallor might have had more to do with the temperature in the freezer. "Hello, my friend," Ocelot said in Spanish. "I am sorry to have interrupted your eternity."

Those blind eyes turned on him, and actually appeared to *see* him. "Am I really dead?" it asked; Ocelot felt the voice more than heard it.

"I am afraid so," Ocelot replied. "We don't have much time," he added, fighting a powerful fatigue as he spoke. Ocelot wanted nothing more than to curl into a tiny little ball and sleep for the next twenty years. "Who were you in life?"

"I am..." it started before pausing. "I was Sebastian Montclair."

Shit, Ocelot thought. "How did you come to be in the rail yard?"

"I wasn't in the rail yard," it said, then cocked its head slightly. "Oh," it added. "I guess I *was* there, wasn't I? I don't remember that."

Ocelot looked at Kate, who was clearly freezing to death. "He was killed elsewhere," he said.

"And mo-mo-moved to the rail yard," she nodded. "That explains why we di-di-didn't find—"

"Exactly," Ocelot replied, cutting her off. Turning back to the skull, he asked: "Do you know who did this to you?"

"It's so weird how I can see *here* and yet also be *there*," the skull said.

Ocelot felt his ability to keep the spell going beginning to slip; the marigold in his hands was quickly fading. "Focus for a moment," he said, gritting his teeth as he tried to pour just a little bit more into the link he had made. "Describe what you saw in your final moments."

"I have so many regrets. I never went to Venice, never hiked in the Himalayas—"

"*Please*," Ocelot hissed, the pain of keeping the spell going now quite physical. "*Who did you see?*"

"I think I understand your question," it answered, and then promptly slumped back into body bag.

Ocelot wasn't fairing much better, for he sagged against the gurney when the spell broke; trying to steady himself against it, he instead missed the edge and tumbled to the cold tile of the floor. Gasping, he struggled to get up only to feel like the room had begun to spin around him. Blinking hard to try and steady his vision, a bolt of fear shot through him when he saw that a portion of his costume along his thigh had disappeared, exposing the skin beneath to the frigid air. Rolling slightly over to hide it from Kate as she bent to help him up, he felt another wave of nausea roll over him, harsh enough that he sagged back down onto his knees.

"Ocelot," Kate said as she dropped to her knees. "What's wrong?"

"I'm fine," he lied as he tried to stand again and fell into Kate.

"Clearly you're n-n-n-n-ot," she stuttered as she held him against her compression bra. "You can't open a por-por-portal to get us out of here, can you?"

He squeezed his eyes shut. "I don't think so, no."

"Shit," she breathed. "All right, let's do this the old fas-fas-fash-ioned way."

Carefully helping him up, he made no attempt not to lean against her as they moved to the massive door of the freezer; he didn't need to see the expression on her face when she pressed the handle to exit, and nothing happened. "It's locked from the outside," he groaned. "Who makes a freezer like that?"

"Someone protecting against god-like superheroes who can tele-port in but not out," she chuckled, despite the chill.

"For the last time, I'm not a god—"

"I know," she said softly. "And for wh-wh-what it's worth, after that little stunt, I believe you."

"Thank you," he said. Swallowing hard against the vomit that was threatening to erupt, he tried to focus on the door in front of them. "I might have an idea," he said as he tried to slip her grasp.

"You can barely stand up," she said, holding him tighter. "Are you sure?"

He nodded. "You might want to step away from me."

"Not on your life," she said. "Do what you need to."

"You've been warned," Ocelot replied. His vision swam again, then steadied as he focused on the handle. It took more effort than he would have expected to press both hands to the handle; taking a deep breath, he knew he was on fumes as he reached out into the room with his senses and located a power line running in the wall behind the door. Bracing himself, he focused on the electricity flowing through those wires and then gently, oh so carefully, begged it to shift directions slightly.

The sizzle that moved across his body shocked some life back into him, and for a moment, chased away the fatigue that threatened to overwhelm him. Guiding the current as best as he could, he forced just enough of it through the circuitry of the door that whatever fail-safe had been programmed into it was triggered; the loud *click* of the lock disengaging saw him collapsing against the door in relief. And that seemed to be the last of his strength; slumping against the handle, he fell against the door as it swung open and found himself in short order splayed out along the tile of the exam room, up close and personal with the grit of the grout. Ocelot felt his eyes close, and his body willingly reaching for the slumber he so desperately needed.

"Ocelot," whispered a voice that he seemed to recognize. "We can't stay here. Get up."

Another, smaller, jolt of adrenaline shot through him as he remembered where he was and what was happening; lethargically, he opened his eyes again and tried to push himself up. Looking at his arms, it appeared other than the one spot on his thigh, his costume was still intact — for now. Fear of discovery shot even more adrenaline into his system, enough to get him to his feet. "I can't get us back to your house," he heard himself saying as Kate ducked under his arm to support him.

"I've got you covered," she replied. It felt like she was at the end of a long tunnel. "Just stay with me a little longer."

The world winked out for him before he could reply.

SEVEN

When the world came back to Ocelot, the first thing he noted was the crisp smell of bacon being fried somewhere close at hand. The latent predatory instincts that he always fought against seemed to sense his weakened state and took over for a moment; his eyes snapped open and his nose began sniffing at the air, confirming the directionality of food. In the blink of an eye, he'd flipped off of the bed he was on and was halfway to satisfying his suddenly ravenous hunger before coming up short: while the space was itself familiar, he knew with a cold dread that he shouldn't be there. The shock from understanding *that* allowed him to regain his sense of self; instead of turning the handle for the door, he paused and took in his reflection from the full-length mirror mounted to the back. Twisting slightly, he was relieved to see his costume appeared to still be intact; even the small section on his thigh that had thinned out in the morgue seemed to have been restored. His hair was all akimbo, though, for the leather thong tying it back appeared to have disappeared. Moving back to the bed, he sorted through the bedclothes and located the missing strip of leather, then frowned when he saw various tears in the sheets. Holding his claw-tipped hands up, his masked eyes narrowed; now he had an expensive answer as to whether the magic keeping him as Ocelot would hold even if he was unconscious. Pulling his hair back and running the thong through it, he made a mental note to replace Kate's sheets as soon as he could.

For as he made a slow revolution of the room, he knew with cold certainty that he was in *her* room — or at least, what had once *been* her room before she'd left for college. It hadn't changed much since the last time he'd been there; from the bookcase of science fiction paperbacks and thick detective novels to the wood dresser topped by plastic starship models, it felt a bit like a time capsule, one that he never thought he'd ever see again. Moving over to the dresser, he gently ran a claw tip along the base of the starship *Voyager* and smiled. While Ocelot hadn't been very enthusiastic about fiction of any kind while growing up — nothing could truly compare to his *actual* reality — he *had* made the effort to watch the show that had so captured the imagination of Kate's parents that they would name their child after the main character, the brilliant and equally as compassionate Captain Kathryn Janeway.

She's so much like Janeway, in many ways, he thought as he continued to roam the room. *Her parents were quite prescient.*

There was a small shadow box hanging on the wall beside the window that faced the street, and leaning in, he smiled as he picked out the gold medals Kate had won at various cycling competitions over the years; based on the empirical evidence from the prior evening, he had a feeling she was still quite active in the sport and wondered if her most recent awards were at her home. A small basket was beside the bed and held several softball gloves and a random assortment of soccer pads and socks, underscoring just how much of an athlete the younger Kate had once been. In the far corner of the room was a small console holding a modest widescreen televi-

REFLECTION IN THE SHADOWS

sion; a now ancient looking gaming station was snugged in beside it, along with a dozen DVD-sized holders containing quite the variety of video games. Ocelot tapped each with a claw, and then carefully pulled out a particular title that brought a soft smile to his masked face.

I've not played any of these in years, he thought as he slid it back in. *It would be fun to fire up my old console and see if I still have what it takes to take down an array of bad guys driven by artificial intelligence,* especially *if I can't use my magic...*

Returning to the mirror behind the door, he did a self-check and thought the rest he'd gotten had recharged him enough to open a portal, but found himself reluctant to do so; it was clear that Kate had gone to great lengths to get him to safety, though he was somewhat at a loss as to why they were in her parent's house. Granted, it was at the southern tip of Santa Marcel, closer to the Orange County complex where they had been; his reflection smiled at him when he realized that maybe the detective was unwilling to be alone with him back at her place, and had opted for some measure of security by crashing with her parents. Either way, his breeding at a minimum required him to make an entrance so he could, at the very least, thank them for their hospitality. As the scent of bacon hit his nose again, his stomach pointed out that he might find other benefits should he venture forth into the day.

Twisting the handle to the door, he quietly pulled it open and peered down the hallway of the ranch-style home; the plan was a familiar one, considering how many houses like it had been built in that part of Southern California from the late 1970s to the mid-1980s. Following his nose, he carefully walked down the hallway and out into the living room with its massive bay window looking out onto the patch of grass fronting the street; the angle of the sunshine pouring through the glass was a leading indicator that the morning was well underway. A small archway led into the cramped kitchen just behind the living room, and there he found Kate working over the stove, her back to him. She had her blond hair up in a casual bun, with strands haphazardly sticking out here and there, and was wearing a gray hoodie over what appeared to be the same workout tights she'd had on the prior evening. In classic SoCal fashion, she had on seriously hot pink flip-flops, exposing toes that had expertly applied dark purple nail polish. Glancing at the clock on the microwave over the stove, he tried not to groan when he realized his alter-ego would soon be missed.

"Good morning," she said without looking over her shoulder. "I'm doing scrambled eggs, bacon and wheat toast if you'd like to join me."

"I would, thank you," he said. "Can I help in any way?"

"Orange juice is in the fridge," she said, pointing to the device with her spatula. "Glasses are over the sink."

He nodded and retrieved the orange juice, smiling slightly to see the gallon of chocolate milk was still residing on the door. Kate's mother had an insatiable sweet tooth that started with a glass of the confection even before brewing her first cup of coffee for the day. Moving carefully around Kate in the tight space, he opened the cabinet door and paused for a moment, his claw-tipped fingers hovering over glasses bearing the Disneyland logo. Too many memories were attached to those, so he grabbed two small plastic tumblers instead.

"Thank you," he said as he poured out the juice. "I was in serious trouble there."

"You were," she said, looking at him. Her eyes were filled with concern. "What happened?"

Ocelot glanced at the hallway. "Are we alone?" he asked.

"Mom is at work," she nodded. "Left about an hour ago. Dad has been dead for about five years now."

He was thankful the mask hid most of his shock at discovering the gregarious man was no longer among them. *I've missed more than I realized while I was in the jungle,* he thought morosely. *She could probably have used a friend, and I was nowhere to be found.* "I'm sorry to hear that," Ocelot replied softly.

She shrugged. "Heart attack," she replied. "Dropped dead as he got off the elevator at his office. At least he went quickly; that's better than most of us will get."

He decided not to pursue her odd view on death. "How did your mom react to me...?"

"Aside from being thrilled that I had a boyfriend — don't look at me like that, it was the only thing I could think of in a pinch — she was quite happy to be our designated driver after we'd had one too many at Spenser's."

Ocelot shook his head as he put the orange juice back in the fridge. "You let her think I'd passed out from alcohol? And she *bought* it?"

"I've been known to drink my dates under the table," was the rejoinder.

"Good to know," he rolled his masked eyes. "Especially if we ever do go on a date."

"That would be a *big* if," she chuckled.

Feeling unusually curious if there happened to be someone else out there for Kate, Ocelot pressed. "Why? Would I have to stand in line?"

"Hardly," she sighed. "There's very little time for a social life in my line of work. I would presume that's also the case for a superhero."

I wouldn't know, he thought to himself, *since this is all a bit new to me.* "And your mother didn't think my outfit was odd?"

Kate shrugged. "It's Southern California," she said, looking at him. "We've *all* seen stranger."

"Good point," he laughed.

Kate took some plates down from another cupboard, then spooned equal portions of the eggs she'd cooked onto them. The bread happened to pop from the toaster at that moment, which she also divided evenly among the plates. Handing him one, she then led him to the small circular table that was nestled into a windowed nook looking into the backyard. Taking their seats, she picked up a fork and then paused.

"You avoided my question."

"Which one?" he asked innocently as he snagged some bacon from the plate she'd put between them.

Kate just looked at him.

Munching on the bacon, he sighed. "You want the truth?"

"Yes," she replied. "Especially after I wound up having to carry you. Those muscles of yours make you kind of heavy, by the way."

"Ah," he said. He crunched on more bacon, managing to delay only slightly. "There is a long explanation, and then a shorter one."

"Just give me the précis," she said, glancing at her watch. "I don't know about you, but I am already late for work."

"Yeah." He picked up the fork and then put it back down. "So... while there aren't any practical limits to my abilities, I've not yet reached the age where I can fully use all of my powers."

"Are you telling me you're like a teenager with a learner's permit?" Kate teased with a slight smirk.

Ocelot felt his face warm. "I'd not thought of it in those terms, but, yeah, that about covers it."

"When do you unlock everything?"

"Remember that Aztec calendar we were talking about last night?"

"The one that has both a solar calendar and a ritual one?"

"Yes," he nodded. "I'll be able to access my full abilities eight of our year-cycles after I ascended to my role. That happens to be in a few weeks, though like I said earlier, it's often hard to align the Aztec calendar with our modern one."

"That only tells me how powerful you *might* be," she correctly observed. "Last night, you were doing fine until you got those bones to talk to you; is there a limit to how *much* you can do at any given moment?"

Ocelot smiled. *Like you really needed a reminder of how smart she is,* he thought. "Your insights serve you well; I can see why you are a top investigator. In this case, though, the issue has more to do with *me* and less to do with my magic."

"What do you mean?"

"Let me put it this way: I saw that you had a stationary cycle at your home — how long have you had it?"

"Quite a while, but I prefer to actually use a *real* bike."

"How far do you ride?"

"Depends on the workout, but between twenty-five and fifty miles; some weekends, I'll do even more."

"And were you able to put in that much distance the very *first* time you rode your bike?"

"Hell no," she said as she picked up her toast and buttered it. "It took me months to get the stamina to ride ten."

Ocelot nodded. "That's *exactly* what's happening with me," he continued. "I have access to all of this power, but I've only recently been *using* it. In a very real sense, the 'muscles' I need to wield magic are still being developed."

Kate cocked her head. "And if you push that limit — push yourself beyond what you can physically handle?"

He felt his face heat up again. "I crash. *Hard.*"

"That could get you into trouble," she mused.

"You think?" he chuckled. "I was starting to spiral down when you surprised me at the rail yard, though I still managed to open a portal to escape. Last night, I had nothing left; I'll be honest, I was weak enough, I wasn't entirely sure I'd be able to even keep my costume going."

"Who says you did?" Kate smiled slyly.

Ocelot felt his masked eyes go wide. "Did I lose—?"

"Calm down," she chuckled. "Your magical mask remained firmly in place, along with everything else. I still don't know who I am really talking to."

"But you are clearly more comfortable about that than you were yesterday," he pointed out, somewhat relieved his secret hadn't yet been revealed.

"Yeah," she said as she polished off the last of her juice. "I suppose I am. So, who was our victim?"

"Sebastian Montclair," Ocelot replied. "My mole at Vasquez Industries."

"Shit," Kate breathed. "A whistleblower?"

"Of a kind. I had... suspicions of what was going on internally and approached him; he confirmed just about everything, and then continued to provide me with ongoing intelligence."

"That supports your hypothesis that the fire might have just been cover," she mused. "Someone found out about what he was doing and silenced him."

"Maybe," he nodded. "Unless you feel differently, I was going to dig into that next."

"No," she shook her head, "I think your instincts are good on this." She paused. "I actually have a contact there myself, one who offered to help me earlier. I think I'll visit him today and see if the offer is still good."

"Sounds like we can work this from multiple angles," he nodded. Glancing down, he was surprised to see he'd managed to empty everything on his plate, though he didn't have much of a memory of eating. Looking back up, his masked eyes caught her smiling.

"I'd offer to make more, but I *truly* need to get going."

"I appreciate what you did," he smiled back as he stood and piled her plate onto his. "And thank you for your impromptu hospitality."

"Oddly, I'm glad it worked out this way," she said as he began to run the plates under the hot water. "I don't know if I should admit this, but you're officially off the suspect list."

He smirked at her. "Of course I am," he replied cheekily. "No one this handsome could ever be considered a murderer."

Kate suddenly reached up and pulled him toward her; before he fully understood what was going on, she'd gently pressed her lips to his, pushing his back against the sink in the process. Ocelot tensed and tried to pull back; his masked eyes widened in panic when he couldn't easily wriggle out of her grasp. Panic then shifted to shock when the light kiss became something more urgent; her hands moved from the back of his head to the small of his back, tentatively pulling him closer. To his surprise, he found that he didn't want her to stop, despite how his brain was screaming at the top of its lungs there were a million reasons why he needed to get off the path they were quickly headed down. Kate felt him tensing up again at the conflict within him, and leaned back enough that her eyes met his.

"Go with the moment," she breathed.

"I'm not sure this is a good idea," he said; the huskiness to his voice, though, undercut the sentiment. His masked eyes searched hers. "You don't even know who I am beneath this mask."

She reached up and pressed a hand to the side of his masked face; he was surprised at how electric her touch was against his skin. "I can't explain it, but I feel like I *do* know you," she replied softly. "Is that crazy?"

"It's probably the stress we're under," he replied weakly as he once more tried to disentangle himself from Kate. "And as flattered as I am—"

Kate leaned into him and smothered the final part of his protests with a kiss that made his toes curl; when she pulled away again, they were both breathing hard. "We do this," he whispered as he felt the last of his resistance crumble away, "you need to know there's no going back."

"I don't care," she replied.

As she tugged him out of the kitchen and back down the hallway toward her old bedroom, he wondered if she soon would...

EIGHT

I f someone a week ago had told Kate that she'd find herself in her childhood bed with a masked stranger nestled beside her, she would have asked what they had been drinking and ordered them another. As she idly ran her hand through Ocelot's long hair, freed from its binding as a result of their extracurricular activities, she wondered what sort of madness had overtaken her. Not only had she slept with someone who she truly didn't know — and, in fact, despite what she had said earlier, might technically still be a suspect — she'd done so when quite literally being on duty. And then there was the little matter of more-or-less having *seduced* said stranger; closing her eyes, she wondered where that side of her had been hiding. Sure, she'd picked up more than a few guys for an entertaining one-night-stand over the years, but that had always been the end result of a fairly typical dance between her and the flavor du jour. What she had done to Ocelot had gone well beyond that, and yet, as she relished in the warmth of his body against hers, she couldn't find any trace of regret in having pushed him over the edge.

Then again, other than those first few moments when he'd

looked ready to bolt from the house like a frightened animal, Ocelot had quickly demonstrated it wasn't exactly his first rodeo; while not unexpected, she'd been surprised by the ferocity of the experience, almost as if *both* of them had been far more desperate to make a deep connection with another than *either* had realized. Opening her eyes to find his masked brown ones gazing up at her, she found herself curious about *why* that might be for Ocelot; assuming the man she'd come to know over the last day was as authentic as he appeared to be, under ordinary circumstances, she'd have found him quite the engaging individual — someone she could easily see herself looking forward to spending time with. That others *hadn't* might mean he'd been reluctant to put himself out there, socially; or, as she suspected was more likely, moonlighting as a masked hero might have simply crimped his schedule. Watching him watch her, and seeing those masked eyes narrow slightly, she knew one thing: something had shifted deep in her heart. Reaching down to push his hair back behind an ear, Kate felt the first brush of fear that she'd stumbled into something good that she might ultimately lose.

It wouldn't be the first time.

Ocelot grabbed her hand and pulled it to his lips, then kissed the back of it gently before looking at her again. "What did we just do?" he asked quietly. "And where do we go from here?"

Kate smiled slightly. "You really know how to get to the point."

He smiled slyly. "Only when I need to," he said as he kissed her hand again.

Feeling her face flush slightly, she nodded. "True. And to answer your question, I've not got the faintest clue." Wanting to put off that discussion for a bit, she ran her fingers along the back of his neck, smiling as he closed his eyes and leaned into her touch. His chocolate-colored skin reminded her of something she'd wanted to ask earlier but had been rather distracted by what had been going on at the time. "I guess this answers what's under your costume," she observed.

She was starting to love the smile when it appeared on his face. "I'd appreciate it if you'd keep it between us," he said. "Not sure I want people to know I'm essentially running around commando style."

"Your secret is safe with me," she chuckled. "Though I'll never look at you in costume quite the same way, now."

"Great," he rolled his masked eyes dramatically.

Her fingers came to the leather thong tied behind his neck, and her eyes moved to the small obsidian disk it was attached to. "Where did it go, by the way, and what is this?"

"My costume?' he asked. "The magic is selective, which is how I could keep the mask and — well, some other ways I've hidden my identity."

"Like your tattoo of your mother?" she teased.

"Something like that," he laughed.

"And the amulet?"

Ocelot's eyes dropped to the reflective object and frowned slightly. "That's not entirely my secret to share," he replied softly. "Let's just say it's extremely important to me and my family."

"It must be," she said as she let it go and watched it bump down against his muscled chest. "For you to wear it even as Ocelot."

He nodded. "It is."

Kate glanced at her phone sitting on the small side table by her childhood bed. "I've really got to shower and get going," she said, looking back at him. "I imagine you do, too."

"Yes," he nodded before that sly smile appeared again. "We could speed things up and shower at the same time."

She pushed his masked face away with a finger as she rolled out of the bed. "I think that would have the opposite effect," Kate said as she pulled on her tights and then shrugged into the hoodie. It wasn't lost on her that she had Ocelot's rapt attention. "If you want to go first—"

Ocelot leaned on his arm and smiled; the sheet had fallen away to expose more of his ripped abs, which she tried to ignore. "I suppose you're right," he sighed dramatically. "In that spirit, I'll just pop back to my place instead."

"Off to your secret lair?" Kate teased. "Buried deep beneath the streets of Santa Marcel?"

Ocelot smiled slightly. "Nothing quite so grand," he replied. "At least, not yet. I think you get the secret lair after being a hero for a few years."

"Or a wealthy benefactor."

She nearly missed the slight hardening in Ocelot's expression. "I'm not sure I'd want to be beholden to anyone," he said before softening his look. "Well, not just *anyone*."

"Good to know you've already developed your moral code," Kate smiled as she pulled her hair into a quick ponytail.

He waited a beat. "Would you be... okay... with my appearing at your place later tonight?"

Kate sat back down on the bed. "Yes," she nodded. "What time?"

He frowned. "I guess it depends on how the day goes," he sighed.

"Don't all heroes work at night?" Kate asked.

"Heroes, maybe," Ocelot sighed again. "Just not their alter-egos. How about ten?"

"Ten it is," she smiled.

"All right," he smiled back.

There was an awkward moment where they looked at each other.

"I should go," he said.

"Yes," she nodded again.

"All right," he laughed again.

Kate wasn't entirely sure what happened next, for one moment Ocelot was there, smiling like the Cheshire Cat; the next, the sheet that had been covering him was slowly drifting to the mattress. Save for the heavy scent of their activities hanging in the air around her, she could nearly have talked herself into believing it had been some sort of dream; frowning slightly — and to try and avoid questions from her mother she didn't want to answer quite yet — she stripped the bed and remade it with clean sheets from the hall closet, then started a wash in the ancient front-loading Maytag that had been old twenty years earlier. As she had nothing at her childhood home remotely close to professional attire, she hauled out her phone and ordered up an Uber before checking in with the station; fortunately, the Chief was still out of town at some sort of quasi-quarterly statewide meeting, which in turn meant she'd not truly been missed — yet.

The Uber driver arrived a few minutes later; as her dalliance with Ocelot had pushed her beyond the normal rush hour window, she arrived at her place in record time. She was halfway through her shower when the insanity of the morning's events hit her all over again; sagging against the tile of her shower for a moment, that pit of... something... reformed in her stomach. It wasn't exactly a warning — and if it were, it was way too late; no, it felt more like the fear that had brushed her heart when she'd had his head against her side. And yet, even that wasn't quite the same — it wasn't fear of having *done* anything, but fear that it might not *continue*. Shutting off the water and reaching for a towel, Kate shook her head once more, trying to fathom what exactly had happened to her in the twenty-four hours since Ocelot had literally dropped into her life.

Tying her damp hair up in a businesslike bun, she opted for the more professional outfit that she normally wore to court appearances; after her last meeting with Tenoch, Kate had a feeling that appearing in her conservative navy-blue pantsuit might garner her a few points, especially given how she'd ended her last visit. As she quickly applied her makeup in the bathroom mirror, she thought a bit about what she wanted to accomplish during her return visit to Vasquez Industries, then realized she was blanking on the name that Ocelot had given her. Glancing at her phone made her frown, for getting the hero's contact information hadn't exactly been high on her list, so reconfirming that rather significant tidbit was completely out of the question. Kate wondered if Ocelot even *had* a phone, and smiled slightly to think that she might have to build some sort of Batman-esque signal to catch his attention.

Didn't he say he could travel through mirrors? she thought, pressing her hand to the cold surface of hers. *I wonder if that is another way to reach him — though I'm not certain I like the idea he could be watching me.*

Shaking her head again, she finished up and made her way out to her driveway and the departmental SUV she'd brought home the night prior. For once, she was glad that she'd taken advantage of the perk, for she was in no mood to bike to the station to pick up her ride. Firing up the vehicle, she backed out onto her street and then made her way across Santa Marcel to the world headquarters for Vasquez Industries. Kate found the small visitor lot was as empty as it had been on her first visit; the guard that issued her the guest pass was also the same, a handsome guy that seemed a bit skinny to be in that particular line of work. It wasn't lost on her that he seemed to be falling all over himself to show her how to work the elevator, despite there only being a single button beside it. Another minder met her when the doors opened on the floor housing the executive suite; the unsmiling older woman made it clear with her dour expression that Kate's unexpected appearance was throwing an otherwise perfectly scripted day into unsuitable disarray. That frown grew deeper when she threw open the door to Tenoch's office to announce Kate's arrival only to find the grand space was empty.

"Mr. Vasquez will be here shortly," the woman said tersely,

waving Kate to one of the guest chairs. "Please make yourself comfortable."

"Thank you," Kate smiled as the woman bowed and removed herself, closing the door behind her.

She'd barely settled into a chair when the door behind her opened again. "Kate?"

Turning, she saw the elegant figure of Tenoch framed in the doorway. "Hi," she answered. "I'm sure you weren't expecting me to turn up so soon after what happened yesterday."

Closing the door behind him, he walked over to the guest chair beside her and sat down. "I'll be honest," he smiled. "I wasn't entirely sure you wanted to be in the same ZIP code with me."

"There might have been a few moments when that was true," she nodded. "In my defense, it was quite a bit for me to take in."

"That's on me," he replied. "I should have immediately gone straight to you when I returned and explained everything."

"It wouldn't have hurt," she said. "Look, last night you hinted that you might be willing to help me with the investigation. Did I read you correctly?"

Tenoch smiled. "As well as ever," he replied. "Is that why you're here?"

"Partly. I did want to apologize for how I walked out on you. I could have been a bit more adult about the whole thing and instead reverted to my inner teenager."

Tenoch held up his hands. "No one could blame you," he said before smiling again. "I've already forgotten about it. Aside from going to Oaxaca for you — which is already scheduled, I might add — what else can I do?"

Kate looked at him closely. "I have a confidential informant who in turn appears to have had a source here at Vasquez Industries," she began. "I want to preface this by saying that I'm not investigating your company at this time, but I should also warn you that I will follow any leads that might crop up as I look deeper into what happened at the rail yard."

"I would expect nothing less," Tenoch replied. "What did this source-of-a-source tell you?"

"They pretty much confirmed what you more-or-less tried to tell me last night," she answered. "That Vasquez Industries has been a conduit for human trafficking for some time. They also provided the exact details for the timing on the container we found at the yard."

Tenoch nodded and sighed. "I've been looking into this for a while, now," he said.

"I gathered that much from what you said last night."

His eyes widened. "Last night?"

Kate looked at him. "When I was here?"

"Oh, right," he nodded as he pinched at the bridge of his nose for a moment. "Sorry, it's been a long day."

"Tenoch, it's not even eleven," Kate said before noting how puffy his eyes looked. "Did your girlfriend keep you up all night?" she teased.

"A gentleman never kisses and tells," he replied, but the smile in those green eyes told otherwise. "And yes, that was exactly what I was trying to get across when we last spoke. I didn't think you'd have too much trouble picking up on my inference."

"I'm flattered you think so much of my investigator skills," Kate smiled.

Tenoch shrugged. "It's clear you're really good at what you do," he replied. "Can you tell me who this source is within my company? I feel like we should bring them into our little circle of trust."

"That would be hard to do," Kate replied. "For they are sitting in the Orange County Morgue right now."

Tenoch blanched slightly. "The victim from the fire?"

"Yes," Kate nodded as she frantically tried to recall what Ocelot had told her. "Someone from your Operations department, I think.

Sebastian Montclair," she added when the name finally popped into her head.

Those brown eyes widened again. "Sebastian..." he said slowly.

Kate saw something in his expression. "You know him, don't you?"

Tenoch nodded. "Yeah, I do. He's one of the first people I hired when I came back to the company — right out of the Marshall School of Business."

"Did he report to you?"

"Technically, yes," Tenoch smiled. "Seeing as though I'm the VP and all."

Kate looked at him. "But your mom is really running everything, isn't she?"

"As much as I let her," he smiled ruefully. "Come on," he said as he stood.

"Where are we going?" she asked as she followed him to the door for his office.

"If Sebastian was feeding your source-of-a-source information, he may have left some breadcrumbs behind." Tenoch paused with his hand on the door and looked at her with a slightly conspiratorial grin. "You'll need to keep this between the two of us," he said. "If *madre* finds out that I'm helping you, it might be the end of my career."

Kate arched an eyebrow. "She's not likely to fire her own flesh and blood."

"No," he said as he pulled the door open, "it would be something far worse, actually. This way."

Wondering exactly what Tenoch had meant, Kate found herself hustling to keep up with her host. He led her down a long hallway that had tall windows set into one wall, and then with a sudden swift move, diverted them into a small alcove just as two well-dressed employees of the firm rounded a corner. If she'd thought he'd been joking about avoiding detection, the way Tenoch carefully scanned the corridor before taking her hand and leading her back out into it confirmed he was deadly serious about staying off his mother's radar. What was more fascinating was how attuned to the environment he seemed to be, easily ducking into what shadows there were long before Kate even heard footsteps approaching.

Ultimately, they reached an elevator lobby; unsurprisingly, Tenoch eschewed the devices and instead pushed open the door to the stairwell just beside them. Nodding toward the shiny metal doors, he held the door for her. "The department Sebastian was in is down on two."

"Lead on," she smiled as he let the door slowly shut behind them.

He started down the concrete-and-metal steps, and she fell in behind him. The bright lights emphasized the utilitarian feel of the stairwell, and made for quite a jarring dissonance with the far more tastefully designed public spaces of the building. Their combined footfalls echoed as they continued downward, something that seemed to concern Tenoch if the expression on his handsome face meant what she thought. Though he tried to hide it with a smile, she didn't miss how he was carefully ensuring no one was above or below them each time they came to a landing. What struck Kate as odd, though, was how he appeared to be paying little attention to the bubble security cameras that had been placed to cover every possible angle; unless someone had fallen asleep wherever the system was being monitored, their passage would likely be noted and recorded.

Why is he so worried someone might be following us? Kate thought as they passed a door with a large number three painted beside it. *Given the security posture for the building, why isn't he more concerned about the cameras?*

Almost as if he had sensed her thoughts, Tenoch paused on the landing, and nodded at the camera closest to them. "They aren't working at the moment," he said. "The security arm of our organization has been upgrading the system, but it seems to have uncovered a bit of a software glitch — one that has knocked out portions of the building. Certain hallways, a few offices, and," he smiled a bit, "the eastern emergency stairwell along with its exterior door."

Kate's eyebrows went up. "That's amazingly convenient."

"Isn't it?" Tenoch replied. "I only found out about it this morning when our security chief grudgingly admitted to us they were still having trouble." He frowned slightly before continuing down the steps. "They only revealed there was a problem because they want me to pay for an outside contractor to fix the code." He looked at Kate. "My mother has a unique emphasis on doing everything in house, so it's a package developed here at headquarters that ties into our other systems. We also use it at our other locations worldwide. Our security chief is concerned that this glitch might be the software version of a canary in a coal mine, indicating that we have a back-door open into the code that can be exploited."

"Hence the outsider," Kate observed. "You think the system was hacked?"

"Maybe," Tenoch nodded again.

One of his long, curly bangs suddenly swooped down into his face as he nodded; Tenoch casually brushed it out of the way and behind an ear in a movement that seemed strangely familiar to Kate. Taking a closer look at her friend, she saw he wasn't nearly as put together as he'd been the day prior; his hair hadn't been gelled into Fortune 500 submission, and was instead as free-flowing as it had been when he'd been a teenager. She decided it was a better look for Tenoch, one that made him far more like the person she knew than the corporate titan he seemed to be pretending to be. Lost in her thoughts, it took a moment before she realized he'd been speaking.

"...when I discovered the outage this morning, it made me think it might be how your source-of-a-source was able to meet with Sebastian, and keep it off the radar."

"Wouldn't that be pretty risky?" Kate asked. "Coming here directly?"

"Maybe," Tenoch said as they continued downward. "On the other hand, it's rather brilliant."

"How do you figure?"

Tenoch put his hand on the door to the second floor and paused. "My mother would never have expected such espionage beneath her own roof," he said simply. "Other companies? Sure. But not here." Tenoch smiled oddly. "And not so close."

As he pulled the door open, Kate had a wry observation about Tenoch's domineering mother teed up only to have it die on her lips when she caught the woman herself standing in the hallway outside of the stairwell. While it had been over a decade since the last time she'd seen Reyna Vasquez, she'd never forgotten the quiet power that had always seemed to surround her like an invisible cloak. Kate wasn't *completely* confident Tenoch's mother had approved of his relationship with her, but neither had she done anything to directly prevent it from continuing, either. Standing there toe-to-toe with her, though, Kate suddenly had the damndest feeling that Reyna had played an outsized role in whatever had prevented Tenoch from living his dream as a professional soccer player.

Much as she'd been eyeing the current head of Vasquez Industries, Kate found that Reyna had been equally as appraising; the slight frown that formed on the elegant face was the only indicator Kate might not have measured up as expected. Turning toward Tenoch, Kate caught the small flower that had been pinned tastefully beside the bun of her silver hair; it appeared to be an orchid of some sort, with an intensity of color that matched the woman's personality. Pressing her hands together where she was holding them oddly at her waist, Reyna's expression shifted into something far more professional.

"Still assisting the police with their investigation?" Reyna asked. "I can't imagine we have much more to share that would be of interest to them."

While it was said pleasantly enough, Kate could feel an undercurrent of disapproval in her tone; it spurred her protective instincts and had her speaking up before she realized what she was doing. "Actually, I was just giving Tenoch an update. As a courtesy," she added after glancing at Tenoch. "Your son has been extremely helpful in filling in some of the blanks with respect to what goes on around here."

While his expression remained pleasantly neutral, she had the strangest sense that he appreciated her slight bending of the truth. "We were just wrapping up," he said before nodding to something behind his mother. "I was about to pull the manifest for the container so she could add it to the evidentiary file."

Reyna looked over her shoulder and then back at Tenoch, arching a sculpted eyebrow in the process. "Can't you just email that to her?" she asked. "I'm not sure I want any of our physical records to leave the building."

Kate picked up the thread. "There's no way around it, I'm afraid. Courts prefer the physical when possible. You will get it back after the case is closed, if it helps."

There was a long moment when it seemed like Reyna wasn't buying what they were selling, but then she nodded. "It was good to see you again, Kathryn. Can you find your way out after Tenoch provides what you need? We have an urgent matter to deal with, and I need him upstairs."

"Yes," Kate replied before eying Tenoch. "I have a feeling if I get lost, someone will escort me to the exit."

"That they will," Tenoch smiled at her before looking at Reyna. "Five minutes?"

"Less, please," she replied crisply before turning and striding down the hallway.

Tenoch waited until his mother had disappeared around the corner, then pitched his voice low. "Sorry about that."

"No worries," she replied. "I take it searching for the bread-crumbs will have to wait?"

Those green eyes met hers for a moment. "For now. But something makes me think you'll find a creative way to continue our quest."

"I can return tomorrow—" Kate started to reply before Tenoch started to shake his head.

"*More* creative than that," he smiled before reaching into his pocket to retrieve a slim wallet. Opening it, he sorted through the contents before withdrawing a small card. "Here's my direct line if you need to reach out to me," Tenoch added before handing the card to her.

Kate gave the card a perfunctory glance before shoving it into her own pocket. "I guess I'm dismissed, then?" she asked, feeling a strange sense of dismay as she did so. The longer she spent with Tenoch, the less it felt as though there was a decade-long gap in knowing him. Leaving his presence felt almost painful.

"I wouldn't put it quite like that," he said as he reached for her hand and then gently brushed his lips to the back of it. "Until the next time we meet?"

She nodded. "Is your offer of dinner still on the table?" she heard herself ask.

Tenoch glanced in the direction his mother had gone. "Of course it is," he said softly.

"Are you free tomorrow night?"

"I can be," he answered. "Text me your address and I'll pick you up, say, around six?"

Kate's initial impulse was to insist she could drive herself to their destination, but the earnest look on Tenoch's face had her slowly nodding. "Sounds good," she replied as she finally pulled her hand from his. "The exit is that way?"

He nodded and she started in that direction before his voice stopped her. "Kate — be careful."

She looked over her shoulder, intending on a snarky reply; his look of genuine concern gave her pause. "Don't worry about me," she smiled slightly. "I know how to take care of myself."

Tenoch eyed her. "Yes," he replied at length. "I think you do."

NINE

Ocelot landed with practiced ease on the rear wall of Kate's small home in Santa Marcel and then crouched there for a moment, allowing his senses to rake over the space. The first thing that hit him was the unique scent of the owner, something that he'd only been vaguely aware of when he'd visited initially. It was an unusual combination of orange blossoms and cacao, incredibly evocative of the botanical lushness of the jungle where he had done the bulk of his training. Sniffing at the air carefully, he realized she'd recently been out on her patio but appeared to have returned inside; he smiled slightly at the thought of her expectantly pacing as she awaited his arrival. He was a bit later than promised, owing in large part to his alter ego's inability to extricate himself from obligations that had, in the end, proved more punitive than meaningful.

His sensitive hearing picked up the strange *plink-plink-plink* noise coming two yards away; despite the late hour, there was a teenager repeatedly kicking a soccer ball against a small net. Squinting, his superior night vision let him watch for a few moments as the teen darted one way and then another, repeatedly taking shots from various angles. Ocelot wondered if they were dreaming of the crowd roaring as they raced down the pitch to line up for a goal that would win the day; he knew he certainly had, for years. Right up until reality had intruded, a reality that had turned his dreams into nothing more than unreachable fantasy. Still, a part of him itched to leap over the fences and join the kid in a quick pick up match; despite how he ached for the freedom the sport had once offered him, he knew his obligations that evening trumped such frivolities. Looking back toward the small home and the cozy light spilling onto the patio from Kate's kitchen, he figured there could be worse things than spending time with the detective.

Scanning the space with augmented senses once more, he recon-firmed he was completely alone in her backyard save for some sort of mouse busily digging in her flowerbed. The sudden predatory instinct to go after the rodent was hard to ignore, reminding Ocelot that he was still not in full command of his powers. Taking a moment to tamp down the worst aspects, he slipped off the concrete wall and dropped to the lawn on all fours, then waited to ensure the kid hadn't detected his presence. Satisfied, he nonetheless crept along on all fours until he reached the patio; there, he moved into a crouch before gently tapping one of his claws against the glass.

The patio door slid back almost immediately. "You're late," Kate admonished with a smile. "I was starting to think you'd forgotten about me."

Ocelot smiled and started to reply, but found himself distracted by the potency of Kate's personal scent. This close to her it was suddenly overwhelming, enveloping him in an almost physical embrace that was difficult to ignore. The harder he tried to focus, the faster his heart began to beat, much as it had when he'd run through the treetops of the jungle, side-by-side with those that had trained him. Puzzled at his reaction to Kate's appearance, he struggled to regain his composure; it was a fight that she apparently could see as it played out on his face — despite the mask covering most of it. Instantly she was on her knees beside him, a look of concern creasing her brow.

"What's wrong?" she asked. "Are you having trouble with your magic?"

"No," he managed to reply, shaking his head to try and clear it. Everything suddenly seemed fuzzy, *except* for Kate; she was crystal clear in his vision, almost painfully so. All of his enhanced senses were solely focused on her, generating so much feedback that he was starting to feel a bit lightheaded. "I... I think I need some air..."

"Ocelot, you're already outside," Kate pointed out as she pressed the back of her hand to his forehead. "You *do* feel a bit warm..."

Whatever else she said was lost in the rush of blood that filled his ears; her touch against his skin was electric in a way that he'd only felt one time before. In an instant he realized what was happening — and what *had* happened — and felt a surge of panic bubbling up around the edges of his consciousness. Blindly he tried to back away from Kate, but that only served to have her pull him *toward* her protectively, wrapping him in a hug that felt so electric, it threatened to short out his last set of functioning brain cells.

The world went completely white; when it reformed, he found himself standing where he had often stood, in that strange between-the-worlds space that connected the gods to those who served them. It was full of warm light and a gentle mist that served to obscure anything more than a few meters away. When he held out a hand to test the density of the mist, he noted with some surprise he was still wearing his Ocelot costume; as all of his prior visits had seen him attired in the traditional loincloth, face paint and feathered headgear of his heritage, he knew it was significant that they were departing from generations of tradition, but could also sense this wasn't the time to delve into the reasons behind it.

Ocelot intrinsically knew he wasn't alone; he never was when summoned. He had a fleeting moment of concern of how Kate might be reacting to his sudden trance-like state, though given the timeless nature of what was happening, from her perspective it would only seem like a few seconds of unresponsiveness. Reaching out into the mist with his enhanced abilities, he felt more than saw his patron materialize. The codex he consulted regularly ascribed very specific meanings to how Tezcatlipoca chose to make its appearance; wars had been started — or ended — based on the form viewed by the adepts. So it was extremely startling when the mists parted to reveal the god in its full jaguar form; Ocelot felt himself take a protective step backwards despite knowing that if Tezcatlipoca wanted him dead, there was very little he could do about it. Taking his *nagual* form was deeply unusual, though; a sign, perhaps, that the situation was far worse than Ocelot had realized. Carefully watching as the animal slowly began to pace back and forth in front of him, he braced himself for what was coming — and still wasn't remotely prepared when the familiar voice boomed in the back of his head.

It was too soon! There is a time for everything!

"I didn't think it was possible for it to happen," Ocelot replied. "My cycle is not yet complete."

It was complete enough. The jaguar paused in its pacing and actually stared at him; it was the unsettling glare of a predator considering the tastiest body part to rip away first. *You should have realized this was a possibility; now we have a distraction that must be dealt with before we can return to the matter at hand.*

Ocelot felt the first shiver of fear brush his heart. "Kate has no idea," he replied, though he was aware how little point there was in arguing with the deity. "She has a life — and an important role in this reality. It would go against everything you represent for me to do what you are asking."

There is no justification for allowing her to continue, the voice boomed in his head. *This is not the time for such complications.*

"Kate can be an asset," Ocelot said. "She has access to things I need — *we* need — to prevent what must not happen. My task would be *greatly* complicated were she not... available to me as a resource."

Your heart is clouding your perspective, mijo. What is done is done and cannot be changed.

"My *heart* is why you chose *me*," Ocelot said firmly. "It has always led me true." He waited for a long moment, then boldly took a step forward. "And you cannot deny I've never let you down."

The jaguar actually looked thoughtful. *No, we cannot.*

"You need me," Ocelot pressed. "And I need *her.*"

In more ways than you know, mijo, the voice replied; for the first time, Ocelot felt a touch of compassion, something he'd never experienced from the deity. *Be warned: there is a price to pay for her to continue on this path with you.*

"Have I not *already* paid the ultimate price?" Ocelot asked. "What more would you ask of me?"

That will become evident.

"There are times when I wish you would be less circumspect," Ocelot sighed.

He thought the jaguar smiled — though it was more like a grimacing precursor to a growl. *And where would the fun be in that?*

"We appear to have different definitions of 'fun,'" Ocelot replied. "How much am I allowed to tell her?"

Only what is necessary, was the immediate reply. *You must guard your secret until I release you from your vow; do not forget what awaits you if you break it early.*

That chill of fear washed over his heart again. "I'm unlikely to do that."

Then I will return you. Until next we meet, mijo, remember: time always comes full circle, and the universe does as it will.

Ocelot rolled his eyes. *What is it with gods and their propensity for cryptic statements...?* he thought as the world went white once more.

Ocelot blinked and found himself staring once more at Kate. "Hey," she said, her eyes wide.

"Do you welcome all of your masked guests this way?" he quipped, smiling slightly.

"Hardly," she frowned, though it accentuated her worried expression. "You checked out there for a moment. Are you sure you're okay?"

"I am now," he said. Oddly, he felt no compunction about continuing to allow her to hold him; her scent, while still potent, seemed be tolerable now, possibly owing to now knowing *why* he was suddenly so sensitive to her. "I'm sorry for the scare."

"I'm not accepting your apology until you tell me what the fuck just happened. And who the hell were you talking to just now?"

He frowned slightly. "I was talking?"

"Yes," she nodded. "In an odd language I've never heard before."

Oh crap, he thought. *I assumed I was a zombie; thank the gods she doesn't understand the old tongue.*

"Uh," he started, sorting through various explanations before deciding some version of the truth was best. "Tezcatlipoca, actually."

Kate's eyes widened. "Tezcat-*who*?"

"Tezcatlipoca," he repeated, carefully pronouncing the name.

"Is that the... god you work for?"

He nodded. "That is one way to look at it, yes. They come to me at the damndest times, and I pretty much have to drop everything and listen when they do."

She ran her hand over his head in a not-very-subtle effort to look for an injury. "If it were anyone else, I'd wonder if you'd bonked your noggin and needed medical attention."

That would be far easier to deal with than what has actually *happened,* he thought. "No, I'm fine," he replied after doing a quick self assessment. "And you are right, I *am* late; I'm afraid I never got your number, so I had no way to let you know I'd been delayed."

Kate smiled slightly. "I could say the same thing," she said, then made a show of examining his form-fitting costume. "I don't see a phone hiding on your person, though."

Ocelot smiled slightly. "Because I don't want you too," he replied as he held up a gloved hand. Taking a moment to center himself, he quickly snapped his fingers and was rewarded when a small whorl of energy opened beside him.

"What is *that?*" Kate asked with awe.

"My backpack, essentially," Ocelot laughed as he reached into the space and felt around for a moment. "The complexity of the interaction between time and space creates unusual folds; I use a few as storage compartments when needed."

"You... use a fold in the fabric of the universe... as a *locker?*"

"Pretty much," Ocelot smiled as he withdrew the burner phone he'd picked up earlier that afternoon. The whorl disappeared a moment later. "I'm going to give you this number, but only if you promise not to reveal your knowledge of it — or of *me* — to anyone."

"I wouldn't do that," Kate said.

"Good," he smiled. "Now, what's your number?"

"It would be faster for me to enter it for you," Kate said as held out her hand. He placed the phone in it and watched as she navigated to the contact list. "What, exactly, did this Tezcatlipoca want with you, anyway?" she asked casually.

Ocelot sighed; it had been overly optimistic that his little pyrotechnics show would have distracted Kate. Again deciding that it would be easier to stick as close to the truth as possible, he answered, very simply, "You."

Kate's eyes moved from the phone's display to his masked visage. "Me?"

"Yeah," Ocelot replied. "What happened between us earlier today... has complicated the situation just a bit."

"Which part?" she asked with a smile. "Having breakfast together or making love to each other?"

Always straight to the point, he thought as he felt his face heating up. "The latter," he said.

"Seriously?" Kate asked as she rolled her eyes. "Do you work for some sort of puritanical deity?"

"Not exactly," he replied, shifting uncomfortably.

Kate caught something in his tone. "Ocelot, you don't have to worry — I'm not planning on having any kittens. I took precautions."

Ocelot felt like his face was on fire. "You don't understand," he said quietly. "We... we *mated*."

"That's an equally as outdated way of looking at it, too," Kate replied a bit testily. "We had a one-night thing, and it was lovely; I won't lie, I'm somewhat hoping it will happen again—"

"Kate," Ocelot said, catching her eyes and holding them.

He watched as dawning realization appeared on her face. "You're serious? Like, *mated* in the full animal kingdom sense?"

"Yes," he nodded. "I thought it couldn't happen until *after* I reached my ascension. Turns out, it, uh, can." Ocelot smiled wryly. "Like I said, our calendar doesn't quite align to reality."

Kate considered him a moment. "Which is why Tezcatlipoca summoned you?"

"Yes."

The frown on her beautiful face spoke volumes. "Are you in some kind of trouble?" Kate asked. "For, uh, mating prematurely?"

"Honestly?" Ocelot replied before settling on a tiny white lie.

"I'm not a hundred percent certain. Tezcatlipoca was a bit opaque on that point."

"That sounds a bit like a 'yes,'" Kate correctly intuited.

Ocelot smiled slightly. *Too clever by half, indeed.* "Maybe. Whatever penance I might have to pay will happen *after* we deal with the current crisis, though. That much was certain."

Kate frowned deeper. "You shouldn't have to pay *anything,*" she said firmly. "I'm the one that forced the issue. If anyone should be in trouble, it's me."

"I wasn't exactly an unwilling party," Ocelot reminded her as he gently placed a gloved hand to her cheek. The heat of her skin against the magical fabric sent a thrum of electricity through him, another indictor of how things had changed. "This will take some getting used to, though."

She sat back. "What, exactly, does *this* mean?"

Ocelot smiled and diverted from the actual answer — for now. "I suspect you already know."

"I—" Kate started before getting a strange look. "Holy *shit.*"

He smiled a bit wider as he felt her first tentative exploration of the connection that now existed between them. No words could adequately explain the glowing filament that stretched from his heart to hers; now that he knew what to look for, his keen vision could see how it hung there between them, a vibrant reminder they were joined in a way that was nearly impossible to break. Ocelot understood how it would complicate his alter-ego's ability to hide from her when necessary; still, his training in the jungle had included the appropriate magic for just such a situation. As he reluctantly withdrew his hand from her warm cheek, he also understood the strange purgatory he'd placed himself into, for it meant that Kate could never truly know who was under the mask. Revealing his identity to her before being released from his vow to Tezcatlipoca was a one-way ticket to an oblivion straight out of his worst nightmares.

"I'm sorry," he said simply. "This isn't exactly how I expected it would happen when the time came."

Kate cocked her head. "No," she said after a moment. "I can feel that. And... something else..."

Ocelot felt his face heat again, for he'd once more underestimated Kate's abilities and had left himself far too open. Hastily erecting some mental barriers around the truth she could not yet know, he simply nodded and deflected. "Yes."

Kate frowned. "Are you blocking me from seeing what it is?"

"Only until the time is right," he said.

Kate's frown deepened. "And who gets to decide *that*?"

"Someone *way* above my pay grade," he smiled.

"I'm not going to let this go."

"I would expect nothing less," he smiled wider before nodding at her house. "Would it be too much to ask for a cup of coffee?"

Kate rolled her eyes. "Are you trying to distract me?"

"Yes," he replied honestly.

She sighed. "Come on," she said as they stood. "I need to ask a favor, anyway."

He followed her through the sliding glass doors and immediately caught the smell of a freshly brewed carafe of coffee. Smiling, he waited patiently at the breakfast bar while she retrieved two mugs and filled them, then pushed one across the surface toward him. Ocelot gratefully accepted the beverage; sipping at the flavorful cup, his sharp eyes watched as Kate retrieved something from the oven and placed it on potholders she'd staged beside the sink. Surreptitiously sniffing at the air, his eyes widened slightly when he realized she'd actually baked cookies — oatmeal raisin, to be exact, with the surprising addition of semi-sweet chocolate bits. Pulling down a pair of plates from a cupboard beside the sink, she deftly grabbed several cookies and split them among the china, fanning her hand between trips ostensibly to offset the minor burns she was incurring in the process. Carrying the plates to the breakfast bar, she slid one toward him.

"My grandmother's secret recipe," she said as she nodded at the fragrant stack. "I thought you might want a snack after your travels."

He wasn't certain whether she'd detected over their shared connection that he was, actually, rather hungry; there were all sorts of costs to using his magic, with the most prominent one being how much energy it took. Smiling to cover his unease that she might know more than she was letting on, he reached for a cookie and made a show of sniffing it. "I'm not sure I should indulge; I have a figure to maintain, after all."

"Something tells me you burn more calories in your day than a normal human," Kate laughed. "One cookie won't kill you."

"Probably not."

Kate eyed him a moment longer. "Mated, eh?"

Ocelot nodded as he took a bite of the surprisingly good cookie. "With all that implies, yes."

Something flickered across her face as she considered what he'd said. "Well, so much for being wooed with roses and chocolates," Kate sighed. "I hated dating, anyway."

"Really?" he asked as he reached for a second cookie. The first had disappeared faster than anticipated.

"Yeah. Not really my thing."

"Maybe the right cat hadn't come along," Ocelot replied with a sly smile.

"Maybe," she smiled slightly. "So, I need a favor."

"I owe you at least that much," he nodded. "Name it."

"I want to break into Vasquez Industries."

Ocelot tried to look surprised despite expecting that particular ask. "It's a pretty big favor," he replied slowly. "Especially since the world headquarters for Vasquez Industries are not an easy place to gain access to, magic or not."

"You *have* gotten in before, haven't you?" she asked. "When you met with your mole there."

"Yes," he said after a long moment. The triumphant smile on her face told him he'd confirmed something for Kate. "Only on one occasion, though," he added. "And only after I hobbled their security system."

She looked at him. "I was told their software was undergoing an upgrade."

"It is," Ocelot said before smiling slyly. "There are all sorts of enhancements in the software, including a nice blind spot for someone to slip in and out undetected."

"You had a hand in that?" Kate asked before eying him.

He nodded. "Yes."

"Is that mask hiding a software engineer, or did you just whip up a spell?"

"I am a cat of many talents," he replied enigmatically.

"How on *earth* did you hack into their system?"

"The same way we got into the morgue," he answered. "Though the less you know about the *how*..."

"Good point," Kate agreed.

"What's so important that you need to get into Vasquez?" Sipping at the coffee, he eyed her. "Weren't you going to meet with your contact there, anyway? Can't they get what you need?"

"I did meet with Tenoch earlier today, but he wasn't as helpful as I think he wanted to be," she said.

Ocelot narrowed his masked eyes. "The son of the woman running the place is your contact?"

"Yes," she nodded. "He knows something — something he's not telling me."

"It might be more the case that he *can't* tell you," Ocelot offered. "He probably doesn't want to cross his mother."

"I don't blame him," Kate said. "She's a force of nature."

Not wanting to overplay his hand, Ocelot simply nodded. "The question remains, however. What's inside that building that you're asking me to help you do something that's quasi-illegal?"

"I think your mole there might have left behind some bread-crumbs," she replied. "Tenoch isn't in a position to help in discovering whether that's the case. I get the sense he knows how closely his movements are being watched."

"So you want to break in and, what, liberate the evidence?" Ocelot arched a masked eyebrow as a claw tapped against his ceramic mug. "How, exactly, would you explain that in court?"

"I don't know," she replied with a sigh. Reaching for her own cookie, she held it for a moment. "I need to wrap my arms around what we are dealing with; this might help jumpstart that understanding. If I have to pull it in later as evidence, we'll just have to find a creative way to do it."

"That doesn't sound very lawful to me," Ocelot observed. "Are you comfortable crossing that line?"

"No, I'm not," she replied. "I'm already halfway down that slippery slope, though, aren't I?"

"How do you mean?"

Kate smiled. "I'm working with a masked vigilante," she said. "Someone I willingly snuck into the Orange County Morgue and, frankly, allowed to tamper with the evidence we'd collected."

"Sebastian was only telling us what he knew and saw," Ocelot reminded her. "That's not *really* tampering — it was more like interviewing a witness, right?"

"No court would allow into evidence an interview obtained after the witness died, Ocelot."

"*Touché*," he laughed.

"Regardless," she continued, "I'm well outside of the normal boundaries already. What's one more transgression among friends?"

"Well, when you put it *that* way," Ocelot laughed as he dusted the crumbs from his gloves. "How can I refuse?"

"You'll do it?"

Ocelot held out his hand. "We can go tonight, *princesa*."

"I assumed it would take more to convince you to help," Kate said as she came around the counter and then took his hand. "Hence the dozen cookies."

"I would do anything for you," Ocelot said easily before realizing he'd slipped; he covered his gaffe with a grand bow. "Ready?"

"Does this ever get any easier?" she replied. The slight trepidation at going through a portal again seemed to have prevented Kate from picking up on his accidental admission.

"No," he answered honestly.

"Then I'm glad we're not doing it alone."

So am I, he thought as he squeezed her hand and then opened a portal.

TEN

The vertigo wasn't quite as bad for Kate the second time around, but she did find herself leaning against Ocelot for a moment once the world resolved itself around them. Blinking to clear the stars from her vision, she found that they were in the very stairwell Tenoch had used earlier that day; glancing around the space, she felt herself frowning for there didn't seem to be anything remotely reflective that would have worked with Ocelot's spell. Turning toward him, she started to ask the obvious question and then paused; her close proximity to the costumed hero seemed to be exacerbating the vertigo just a bit, a reminder that the strange undercurrent running between them had only continued to grow stronger. Closing her eyes for a moment, she replayed the conversation from her home and the emotions that had come with it; finding out her one-night-stand had actually been far, far more consequential was an unquestionable shock to her system, one that she was barely keeping a lid on. Just *how* consequential remained to be seen, but based on the nonverbal cues she kept seeing from

Ocelot, she knew there was far more to the story than what he'd told her.

And yet.

Tugging slightly on the unseen gossamer thread that seemed to connect the two of them now, she found herself becoming less surprised at his immediate response; the unusual feeling they were two parts of a new whole would take some getting used to, for sure, but there was a strange comfort in now knowing she would never truly be alone any longer. The feelings that brought to the surface were hard to describe; the only other time she'd felt something close had been those final months with Tenoch before the prom. After his abrupt disappearance, she'd written them off as a typical teenager-in-love nonsense, but now, feeling the gentle warmth of Ocelot's body through his costume, she realized those feelings had been very real. Years of being a detective had made Kate rather cynical when it came to concepts around love and relationships; still, the odds that someone would come along and recapture her soul a *second time* felt impossibly long — long enough that maybe, just *maybe*, she found herself believing that deities existed and were completely capable of righting the wrongs of the past.

Opening her eyes again, she saw Ocelot's masked brown eyes watching her with concern. "Are you okay?"

"Yes," she nodded. "I think I'm still digesting all of this."

"It's a lot to take in," he nodded.

Kate waved to the stairwell. "This isn't what I expected," she said. "I thought you needed a mirror to transport yourself."

"I need a reflective surface," he corrected. "A mirror is always nice but is sometimes a luxury."

"Then how—"

"The reflector in the florescent lights," Ocelot interrupted as he pointed a claw tip to a fixture hanging just above them.

Kate squinted. "That seems awfully small."

Ocelot shrugged. "I don't need much. You saw the size of the puddle I used at the rail yard."

"Huh," she muttered before seeing the floor indicator beside the door they were standing next to. "I don't suppose you can tell if anyone is on the other side of that door?"

She watched as his eyes focused on something only he could see; the frown that appeared underscored what he said. "Damn. The security guard is actually doing rounds tonight."

Kate groaned. "Reyna must have suspected something," she said softly as she glanced at the door. "Tenoch took me this far earlier today, but we were intercepted by her before he could get into Sebastian's office."

Ocelot arched a masked eyebrow. "That's a bit of a leap to suggest she anticipated a break in this evening."

"You don't know her like I do," Kate said darkly. "I wouldn't put it past her to spy on her son; she was epitome of a helicopter parent when we were growing up."

"Sounds like you have some serious history with Tenoch," Ocelot said carefully.

Kate turned, for she'd detected just a hint of iciness in the otherwise neutral statement. "Jealousy doesn't suit you, Ocelot," she said.

"What—me? Jealous? Hardly," he replied with a hasty laugh before eyeing her. "Unless I have a reason to be. Is he encroaching on my territory?"

"We were a thing years ago," Kate replied. "I thought he was dead until he magically appeared in my life again this week." Her eyes narrowed when she realized what Ocelot had said. "Despite what you might think, I'm not something to be owned or traded between lovers."

That slight flaming to his cheeks appeared again, darkening his already chocolate-colored complexion another hue. "That's not what I meant," he said, masked eyes widening. "I mean, not really—"

Kate felt her eyebrows go up. "Not *really*? What the hell is that supposed to mean?"

Ocelot's cheeks went crimson. "I think I'm digging myself a bit of a hole here," he said weakly. "Maybe we could discuss this in more depth later?"

"Agreed," Kate replied tightly.

Her anger was tempered slightly by the strange wave of feelings flooding the connection between them; it was clear Ocelot was very worried about what he had said, enough that the barriers she'd felt him erect around their connection had crumbled slightly. Before she realized what she was doing, her investigative mind took the opportunity to probe a bit further, and immediately felt herself enveloped by a deep sense of fear — but not one generated by their current activity. No, it was something else, something far more elemental and intense; pulling at the thread, Kate tried to follow it to the source only to suddenly feel the mental barriers crash down around the connection once more. Blinking, Kate found herself staring at a very uncomfortable Ocelot, mute confirmation that she'd stumbled into something he'd desperately not wanted her to know about.

Deciding it might be best for both of them to simply ignore what had just happened, Kate nodded back at the door to the hallway. "What are we going to do about the guard?"

Looking a bit relieved, Ocelot's face took on a sly expression. "Wait here."

Kate put a hand to his costumed bicep, arresting his movement. "You're not going to hurt them, right?"

Ocelot smiled dangerously. "While I am a predator, *princesa*, you of all people should know that the last thing we need right now is another dead body."

A slight thrill of terror whisked up her spine at his facial expression; it didn't take much to imagine a far deadlier side to her companion than the one she'd gotten to know. The certainty she had felt at knowing the kind of person hiding behind the mask suddenly felt a little less so; a sense of having rushed into something a bit precipitously was tingling at the back of her mind, right beside that very alive and very vibrant reminder she was connected to this stranger in ways far more intimate than she could have ever imagined possible.

What have I done? she asked herself. *And what the fuck is yet to come?*

Feeling more than a little unsettled, Kate tried to hide it behind the professional mask she often used when dealing with her peers. Ocelot seemed to sense her shift and stiffened slightly when she finally spoke, hearing an unintentional rebuke in her terse reply. "Agreed."

"Wait here," he said again before simply vanishing.

Unsure of what to expect, Kate crept toward the door and pressed her ear to it; unsurprisingly, there wasn't much to hear beyond the low hum of the building's HVAC equipment in the background. The truth was Kate didn't do waiting well; after a few seconds of consideration, she carefully put her hand to the latch and gently pulled the door open just enough to be able to see into the corridor beyond. She nearly jumped when the entire view was taken up by a particularly handsome man in a feline costume. Ocelot pushed the door open further, exposing his knowing grin fully.

"I figured you'd get impatient," he said quietly. "Come on, the coast is clear."

Kate eyed him as she stepped in the corridor. "What did you do?"

The knowing smile turned a bit sly. "Are you sure you want to know?"

"I suppose not."

Kate pulled out her phone and scrolled through the notes she'd made earlier that afternoon; while Tenoch hadn't given her an explicit office number, she had combed through the official website for Vasquez Industries and learned the Operations Department was in room 240. Taking her bearings, she started down the left side of the corridor, then glanced at Ocelot who had taken up position beside her. It wasn't lost on Kate that while he had adopted his usual air of nonchalance, his eyes were very carefully scanning every square inch of space, nor the fact that he was taking pains to be a half step in front of her. The sense that he was intentionally ensuring he'd be able to shield her from anything they might encounter was more than a little insulting, considering she was a police officer — enough so that she attempted to lengthen her stride. To her frustration, he matched her step-for-step.

Ocelot glanced at her. "For the record, he's not dead. I whipped up a distraction that sent him to the executive suite; we have about ten minutes at most before he returns."

"What kind of distraction?" Kate asked, oddly curious. "For the record."

They came to a junction in the corridor; Kate followed the small, numbered placards beside the doors and turned left again. As they walked, she got the sense they were close to the exterior of the building, though without any windows, it was hard to know for sure. It was also quite clear that the sense of style she'd seen in the executive suite hadn't been extended to the rest of the building; the off-white walls of the corridor and standard industrial carpet would have looked perfect in a hundred other corporate offices. Kate wondered if it was a reflection of how Reyna felt about her employees.

"Malfunctioning smoke alarm in the men's room," Ocelot said, his eyes still scanning the hallway.

The proper room number finally appeared beside a set of double doors, ending any further inquiry. Kate's eyes narrowed when she saw the small badge reader with its glowing red indicator. Despite knowing it was fruitless, she nonetheless reached for the handle and confirmed the obvious. "Damn."

"This is the spot?" Ocelot asked.

"Well," Kate replied grudgingly, "I *think* so. I don't have the specific office number Sebastian was working out of, but this is the department he was a part of."

Ocelot nodded, which seemed to loosen a bang of his long hair from the leather thong. He ignored it as he knelt to look at the badge reader. "I should be able to do something with this," he said as he pressed a gloved hand to the device. "Hang on."

She watched as his mouth moved, silently making some sort of incantation; a fraction of a second later, the light flipped to green and the door in front of them clicked open. Kate pushed through without any hesitation and then was brought up short by an arm to her shoulder. She glared over her shoulder at Ocelot, who looked genuinely concerned. "What the—" she started before he quickly put a finger to her lips.

"Cameras," he whispered while pointing with a claw to the bubble-shaped devices hanging at intervals between the overhead lights. "With audio. None are affected by the bug in the security software."

Kate reconsidered her moment of ire — and pressed herself into what little protection the entrance alcove was providing. "Oh," she said just as quietly. "I wasn't thinking. Thanks."

He nodded. "I'm obviously not a huge fan of surveillance," he continued. "But this firm seems to take it to a new level."

"They certainly don't seem to trust their people, that's for sure. Can you obscure us from them?"

"Already doing so," he replied easily, "but it's not foolproof. Someone looking carefully at the tape will be able to see the negative void I'm creating."

The tension in Ocelot's voice told Kate how much effort it was taking to weave whatever spell he was using; the clock was now clearly ticking. "Then we'd better be quick."

He nodded. "Which way?"

That's a good question, Kate thought as she eyed the cubicle farm they had stepped into. Multiple rows stretched out between the two of them and a set of windows that showed little beyond confirming it was still dark outside. "This department is far bigger than I expected."

"Maybe I can narrow things down a bit," Ocelot whispered.

Whatever anger she'd felt toward him a few minutes earlier had melted into concern. "Are you sure?" she asked. "You still need to get us out of here--"

"Yes," he replied, cutting her off.

Kate simply nodded.

Ocelot held his hand up and snapped his gloved fingers again, opening that strange whorl of energy he'd used to stash his burner phone; Kate's eyes widened when he reached in and pulled out a small notebook. Seeing her questioning look, Ocelot smiled slightly. "This is one of many notebooks Sebastian shared with me while we were working together," he said. "It should have enough of his *alma* on it to use as a tracker."

Kate's Spanish was good enough that she recognized the term for *soul.* "It's worth a shot," she said, though it was hard to hide her skepticism.

Ocelot ignored her and instead focused on the notebook; Kate realized she was beginning to get used to his parlor tricks when the small notebook rose into the air on its own and it didn't even phase her. Ocelot leaned close to the spiral binding and whispered to it: "*Vete a casa!*"

The small book rotated for a moment, then very slowly started down the narrow aisle directly in front of them. Kate waited for Ocelot to take off behind it before following; much like any decent digital navigation software, the notebook deftly picked the shortest path and ultimately came to rest in front of an otherwise nondescript cubicle three-quarters of the way down the aisle. Unlike most corporations she had visited, Kate was surprised to see that no name was hanging on the dull fabric of the cubicle; scanning the rest of the aisle, she quickly determined none were identified at all. Sliding into the cramped space behind her companion, Kate noted that the desk was similarly austere save for a small orchid beside the computer monitor; leaning closer, she was duly impressed when she discovered it was comprised entirely of LEGOs. Her eyes flicked to the bottle of water sitting beside it, unopened and forever doomed to wait for its owner to return.

"This is the spot," Ocelot said with a certainty Kate didn't feel. "What are we looking for?"

"You'd know better than I," Kate said. "He was your mole, not mine."

"True," he nodded. "So we want the files he created connecting the dots on the trafficking ring. Once we have that—"

"We'll have a better sense of why he was killed," Kate finished. Scanning the cubicle, her eyes landed on a small lateral filing cabinet. "I'll check the physical files."

"And I'll see what's on his computer," Ocelot said as he pulled out the office chair and sat down at the keyboard.

The image of the feline-themed hero-in-training tapping away at the computer was not one Kate would soon forget; smiling slightly, she pulled open the top drawer of the lateral and began scanning the manilla folders. Most seemed to hold duplicate shipping manifests dating back ten years, though when she flipped through them, none dealt with any sort of routes going through Central or South America. Kate began to suspect that geographic region wasn't part of Sebastian's purview when the second drawer had even older records dealing mostly with items going to and from Canada. Standing up with a heavy sigh, Kate began to go through the files that were carefully stacked on the work surface; she finally hit pay dirt in the final folder on the bottom of the stack, the only one holding a shipping manifest that included waypoints in Oaxaca and Santa Marcel. Sliding the paperwork out, she began to flip through pages of the form; while most of it was Greek to her, at the very least the dates lined up with the arrival of the container that had held the women Ocelot had rescued.

"I've got something," she whispered as she placed the paperwork back on the desk.

"Same," Ocelot replied. "Take a look at this."

Kate stood behind Ocelot and looked over his shoulder, trying — and failing — to ignore how potent his sandalwood scent was in such close proximity. "How on Earth did you hack into his computer?" she asked when she realized the feline was logged into the main system for Vasquez Industries.

Ocelot let out a quiet laugh and then held up a tiny yellow sticky note. "Password was under the keyboard."

"Damn," Kate chuckled softly. "Internal security won't like that."

"Nor the fact that it wasn't changed when he left their employment." Ocelot tapped at the screen with a claw. "I found the manifest I think you were just reading," he continued. "It aligns with twenty-six identical such shipments over the past year."

Kate felt like someone had just gut punched her. "Twenty-six?"

"Yeah," he confirmed.

"Definitely not a one off," Kate said. "Do we know who's paying for these shipments?"

Ocelot shook his head and changed screens on the computer. "Sebastian seems to have been attempting to do just that, though his spreadsheet is incomplete. Barely a third of these transactions had been mapped, and of those, I'm seeing six different firms from four countries listed."

"Probably shell companies," Kate groused. "Damn."

"It's a start," Ocelot reminded her.

"True."

Ocelot's claw traced a number of lines on the spreadsheet, most of which were outlined in green; he stopped when the claw hit a section in yellow. "These three are in progress; this particular container is due here in Santa Marcel next week. Cross referenced with the manifest system, I can see it belongs to one of the six firms Sebastian identified."

"Shit. Can we stop it? Can *you* stop it?"

"Maybe," he murmured. "Let me download the GPS tracker—"

Kate found herself ducking below the surface of the desk when the overhead lights winked out and were immediately replaced by emergency lights of deep red; a blaring klaxon began to fill the space, loud enough to wake the dead. Her initial thought that the fire alarm had been triggered was immediately squashed when a computer-generated voice began to speak over unseen speakers in the ceiling.

"*Intruder alert, crimson level. Intruder alert, crimson level. All exits fortified, all units activated. Intruder alert, crimson level...*"

"That can't be good," Kate whispered to Ocelot. He had similarly ducked for cover, but not before yanking something from the side of the monitor. "Did they discover us?"

Ocelot's eyes were unfocused. "She knows I'm here," he said quietly. "I've got to get you out of here."

"She? She *who*?"

"I'll explain later," he said. Under the strange shadows of the red emergency lighting, his expression looked extremely grave. Pressing what appeared to be a USB stick into her hands, he leaned closer. "Share this with no one. I'll be on your fence tomorrow night at ten to go over everything."

"Ocelot—"

Ignoring her, Ocelot began to frantically scan the small cubicle;

his eyes finally found the bottle of water, which he reached over and yanked from the work surface. Holding it up slightly, he frowned before turning to Kate. "This might be a bit rough."

Before she had a chance to object, the world around her went wild.

ELEVEN

U nsurprisingly, Tenoch wasn't able to use his badge to get out of the Operations Department. While he was tempted — sorely tempted — to use an alternative method to avoid his mother's wrath, he was well aware that he had once again pushed himself beyond the limit and had nothing left in the tank to even try. The nausea wasn't as bad as it usually was, though, so there was that; the pounding behind his eyes also seemed less intense, but the deep ache in every single muscle of his body was about the same as usual. Wanting nothing more than to curl up into a ball in the corner of the entrance alcove and sleep off the worst of the effects, Tenoch instead pulled himself together and tried to carefully consider how to proceed. Thankfully, the robotic announcement had finally quit, and along with it, the blaring klaxon that had not helped his headache. The deep red emergency lighting was the only clue that the building was still on lockdown, a state that would only be lifted after every square inch on every single floor had been thoroughly searched and cleared. By the time the head of security came through the double doors to the department, Tenoch had a plan and was more than ready to face the music.

The grim expression on the stocky woman belied any chance of talking his way out of the inevitable meeting with his mother; resigned to his fate, he fell into step behind her and tried not to take it personally when two more guards took up position behind him as though he was some sort of common cat burglar. They walked to the elevator lobby and then waited for the head to badge open one of the carriages; the ride to the executive suite was short and ended with the doors pulling open to reveal the very unamused face of his mother.

"*Mijo*, with me."

He simply nodded and followed her down the wide hallway; to his surprise, instead of heading into her office, she continued into his, pushing the door open and then standing back to allow him to enter. Despite being relatively certain of what was coming next, he was still unprepared when the vines encircled his torso, lifted him up and then sent him flying across the room, crashing face-first into his desk. The delicate glass shattered on impact, scattering glittering pieces across the Saltillo of the floor in all directions. His cheek stung where it had been cut by the shards; the pain in his hands as he instinctively tried to push himself up confirmed he'd done similar damage there, too. Rolling to his right, he narrowly missed being caught by a second tendril, but he wasn't fast enough to avoid the third; slammed into his bookcase, he felt a rib crack along with the shelf holding his prized collection of Disneyland antiques. Sliding to the floor, he winced with pain when he tried to take a deep breath, and immediately gripped his side in anguish.

He felt more than saw his mother come to stand in front of him. "I'm only going to ask this once," she said, her tone similar to when she was dressing down a member of the board during a meeting. "Did that detective give you the name of the whistleblower?"

Gritting his teeth against the pain, Tenoch forced himself to lock his eyes onto his mother's. "That detective has a name, *madre*," he said. "And she's interested in the same thing I've been warning you about for months."

"I don't give a damn what she wants," she replied. "Do you know who the whistleblower is?"

Tenoch nodded. "Sebastian Montclair."

She looked at him for a long moment, then stepped away. He followed her movements while trying to ignore just how painful it was to breathe. "I'll have HR fire him in the morning."

"Aside from how illegal that is in California — not to mention multiple Federal laws — that would be rather difficult, since he's lying in the Orange County Morgue currently."

She turned and looked at him. "When?"

Despite his dampened abilities, Tenoch thought he felt a slight undercurrent of deception in the air but decided to play along. "A few nights ago, according to Detective Oliver. He has been tentatively identified as the victim from the rail yard."

"I didn't think there was enough left of the body for that," she said.

"Modern science is amazing," Tenoch said with no trace of irony. "I presume I triggered something when I was searching his computer this evening?"

His mother smiled but there was no trace of humor behind it. "You might be close to ascension, but you still haven't mastered the basics, *mijo*. Getting into the building undetected was one thing, but trying to erase your presence in real time attracted all of the wrong attention." She crossed her arms. "Was she here with you tonight?"

"Who?" he asked as he braced for her inevitable response.

Multiple thick vines studded with small versions of the orchid she favored encircled his body nearly from head-to-toe and immediately began to squeeze; unable to catch his breath nor wiggle so much as his little toe, he saw the darkness creeping in at the edge of his vision. As his body was lifted from the floor once more and then slammed into one wall, then another, Tenoch had an insane moment of clarity; punishment for transgressions at all levels of the Vasquez family had long bordered on the inhumane, making his fellow schoolmates' complaints of being grounded seem like country club vacations by comparison. It took every last ounce of his training to withstand the assault; when she finally released him and he sagged against the wall of his office, breathing hard, he knew he'd not be able to go another round. Still, he met her eyes once more, mustering up as much defiance as he could while also trying to ignore the searing pain of his injuries.

"Was she here with you tonight?" she asked again.

Stick as close to the truth as you can when lying, he thought. "I've not mastered secondary reflective transport, *madre* — at least, not fully. So if she *had* been here with me, you'd have found her, too." Tenoch paused. "Since we're having this conversation, I am going to assume you've not found Kate. Or anyone else besides me."

She eyed him. "No, we haven't."

Tenoch nodded. Every muscle felt like rubber, but he pushed through the lethargy and managed to get back onto his feet. The look of respect that garnered him from his mother was a nice side benefit. "I'm going home."

"How? Your car isn't in the lot. Which begs the question as to *why* you wanted to enter our place of business undetected."

He stared at her. "To avoid this very situation," he said coldly. "At least, until I had enough information to bring to you — I mean, you *were* the one to assign me this task, weren't you?"

She looked at him. "I suppose I did."

"You didn't stipulate *how* I was to investigate, either," he continued. "Digging through one of our employee's files during business hours would have raised suspicions, *madre*. By coming in after hours, and trying to go undetected, I was acting in the best interests of our firm."

"I suppose you were," she grudgingly admitted. "Maybe you *have* learned a thing or two."

The rebuke stung more than it should have, but Tenoch managed not to react. "Good night, *madre*," he said as he mustered up what was left of his dignity and exited his office.

Every step was agony, but Tenoch managed to stay upright and reach the executive elevator; stepping inside, he waited until the double doors sighed shut before sagging against the rear of the carriage. Acutely aware of the camera in the elevator, and more than a little concerned that his personal phone was also now being tracked, he knew there was only one failsafe way for him to contact Kate without attracting undue attention. And he was *genuinely* worried about her, for he'd not been lying about his difficulties mastering the finer intricacies of reflective transport. There was a real chance Kate might have landed in Versailles' Hall of Mirrors instead of her small home; as the doors sighed open to reveal the executive parking lot, Tenoch pushed himself away from the wall and slowly walked out into the night, determined to make good on his promise.

Pulling out his iPhone, he made a show for the cameras covering that portion of the property of looking as though he were calling for an Uber, then walked as fast as he could manage down the access road to the main thoroughfare that ran past the building. Despite knowing he was running on fumes — not to mention having to cradle what he suspected was a seriously fractured rib — Tenoch kept up appearances long enough to walk as far as a particular cluster of bushes just around the corner from Vasquez Industries. As late as it was, there was no traffic to speak of; still, he waited a heart-beat before pushing into the undergrowth to reach a somewhat secluded spot several yards from the sidewalk that opened onto the small brook that ran through that part of the city. An artifact of the County's water reclamation project, it had long suited his purposes as an emergency transit point when the office wasn't a viable option. Taking shallow breaths to try and avoid the pain from the rib, Tenoch grimaced slightly as he knelt by the brook and then leaned over so he could see what little of his reflection as was visible on such a dark night.

Closing his eyes, Tenoch whispered the phrase that only a handful of people had ever uttered, then braced himself for what he knew would be an unusually painful transformation into his alter ego. Considering how badly his body had been battered, and how much of his energy had *already* been used that evening, he was more than a little surprised when he reopened his eyes and saw his masked visage staring back at him. The adrenaline rush that came from becoming Ocelot momentarily chased away the worst of the pain from his fractured rib, but taking a tentative deep breath told him he was still wounded and would continue to be until he took the time to cast a proper healing spell. Sorting through his mental catalog of triage spells designed to patch warriors up while on the battlefield, he hit on one and then carefully stood; running his gloved hands carefully over the damaged rib — and trying not to gasp at the pain when he touched the very visible bump that even the magic couldn't hide — he muttered the proper phrases in just the right cadence and was rewarded when a brilliant electric blue glow began to emanate from his palms. Gritting his teeth, he quickly pressed both palms down on the wounded rib, hard, and immediately let out a visceral scream of pain as the magic sizzled through his injury. Ocelot had used that particular spell more times than he cared to admit during his time in the jungle, and knew the results were nearly instantaneous; pulling his hands away from his torso, he took a tentative deep breath, then another. By the fourth it was clear the worst of the damage had been repaired; twisting one way, then the other confirmed he'd restored nearly full movement with only a minor after echo of the pain that had once existed.

Squatting next to the brook again, he scooped out a handful of water and tossed it on his face, then ran his wet fingers up and through the long black hair he'd chosen as part of his disguise. Glancing once more at his reflection on the surface of the brook, he wondered for a moment where that extra little bit of stamina had come from; by rights, he should have completely crashed after his prior exertions, so pulling off the healing spell had him arching one of his masked eyebrows. Looking up at the sky, he wondered how badly he had miscalculated the *tonalphualli*, for it certainly felt as though he was far closer to attaining his full powers than he had realized.

I'll have to check the algorithm when I get home, he thought. *First things first: I need to check on Kate.*

Now that he had his night vision, the forest around him had burst into full resolution; the shifting colors of the brook told him how fast the current was running through that part of its course, much as the subtle shades of darkness indicated the relative leaf cover he had from the canopy above him. As forests went, it was pretty typical for California — which was another way of saying that, unlike the jungles where he had trained, there was very little cover even for someone wearing a magical costume capable of blending into nearly anything. Glancing back toward the road, Ocelot extended his senses with a slight bit of magical help and determined no one had decided to pursue him from the headquarters of Vasquez Industries; stretching his magical muscle just a bit more confirmed the nearest traffic along the route was a good three kilometers away and heading in the opposite direction.

Dipping his head back to the brook, he began to trail a claw along the surface of the bubbling water, slowly drawing a circle of calmness in the current. By the second circuit, a slight purple phosphorescence began to trail in the wake of his act; by the tenth, he was able to carefully pull his hand back and watch the purple line continue on its own, increasing in speed with each passing moment. The pool of water that had been captured by his actions became still, then crystal clear a moment before filling with a smokiness that hid the small rocks at the bottom of the creek.

Show me what I want to see, he thought with a passion he normally reserved for more complicated incantations. *Show me the one that I love. Show me so I can know she is safe.*

Crouched over the becalmed spot in the brook, his eyes remained locked on the fog within the water; it seemed to take forever, but at length, the fog dissipated in stages to ultimately reveal a lopsided view of a bed. Frowning, he leaned a bit closer and tried to divine what he was seeing, for it didn't seem to be any location he'd yet been in with Kate. While he was aware the observation spell wasn't an exact science (so to speak), Ocelot knew it was one that he wielded particularly well; he wondered if his feelings for Kate — and their new shared connection — had disrupted his abilities in a way that he'd not expected. Scanning what little of the room he could see, he frowned deeper.

Sitting back, he gave a gentle tug to the gossamer connection he shared with Kate... and got nothing back. As he was still negotiating the privacy implications of sharing his consciousness with someone else — someone who still needed to be blocked from parts of his mind that he couldn't share with her yet — Ocelot had avoided reaching out to Kate beyond just knowing she was there at the other end. Tugging harder, he felt a sluggishness that gave him great pause.

Something's wrong, he thought as he looked back into the small circle showing him a portion of a bed. *Where the fuck did I send her? She might be in trouble—*

Without giving it a further thought, Ocelot reached his hand into the small circle, instantly converting it to a portal; the cost of doing a transit in his current condition was more then he realized, though, which made his exit at the other end somewhat less than elegant. Smacking the top of his head against something hard only added insult to injury; bright stars swam at the edge of his night vision, rendering it nearly useless for a few heartbeats. Blinking hard against both the stars and a new source of pain, Ocelot found himself on a rather nice berber carpet, his back against the footboard of what appeared to be a queen-sized bed. Rubbing at his scalp, he thought he could hear voices beyond the door of the room; he tried to use his magic to get a sense of what was out there, but was met instead with a telling wave of nausea. Swallowing the bile rising at the back of his throat, he crawled to the door and cracked it open; the second wave of nausea warned him that the crash he thought he had avoided earlier would not be denied, but like any good feline, he *had* to know what had happened to Kate.

Pulling open the door just enough to slip out, Ocelot pressed his back to the wall of the short hallway he was in, thankful that the only source of light seemed to be from something small at the other end. Creeping with one hand against the textured surface, he slowly worked his way in that direction, straining what was left of his enhanced senses to their max. Only when the hallway emptied into a very familiar living room with a stationary bicycle pointed toward the wall of glass for the patio did Ocelot begin to breathe normally; his heart did a funny *thumpa thump* when he saw Kate completely zonked out on the couch, covered in a quilt bearing the logo for the Rams and facing a television tuned to one of the cable news networks. His puzzlement at why he couldn't feel her gave way to understanding when his feline eyes fell upon the wineglass on the coffee table; the empty bottle of red surprised him, though, for it hadn't felt like he'd been with his *madre* for more than a few minutes. Then again, he of all people knew that time wasn't always linear at Vasquez Industries.

Well, that's one mystery solved, he thought.

Feeling slightly like he had intruded — okay, there was no *slightly* about it — Ocelot carefully withdrew and crept back to the bedroom. The third wave of nausea was nearly impossible to hold back, banishing any thoughts of a quick escape via the small mirror he'd apparently used to enter Kate's home. The window beside her bed was just big enough for him to carefully slip through, though he grimaced a bit at the inadvertent grooves his claws made in the soft plaster of the exterior. He managed to get to the small hedge growing along her portion of the sidewalk before being forced to drop to his knees so he could puke his guts out; he'd gotten to the dry heaves part of the program when the light beside Kate's front door burst into life.

Shit, he thought.

Quickly scrambling away from the light, he tried — and failed — on his first attempt to cast a cloaking shield around himself; pressing into the hedge, he tried again, ignoring the creeping blackness at the edge of his vision that served as final warning that his body was close to shutting down. The third try proved to be his undoing; the moment he uttered the final phrase, he felt himself collapse completely to the slightly soggy lawn as though he were a balloon that had suddenly burst. As the darkness overwhelmed him, the last thing he thought he heard was the door to Kate's house swinging open...

TWELVE

Kate awoke with a start; heart beating in her ears, she quickly took stock of her familiar surroundings and felt slightly chagrined that she'd dozed off on the couch again. Glaring accusingly at the talking head on her television screen that was running down the latest insanity going on in Washington, D.C., she reached for the remote and turned it off, plunging the room into welcome silence. Pulling back the quilt she'd been snuggling under, she frowned when she saw it was well past midnight; while she'd not expected Ocelot to reach out to her that evening, no small part of her had hoped he would if for no other reason than to let her know he'd gotten himself out of Vasquez Industries in one piece. Glaring at her iPhone didn't get her anywhere, nor did dialing the number he'd given her.

He's fine, she told herself as she stood and folded up the quilt. *I'm sure he had other things to do tonight; getting back to me wasn't really a priority no matter how I feel about it.*

Sighing, she stared at the pattern on the quilt for a moment and tried to focus on that strange sensation that represented her connection to Ocelot. Probing it slightly, she *thought* she could feel some-thing at the other end of the line (as it were) but had no clue what it meant or what to do about it. Snapping off the light, she gathered herself and then made her way in the dark toward her bedroom; she'd need a few hours of rest if she had any hope of getting through the next day of digging into the info she'd gathered during their clandestine mission.

The door to her bedroom was closed when she reached it; while not unusual, she felt herself frowning slightly, for she *thought* she'd left it open after changing into her comfy clothes to begin her futile vigil. Pushing the door open, she took a step into the room and immediately had the overwhelming sense that Ocelot was nearby — and in trouble. Kate's pulse kicked up a few beats as she reached for the switch to the overhead light; a quick scan of the room confirmed she was completely alone, and yet a significant portion of her brain was nearly screaming the opposite. With all evidence to the contrary, Kate decided the craziness of the week had finally caught up with her and began to head to the master bath to get ready for bed. Only then did she notice that the window beside her bed was cracked open, enough that the curtain was billowing slightly; that *was* unusual since she, like most Southern Californians, was a creature of year-round air conditioning. Redirecting from the bathroom, she started to push the sash down and then paused.

If I didn't open then, who did?

Shifting slightly, she pulled open the drawer to the nightstand and grabbed her flashlight, then after a moment's thought, went to the gun safe and retrieved her service Glock. Snapping on the light, she moved deliberately back down the hallway and then to her front door; turning on the lights for her foreyard, she yanked open the door and stepped out into her small front yard, flashlight held high enough that she could quickly sweep it across the largest area possible. The sound of violent retching reached her ears before she'd gone more than a few yards; while familiar, the knot of dread that twisted in her gut spoke to a different fear suddenly taking hold. Pausing, she *thought* she heard rustling close to the hedge along the sidewalk and immediately shifted her light in that direction. Had she not been looking for it, the slight shimmer of a reflection would have been easily missed; Kate sprinted across the short expanse of her front lawn and dropped to her knees just beside the prone form of Ocelot. Based on the angle of his body, it wasn't a stretch to deduce he'd been trying to stay out of sight; the puddle of acrid-smelling vomit just beside him had her setting the Glock down so she could search for a pulse.

As she pressed her fingers to a spot just above the raised neckline for his costume, Kate quickly felt the fast but steady beat of his heart and sent up a silent prayer of thanks to whatever deity Ocelot worked for. The insanely hot temperature of his skin was more worrisome; combined with the strange series of cuts on the exposed skin beneath his domino mask that spoke to some sort of fight he'd been in, Kate risked doing a quick examination of the rest of his form. Careful to keep her touch light, it wasn't difficult to find the sizable lump halfway down his ribcage, nor to note how his unconscious body tried to pull away from her when she delicately probed to determine the full extent of the injury. Sitting back on her haunches, Kate felt the first shiver of fear pass down her spine; for whatever reason, she'd assumed Ocelot's magic would prevent him from getting hurt, physically or otherwise. It also didn't help that her heart was reading into the fact that he'd found his way back to her in his moment of need; so much for taking slow steps in their fledgling relationship.

"What the fuck happened to you?" Kate whispered, knowing the insensate form would provide no answers. At least, not immediately.

Setting down the flashlight, Kate managed to find a use for the quarterly emergency responder training the department forced everyone through; her fitness regimen made it barely possible to lug Ocelot's inert form to her front door unaided but getting him to the spare bedroom was more than she could handle. Kate settled for slowly dragging him to the couch and then getting him arranged on the cushions, careful to keep him from lying on what she now suspected was a severely fractured rib. Kneeling by his head, she pushed back his unruly hair and pressed the back of her hand to what little forehead was exposed beyond the domino mask; she wasn't a nurse by any stretch, but it was pretty clear Ocelot was running a significant fever.

Fortunately, she knew someone who was.

Pulling out her iPhone, she dialed the number for her mother and then berated herself for doing so as the line rang. She was on the cusp of hanging up when she heard the warm and familiar voice at the other end. "Honey? Is everything all right?"

"It's my... boyfriend. He's—" Kate started, then paused, wondering how much she could say without accidentally spilling a secret that wasn't hers to share. "He's—" she tried again, only to find herself oddly choked up. *Keep it together!* she thought before finally saying: "I need help."

Her mom, as always, immediately read between the lines. "How badly is he hurt?"

"Lacerations on the face," Kate replied, suddenly feeling a weight lifting. "And I think a broken rib. He's also hot to the touch — I think he's got a fever."

There was a tellingly long pause. "I'm guessing taking him to the emergency room is not an option."

"It wouldn't be my first choice, no," Kate admitted. "If you can walk me through what I need to do—"

"Let me grab my bag and I'll be there in twenty," her mother said, cutting her off. "Run a washcloth under cold water and apply it to his forehead; you might have to change it a few times before I get there. It'll help a bit with the fever."

"Mom—"

"No arguments. I'll be there as quick as I can."

Kate stared at her phone for a few heartbeats, unaccustomed to having her mother hang up on her. Sliding it back into the pocket of her sweatpants, she wondered for a fraction of a second what sort of Pandora's box she had just opened before retrieving a stack of washcloths from the small hall closet. Taking a slight bit of initiative, she pulled out a mixing bowl and filled it with tap water, then carefully stuffed all but one of the washcloths into it before sliding the whole mess into her fridge; the last one she ran a beneath the tap and then returned to the living room cradling it so she wouldn't leave a trail of water behind her. Carefully pushing Ocelot's hair back from his forehead again, she gently placed the folded cloth against his skin, hoping for some sign that it had an immediate effect on her patient. When none were forthcoming, she decided she had time to retrieve her Glock from the front yard and return it to the gun safe in her bedroom. After checking — and changing — the first washcloth, Kate bowed to the inevitable and plugged in her coffeemaker to brew a full pot. It wouldn't be the first time either she or her mother pulled an all nighter; she figured the super premium beans she grabbed from the cabinet might go a long way toward apologizing for pulling her mother out of bed. At the very least, the bottle of Baileys Irish Cream she carefully set beside the chuffing machine would be viewed as a peace offering.

The pot had just finished brewing when there was a quiet knock at her front door; Kate unlocked it and smiled slightly when her mother quickly brushed past her and asked with no preamble: "Where?"

"Couch."

Her mother nodded and disappeared around the corner; Kate

had to hustle to keep up. The fact that she was still attired in the blue scrubs she typically wore while working at the Santa Marcel Emergency Room told Kate that Nora Oliver had likely pulled a double again, something she did with alarming regularity. Pausing at the edge of the couch, she put her small medical bag down on the coffee table, unzipped it, and then retrieved a standard stethoscope that she quickly placed into her ears. Kneeling, she gently pressed the business end in several locations on Ocelot's chest; the frown Kate saw worried her, but before she could ask what was wrong, her mother shifted and placed the circular end against the skin of his neck. The frown shifted into a look of confusion as she pulled the stethoscope from her ears.

"The fabric of whatever he's wearing is muffling his chest sounds, but the pulse is strong. I'll need to get this off him so I can do a proper exam," she added before carefully running her hands along the neck of Ocelot's costume. "Is there a zipper or something?"

"Not that I have ever seen," Kate hedged, hoping her mother wouldn't press her on *why*.

The way Nora tried to tug at the edge of the collar told Kate that hope was in vain. "This almost feels like it's been glued to the skin - I can't even get a fingernail under the edge," she observed before turning to look at her daughter. "No wonder you didn't want to take him to the emergency room."

Her mother's slight knowing smile made Kate's face flame. "It's not what you think," she said.

Nora stood and went over to Kate. "And what, exactly, *would* I be thinking?" she asked softly as she put her hands on Kate's shoulders. "You're a decorated police officer covertly caring for a masked, banged up hunk of a guy twice in the same week. There aren't a ton of explanations that cover that; half of them involve kinky sex, which I'm reasonably sure you're not into—"

Kate's face felt like it was on fire, and she wanted nothing more than to crawl underneath said couch. "Mom!"

"—while the other half points to you doing some sort of off-the-books investigation with shady characters the department might not approve of." Nora glanced at Ocelot. "If I had to choose, and I were a little bit younger—"

"*Mom!*"

Nora turned back to her and smiled gently. "So, who's the hero, then?"

Kate blinked. "How...?"

"Oh honey," her mother laughed softly, "every Batman has to have a Commissioner Gordon — though let me be clear, there's nothing wrong if you also just happened to be into latex erotica." Nora paused for a moment. "I'm not wrong, am I?"

Kate thought for a long moment. "His name is Ocelot," she replied. When she saw the slow nod of approval from her mom, she continued. "At least, that's what he goes by when he appears in this form. I suspect his alter ego lives in the area, though I don't have a clue who that is." Kate frowned. "What do you mean, *twice* in a week? He wasn't injured—"

Nora cut her off. "I've worked in an emergency room for most of my professional career, honey. I can tell the difference between someone sleeping off a bit of excess and a body that has totally crashed. It took everything I had not to examine him that night, but you seemed pretty sure he just needed to rest." Glancing back over her shoulder again at Ocelot, she shook her head. "I wonder now if I should have. If he hadn't completely recovered from those injuries—"

Despite a slight pit of doubt in her stomach, Kate interrupted. "He had; I can't entirely explain why," she added at the raised eyebrow from her mother. "At least, not until he wakes up and I know what I can say and what I *can't*. All I know is that these injures are new; I... was with him earlier this evening, and when we parted, he was fine."

Nora looked at her. "I won't ask what you were doing, then," she said as she returned to the couch. Kate knelt beside her. "Without a zipper, I'll need to cut this costume off him, then."

"I don't think that will work," Kate said cautiously as she watched her mom rummage around in her small bag. "But if you can somehow wake him, he'll be able to help."

"I've done this a million times, hon," Nora chuckled as she pulled out a pair of scissors and a small scalpel. "I could tell you horror stories from the E.R, though I feel bad about ruining this costume; Hollywood could take a lesson or two from how well tailored it is."

Warning bells started to go off in the back of Kate's head as Nora leaned over Ocelot. "Seriously, Mom, don't you have, like, smelling salts in that bag or something? If he's conscious, he can help."

"If you are worried about my damaging his suit, I'll be as careful as I can," Nora said as she set the scissors down on Ocelot's chest and carefully began to press the sharp edge of the scalpel to a spot just above his breastbone. "I just need a small spot here—"

Kate's cry of alarm was nearly instantaneous when she saw Ocelot's masked eyes snap open. "*Mom!*"

Nora had half-turned toward Kate before her head immediately whipped back around, her eyes wide at the sight of her wrist being held tightly by Ocelot; they widened further when his masked eyes narrowed at her. "Who are you?" he growled, every syllable dripping with menace. "And what are you intending on doing with that knife?"

"I'm a nurse," Nora replied calmly, though Kate could see how much effort it was taking to appear that way. "Your girlfriend called me for help."

Ocelot's eyes slid to Kate's; she could read some level of confusion in them, so she stepped closer. "I found you passed out in my front yard," she said, "sporting some pretty serious injuries. I knew I couldn't take you to anyone, so I called Mom."

Those brown eyes shifted again to Nora, then back to Kate. "This is... your mother?" he asked, wincing in pain with each breath.

"Yes. She works in the emergency room at Santa Marcel General."

Ocelot relaxed slightly. "My... apologies," he said as he let go of Nora's wrist. "This is... not the way I would have chosen... to introduce myself, but I'm not... comfortable with a... knife at my chest..."

"I can understand that," Nora said. "I need to check your injuries, and the costume has to come off in order for me to do that."

Ocelot shot a glance at Kate. "How much...?"

"It's not my secret to share," she replied. "But for the record, I trust my mother. I think you can, too."

That seemed to be all he needed; leaning back on the pillow of the couch, he closed his eyes and nodded. "The injury... is my rib," he said. "How much access... do you need...?"

"Your entire torso would be good," Nora said, "but I can't see—"

Before she could complete her sentence, the portion of Ocelot's costume that was above the waist simply vanished, exposing the sculpted torso Kate had become rather intimate with. Unlike their interlude in her childhood bedroom, though, the wide expanse of coffee-colored skin was marred by multiple bruises, including an extremely ugly one about where she suspected the rib had been broken. The extent of his injures concerned her immensely, but she buried her worries under the best compassionate expression she could manage. Those brown eyes saw right through her, though, and he smiled slightly for her benefit.

"I missed my landing," he joked.

"I'll say," Nora whistled as she carefully palpitated around the rib. "How badly?"

"A few stories," he replied casually. "It happens. I'm still... getting the hang of it..."

"Of what?" Nora asked absently as she pressed the stethoscope back to his chest.

"Being a hero," Kate replied quietly. Looking at him, she chanced tugging at their shared connection.

What the fuck happened to you? she asked, testing whether he could hear her.

His eyes widened, and she heard his response clear as a bell in the back of her head. *I wondered how long it would be before you figured out how to do this.*

Kate glared at Ocelot. *You could have told me in advance,* she replied.

Where's the fun in that? he asked, and she thought for a moment she saw a slight smirk on that masked face of his. *How long have I been out?*

About an hour. Why are you here? And, seriously, what the fuck *happened? You look like you were in a battle royale with someone twice your size.*

Might as well have been, was the quick response. Ocelot's eyes flicked toward her mother. *I'll tell you later.*

You'd better, she replied.

I promise, he replied. *And I never break a promise.*

It took a moment for her to realize Nora was speaking. "...without an X-ray, I can't know for sure the full extent of the damage. Normally I would refer you to an orthopedic surgeon, but I'm guessing you don't want that, either?"

"Not if we can help it," Kate said then looked at Ocelot. "I thought you could heal yourself?"

"I can, normally," he said, then glanced meaningfully at her mother.

Why not now? she asked.

I pushed too far, was the reply. *I need time to recover, and until I do, my injuries won't fully heal.*

How much time do you need?

A few hours, at least, Ocelot replied. *Until then, I barely have enough to keep what's left of my costume in place.*

Kate smiled slightly. *I wouldn't be opposed to it completely disappearing.*

Under other circumstances, he said, his laughter in her mind, *I wouldn't mind you ravishing me. But truly, I need to rest.*

Party pooper.

His masked eyes narrowed at her. *You may not think that after I'm back at full strength.*

Promises, promises, Kate smiled before turning back to her mother. "Should we brace it or something, then?" she asked. "I'm sure the pain is keeping him from resting, and when he rests, he can heal."

Nora looked at her thoughtfully. "Accepting for the moment your *boyfriend* appears to have some unique abilities," she began, "I don't think immobilizing his rib will do much in the short term other than annoy him."

"Hear, hear," Ocelot said quietly. Kate stifled a chuckle.

Reaching back into her bag, Nora retrieved a digital thermometer and quickly took a reading from the patch of skin visible on his forehead. "101," she read. "Without running a full medical history, not to mention having any sort of concept of what ordinary pharmaceuticals might do to Ocelot, the most I'd recommend is some acetaminophen." She looked at Ocelot. "Do you have any reaction to over-the-counter medications?"

Ocelot glanced at Kate. "My metabolism runs a bit faster than most," he said carefully. "So the effects of things like painkillers and cold medicines tend to wane quickly."

"That's what I thought," Nora sighed as she rustled around in her bag again and came out with a small bottle of pills. "Tylenol it is, and then we'll see how it goes from there; I'll want to keep an eye on him for bit just in case."

"Don't you have work in the morning?"

"Not until seven," Nora replied.

I guess snuggling is out, then? Ocelot asked with a slight laugh. *Even if it helps me heal faster, it would be pretty awkward with your mother here.*

I cannot conceive of it being any more *awkward than it already is,* Kate sighed. *Especially since I know you can't transit anyway.*

True. There could be worse things than sleeping on your couch...

"The bed is made up in the spare room if you feel like grabbing a nap," Kate offered her mother, then nodded at the kitchen. "And there is also plenty of coffee."

"I saw that. And the Baileys," Nora smiled. "I suspect we both had the same thought."

"Where do you think I learned it?" Kate asked. "I'll get some big mugs and glass of water for those pills..."

THIRTEEN

While it had been a few years since he'd seen Nora Oliver, he'd hung around Kate's house enough as a child to know that fighting her efforts would be to little avail. Still, as he tried to settle into the fairly comfortable cushions of Kate's couch, he found sleep didn't come easily; being tended to by Nora and Kate brought with it uncomfortable echos of his many visits to the healers after a particularly brutal training session in the jungle, visits that had only began to wane once his abilities had begun to truly manifest. There was also a tiny sliver of fear deep within his soul that he was too weak to continue cloaking his identity from the duo should he actually allow himself to fall into the deep sleep necessary for his magical healing processes to fully assert themselves. Kate seemed to sense this across their shared connection, and to his great relief managed to convince Nora to make use of the spare bedroom instead of constantly hovering over Ocelot; only when he heard Kate quietly close her own bedroom door did he feel like he had enough privacy to finally let go and plunge into the oblivion that was more Morpheus' domain than his own.

The dreams, while varied and vibrant, didn't hold any special meaning other than serving as a reminder that he'd fucked up yet again. His encounter with his *madre* was front and center, of course; while he'd expected to get a dressing down for having continued to aid Kate in her investigation, the physicality of her response had reopened old wounds he'd thought had been long healed — wounds he'd been carrying since the day she'd told him *padre* had died. The pain of being at the receiving end of her power was second only to the humiliation of being tossed about like a rag doll, suffering her wrath like he was some sort of recalcitrant teenager. Ocelot had learned early that whatever balance their family had once enjoyed was something his father had been responsible for; with him out of the equation, they had devolved into something far less recognizable. Viewed from that perspective, his relative banishment to the jungle had been a blessing.

If he'd ever been asked to describe how it felt to wield magic, Ocelot knew it would be hard to explain other than it always felt like he was wearing a form-fitting cloak that hugged him with a slightly electric sizzle. How *much* of a sizzle depended on a few factors, none of which were completely quantifiable beyond a strange sixth sense he'd developed during his training. Overall, though, his perception of the cloak was one way he gauged how much was left in his tank (magically speaking) or what sort of strain his abilities were currently under. As he swam up through the layers of slumber toward consciousness, the sizzle had shifted into something closer to the warmth of being wrapped in an electric blanket set to high; every part of his body tingled as though he'd just been scrubbed with some sort of loofa sponge. Blinking his masked eyes open, he smiled slightly at the incredibly erotic image that had sprung to mind at that thought; seeing the object of his desires sitting at the breakfast bar working at her laptop did little to chill his libido, so it was fortunate the quilt Kate had spread over him covered what his costume would be unable to hide.

Shifting subtly, he was able to look out into the backyard and could see the first hints of sunrise; what little of the horizon that was visible had the beautiful light-to-deep blue gradient, presaging the appearance of the sun. It was also a non-subtle reminder of how few revolutions of the Earth were left before he ascended into his full abilities; as he turned back to look at Kate, he wondered for the first time if that was why events had been triggered as they had. At the moment, he was far from completely in control of his abilities, hampering his effectiveness as a warrior; the sense he was close to unlocking his full potential had been hovering in the background for weeks now, and along with it the near certainty that once he ascended, very few — including his mother — would be able to stand up to him.

The codex held a warning, though, for while Ocelot ascended, the balance required by the universe meant their still unknown nemesis was currently at the zenith of their powers, striking while they had the advantage. It wouldn't last long — maybe three weeks, perhaps five at most, depending on how far off he was in his calculations — but it would be a dangerous period. Ocelot had committed to memory most of the stories in the codex from the pre-history of their civilization when one of the minor gods chose just such a moment to implement their nefarious plan.

Stretching, he inadvertently let out a loud yawn; Kate's head immediately swiveled toward him. "Hey," she said as she slid from her barstool and padded over to him. Pressing her hand to his forehead, she smiled. "Fevers gone. How do you feel?"

"Better," he smiled as he mentally scanned his body. "Rib still aches a bit, but that's about it."

Kate pulled the quilt down and looked over his torso. "The

bruises are gone, too," she said before lowering her voice. "What happened after you sent me home?"

Ocelot looked in the general direction of the vague noises he was hearing of someone in the shower. "Your mom's still here?" he asked just as quietly.

"She's getting ready to leave," Kate nodded. "Unlike you, I doubt she can hear us from the bathroom, especially over the noise of the exhaust fan."

My mother could, Ocelot sighed mentally before deciding how much of the truth he could tell her. "I wasn't able to avoid security when they made their sweep," he explained. "Things became a bit... intense, but in the end, I was able to get away."

Kate's expression told him she wasn't entirely buying his story. "That must have been quite a fight."

"I was in over my head," Ocelot sighed. "Not for the first time, either. It didn't help I was running on fumes at that point."

"You should have left with me," Kate said, reaching for his hand. Her gentle touch was unusually calming.

"I had barely enough power to send you home," he said. "Which was part of the reason I was in your front yard — I wanted to make sure you'd actually *gotten* home. When I couldn't feel you at the other end of our connection, I thought I might have sent you someplace else."

Kate frowned. "I did get home — obviously — but fell asleep waiting for you. Despite what you said about meeting me tonight, I assumed you'd want to go through the material we recovered as soon as possible." She eyed him. "Was I wrong?"

"No," he replied. "I did, but I also figured I'd need to recharge before I could appear to you as Ocelot."

"I hate to point out the obvious, but you've been in costume this entire time."

"Yes," he smiled slightly. "My magical muscles appear to be

conditioned enough now that I can keep my form even with hardly any effort. Something I couldn't have done a few weeks ago, I assure you."

"That sounds like an improvement."

Ocelot nodded. "It also confirms my calculations about when I come into my full powers are off, too. I'm going to check into that later today, especially since I think whomever it is we are working against is on a similar timeline."

Kate's eyes went wide. "There's *another* Ocelot out there?"

"There's only one of me, *princesa*," he smiled. "But there are plenty of gods in our pantheon and just as many vassals like me that serve them. I think the one we are chasing is currently at the apex of their powers — or close to it. Which makes them extremely dangerous."

"I don't like the sounds of that."

"With reason," he smiled again. "Have you been going through the data on the USB stick?"

Kate nodded. "Yes, though I'm not sure I have the full picture yet. And there's a tiny problem with it."

"Oh?"

"Yeah," she frowned. "You were right about the shipment dates, but the GPS device IDs have all been scrambled; even if I could get a warrant to tap into the tracking system Vasquez Industries is using, I have nothing to track. Without them, the best I can do is guess at when the containers will arrive, and that looks like a ten-day window."

Ocelot frowned slightly. "It's probably not wise to ask your contact at Vasquez for those," he said after a moment. "We'll need to break in again."

Kate squeezed his hand. "While I concur, I also think they'll be expecting that, especially once they realize what was taken. I don't think it's a good idea for us to poke at that particular bear again; I might have the ability to back door something through one of my contacts at the FBI, but it would be a long shot."

"Yeah," he nodded, for he'd already drawn the same conclusion — and resigned himself to doing something that might well end badly for him. Deciding a bit of a distraction would be in order, he smiled and stretched. "I've got to get going," he said, nodding toward the sunbeam that was just beginning to creep across the floor toward the couch. "If that beam hits me, I'll be trapped for the entire morning."

Kate eyed him. "Good to know I can use your feline tendencies against you," she said. "You want something to eat before you go?"

And are you well enough to transit? she asked across the connection.

"No," he replied, "and yes. My alter ego needs to be seen at the proper time, I'm afraid. I'll grab something to eat on the way."

"Are you sure?"

"Yes," he nodded.

To prove his point, he carefully pulled his hand from hers and then quickly restored his costume; standing, he conjured a leather thong out of thin air and then tied back his long hair. As he held out his arms and then slowly rotated to show Kate he was fine, the look on her face underscored how concerned she remained. Not entirely sure how to convince her, he leaned over and gently pressed his lips to hers; pulling away, he smiled gently as he brushed a stray lock of her blond hair behind an ear.

"I'll be back tonight as promised," he said softly. "And will be healed enough to handle *any* activities you have planned for me."

"Any?" she asked. "Like what?"

Ocelot smiled wolfishly as he allowed — briefly — some of his more carnal thoughts to skip merrily across their shared connection.

Kate's slightly flushed face confirmed she'd gotten them. "I see," she swallowed. "Some of those positions are rather creative."

"You learn a lot in the jungle," he laughed as he kissed her again. "Please thank your mother for her help."

"I will."

"Then until tonight," he said before he carefully walked over to the glass of the sliding door and stepped through his portal.

In less than a heartbeat, Ocelot found himself stepping *out* of the glass from his balcony's sliding door; with his enhanced hearing, the crash of the surf along the beach his condo overlooked made him feel as though he'd instead landed on the damp sand the tide was currently retreating away from. Turning slightly, he smiled at his masked reflection in the window for a moment before turning his attention to the ocean; as early as it was, only the hardy were out in the surf trying to get in a few passes before the day truly got started. The health conscious were running or walking or skating their way along the serpentine concrete pathway that ran along the very edge of the beach; the outdoor gym just beside the sand volleyball courts appeared to also be doing a brisk business, and his gaze lingered for a moment longer than it should have on a shirtless blond flexing his biceps on the pull-up bar. The slight tightness in his groin was an unwelcome reminder Tezcatlipoca shared more than just his power with Ocelot; the closer he got to his ascension, the harder it was becoming for him to ignore how the deity's rather fluid sexuality was affecting him, despite his best efforts. It was part of the careful dance he did with his benefactor, one that described just how much (or how little) freedom Ocelot truly had. His love for Kate had been one of the few things that had pulled him through his time in the jungle — time that had tried to crush out of him the ability to ever love anyone other than the god to whom he served. That his heart had so quickly leapt back into the fray upon his return to California told him that some part of who he'd once been was still there, buried deep below the layers of magic he'd been forced to accept. Still, it was always difficult to avoid acting on the rush of desire that often hit him when something caught Tezcatlipoca's wandering eye; fortunately, the adepts he'd trained with had provided a few not-in-the-codex secrets to help him in such situations.

Sighing, he turned away from the window and let his costume fade away; by the time he reached the master bathroom, the familiar form of Tenoch stared back at him from the mirror, albeit with dark circles underscoring both eyes and a vaguely black-and-blue splotch where his rib still ached. Twisting slightly, he could see the rest of the bruises had faded completely, but as he leaned forward into the mirror, he frowned slightly at the faint red lines from the shards of glass that had hit his face. *It's good that the mask hid the full extent of my injuries*, he thought as he flipped over his hands and frowned deeper at the crosshatched lines on his palms. *I'm not as far healed as I would like, but it will have to do.*

The searing heat of the shower went a long way toward easing a bit of the tension from his body, though it also brought with it memories of having been caught in his mother's powerful manifestation of anger. Tenoch took his time lathering every square inch of skin, using the repetitive movements as a sort of mantra to remove every last trace of what had happened to him; when that failed, he grabbed his razor and shaved away the slight haze of dark stubble that had taken his complexion a shade deeper than usual. He lingered another long moment beneath stream of hot water and the plumes of steam it was creating, then twisted the handle to off and grabbed his towel. Less than twenty minutes later, he was putting the finishing touches on his tie before shrugging into the suit jacket he'd hung on the back of the bathroom door; his curls were still damp enough that gelling them would have made for an impossible mess, so he shrugged and headed for the kitchen.

Only when he pulled open the door to his pantry and found it somewhat lacking did he recall a forgotten intent to swing past the grocery store for supplies; the fridge was in a similar state, sporting only a few bottles of beer and a half-eaten round of blue cheese that might have actually completed its transition to penicillin. Sighing, he railed once more against his inability to conjure up food when necessary, then grabbed his keys and headed for the garage. It wouldn't be the first time he'd eaten a meal at the cafeteria Vasquez Industries offered, though that particular morning he wasn't entirely certain he wanted to be seen there — or anywhere on campus, for that matter. His angst at having to return to the scene of his humiliation was channeled into driving many multiples above the stated speed limit on the freeway, though he'd also had to lean into his superior magical reflexes to avoid becoming a Caltrans statistic; as he pulled into the executive parking lot, Tenoch was actually surprised that Jack smiled and waved him through. He'd half-expected to have been banned from the building by his *madre* for his transgressions, then realized that she'd probably wanted him right where she could keep an eye on him. The only problem with that theory was the obvious absence of her Lexus SUV in the lot; as Tenoch pulled into his spot and killed the engine for his Charger, he realized he had a golden opportunity to make good on his silent promise to Kate.

That didn't mean alarm bells weren't going off in the back of his head, though. He'd spent enough time in the jungle to recognize when danger was lurking just behind a sizable fern or biding its time in the canopy far above. Scratching at his chin thoughtfully, Tenoch knew his *madre* ran the company with the precision of finely crafted Swiss clockwork; save for the rare occasions when she traveled for the organization, it was nearly a universal constant that she was behind her desk checking on their global investment portfolio no later than eight. Glancing at the clock on the dashboard, he tried to divine whether his golden opportunity was actually too good to be true; deciding it probably *was* had him immediately begin to consider using not one but *two* spells that might — if he were extremely lucky — allow him to slip in and out of the logistics department undetected.

But first, he needed to be absolutely sure his *madre* wasn't there. And that meant risking a third spell that, frankly, he'd not entirely mastered; his ability to detect others based on their unique magical signatures was tricky at best, and the very act of reaching out to confirm the presence of another essentially telegraphed his own location — making the benefits of using the spell something of a mixed bag. Looking up at the building in front of him, he decided he was *just* angry enough over what had transpired the night before to throw caution to the wind; closing his eyes, he centered himself and then carefully reached out into the magical ether, hunting like the predator he was for his prey. That he was able to catch her faint essence at the family mansion in Carbon Creek surprised him slightly; it was another sign that his powers were growing, for distance had long been a limiting factor in that particular spell being useful. Drawing back before she could sense what he was doing, Tenoch opened his eyes and felt himself smiling slightly; his *madre* lacked the ability to use the reflective transport spell, meaning she was, at best, at least forty minutes away — plenty of time for him to pull off the impossible.

Exiting the Charger, he casually walked to the elevator for the executive suite and stepped inside. He waited for the elevator doors to close before silently weaving his clone-and-cloaking spell; it took longer than he'd hoped, but by the time the doors sighed open on the executive floor, his perfectly crafted doppelgänger stepped out into the elevator lobby, putting on the perfect show for the security cameras as it headed for his corner office. Carefully creeping out behind it, Ocelot paused at the intersection with the main hallway and pressed his arm against the wall; when even he couldn't tell where the wall ended and his body began, he allowed himself a brief moment of joy at having finally mastered the magic before breaking into a run for the stairwell at the far end.

Dashing around staff members oblivious to his presence, he knew that while the sound of his movement was muffled by the spell, there would be no way to hide the door to the stairwell being opened seemingly by itself. Pressing his back against the door, Ocelot waited for the perfect moment to crack it open just enough he could slip through; once on the other side, he carefully pressed the door shut and then leaned his ear to it to see if anyone had been alerted. After several heartbeats, he assumed he was in the clear and leapt over the railing, sailing down the opening at the center of the stairwell until his claws dug into the soft concrete just above the floor holding his prize.

Flipping himself onto the landing, he dropped into a crouch and then crept to the door; pulling it open enough to peer out, he smiled at the sight of the massive logistics center on the other side. As with other non-public portions of the building, it was a very utilitarian space, with an open ceiling and exposed beams; *madre* had once called it industrial chic while giving a tour to some VIP, but Ocelot had long felt it simply underscored how she felt about those who worked for her — especially given the designer carpets and expensive floral arrangements so prevalent on the executive floor. Glancing upward, Ocelot realized the cost-savings measure might actually work to his benefit. Waiting another heartbeat, he slipped around the opening and then leapt into the open ceiling, landing atop one of the rectangular air conditioning ducts with a soft *thunk*. The ambient noise from those working in the cubicles appeared to cover his presence, but he waited another full minute before carefully beginning to creep along the cold metal toward his destination.

Prior attempts to get at the data he needed had underscored just how partitioned each part of Vasquez Industries was; he'd initially wondered if the artificial firewalls had been due to how the organization was financially structured, but as he'd done more digging, it had finally dawned on him that part of how his *madre* ran the sprawling corporation required that there only be one central source of truth. It also had the helpful side benefit of preventing any one division from attempting a coup over the others. So his quest for uncovering who, exactly, had been using their transportation network for human trafficking had required more than one clandestine visit to specific aspects of the company that managed a portion of the traffic; his computer skills had meant most of those had been done from the comfort of his laptop, but in a few cases the security around the data he required had forced him to get more creative. Sebastian had been one of those unique solutions, one that he now feared had been exposed to those he was trying to stop.

Reaching the end of the duct, Ocelot leaned over and saw he was over the *other* creative solution he had come up with; glancing to make sure the coast was still clear, he flipped off the duct and dropped into a four-point crouch inside a nondescript cubicle that appeared to currently be vacant. That it also happened to be in the one blind spot for the security cameras on that floor was a happy accident that had been built into the new security software he'd had a hand in rewriting. As he crept to the desktop computer, he groaned inwardly at how much tequila it had taken to convince the hacker he'd met during the Black Hat conference in Vegas to share her tricks of the trade; matching her drink for drink hadn't been the best of his ideas, but he'd managed to learn what he'd needed before he'd gently left her snoring atop the bed in her hotel room. His guilt at having to erase their evening together by casting his amnesia spell on her had been slightly offset by the fortune in poker chips he'd left in his stead; with luck, she'd assume she'd had a good night at the tables and had slept off the results of her celebration.

Staying beneath the desk, Ocelot flipped onto his back and then carefully used a claw to unscrew a small panel behind the keyboard tray; removing the panel, he reached in and pulled out an identification card and small fob, then slipped back out from beneath the desk. Taking a brief moment to ensure he still hadn't attracted any attention, he sat down at the computer and tapped the identification card to the small reader on the keyboard; the subtle beep was followed by the monitor winking into life so it could display the second part of the login process. Tapping at the fob with another claw, he carefully typed the ten digits that appeared on the small window into the waiting box on the computer; a moment later, he was quickly running through the logistics database, hunting for the transponders specific to the shipping containers Kate had identified. He only gave a moment's thought to how long it had taken for him to create a series of fake employees in the Human Resources database, unique accounts that had *just* enough access to provide a hidden backdoor to specific areas of the organization. It didn't hurt that personnel management was one of the duties *madre* had delegated to him; if she ever found out what he had truly been up to since returning from the jungle, he was certain he'd be sent right back — possibly in small pieces.

The search took far longer than he'd hoped, for it quickly became clear that someone had wanted to keep those particular shipments out of the main tracking system. An inspired hunch about possible routing landed him in the files of their Indonesian subsidiary; when the three transponder IDs finally appeared on the screen, he sent up a prayer of thanks to Tezcatlipoca before quickly taking a mental screenshot of the data. He was in the process of closing down the workstation and re-hiding his purloined credentials when he felt the first shiver of his mother's presence as it ghosted down his spine; it had been something similar the night before that had led to him shoving Kate into the portal. Focusing for a moment, Ocelot frowned when he realized his *madre* was actively searching for him; while he wasn't entirely able to pick up on the emotion being carried along on the same current, it was strange enough that he could detect the hint of *something* that he decided to risk a more expeditious exit from logistics.

Tapping at the metal that supported the wall of the cubicle, Ocelot could just see the barest of reflections of the overhead lights; the surface wasn't what he would have desired, but it would do in a pinch. Touching it more gently, he watched as the telltale whorl of the portal began to open; he had a brief moment to see that he'd correctly connected with the mirror in the private bathroom just off his office before he lunged through. Leaping over the sink at the other end, he landed in a crouch on the Saltillo tile and held his breath long enough to determine his actual office was vacant. Dropping the cloaking spell, he stood and was momentarily startled by his reflection in the mirror; the Ocelot that was staring back at him had changed, albeit subtly. Gone was the long, straight black hair, replaced by an unruly mop of curls far too close to his civilian persona for his liking. Twisting in the light, his masked eyes widened when they caught the set of feline-looking triangular ears that had also taken up residence on his head; they widened further when he realized they were accompanied by a long tail that had sprouted out of nowhere from his lower back. Both were made from the same magical fabric as his costume, though as he reached up to confirm the presence of the ears, he shuddered slightly at the unexpected sensations generated by the touch of his gloved finger. They — and his newfound tail — appeared capable of independent movement, though to what end he wasn't entirely sure. Placing his hands to either side of the sink, he wondered if they were non-subtle signs that his ability to shift into his *nagual* form was imminent.

Can't worry about that now, he thought.

Closing his eyes for a moment, he whispered the phrase to drop his Ocelot persona; blinking them back open, he was somewhat relieved to see no trace of the ears or tail. Taking a deep breath, he turned and opened the door to his office, braced to relieve the worst of the prior evening. To his surprise, as he stepped into the grand space he found it had been completely restored; there was no trace that anything had happened. Even his priceless Disney antiques were back where they belonged, no worse for having been smashed to smithereens when he'd been hurled against them. Wandering the space as though it were the first time he'd ever been in it, he found he wasn't all that shocked to see the small handwritten card in the center of his rebuilt desk. Sitting down in his chair, he stared at it for a moment before reaching for it and flipping it open. The three lines there had been written many times before — so many, in fact, that he folded the note back in half before tearing it into small pieces. Setting them ablaze on his desk made him feel better momentarily; despite the apology, he knew the pattern with his *madre* was destined to be repeated, making it vacuous at best.

Waving away the small tendrils of smoke as the note crumpled into ash, he caught the flash of something out of the corner of his eye and looked for the source; nothing seemed out of place, though, save for the small piece of flint he'd retrieved from the shipping container. He'd left it beside his phone as an intentional reminder to follow up on his suspicion of its providence, but with everything that had happened since its discovery, Tenoch simply hadn't had time. Picking it up, he held it to the light so he could make out the slim vein of quartzite running through the stone; he found himself frowning when the lighter-colored mineral seemed to flicker, and not just from the early morning sunshine hitting it just right.

Maybe I don't need confirmation after all, he thought. *I'd better keep this close.*

Snapping his fingers, the small whorl of energy appeared and allowed him to quickly deposit the stone in his fold-in-spacetime locker; as he waved away the spell, his better-than-human hearing told him his solitude was about to be interrupted. Pulling out his cell phone, he had just enough time to confirm his dinner plans with Kate before the door to his office was thrown open; his mother sailed into his office as though she owned it, which, in a way, she did. Pausing beside one of his guest chairs, her eyes slipped from his to the small pile of ash on his desk before she spoke.

"We have a meeting with one of our banks at the top of the hour. I need the borrowing expenses for the past two quarters, cross referenced by division."

Tenoch nodded; he'd long since stopped being amazed at how she could ignore what she'd done to him, especially when there were pressing matters of business to attend to. "All right. Anything else?" he asked with more pointedly than he'd intended.

She looked at him thoughtfully. "Not at the moment," she replied before whisking out of the room.

FOURTEEN

After spending the day digging through the data files from Vasquez Industries, Kate felt as though she were no closer to understanding the operation her former boyfriend helmed a part of. In fact, in many ways it almost seemed as though the files themselves were acting as some sort of bulwark against putting together any sort of comprehensive look at what, exactly, the multinational conglomerate actually *did*. The easy part had been tracking down the overall routes most of the shipping containers took when they left Oaxaca; beyond that, though, their ultimate destinations — let alone actual manifests — were buried beneath layers of nonsensical information that she had zero ability to decipher. About the only thing she'd managed to glean from scrolling through the endless number of spreadsheets was how easily those *particular* containers had been buried among very ordinary ones; aside from an unusual tag denoting they were slightly heaver than normal, weight wise, they could easily have been overlooked by anyone attempting to trace them. More than once she'd been tempted to pick up the phone and call Tenoch to help translate —

and maybe confirm — what she thought she was seeing, but the impulse had been quelled after his text confirming their dinner plans for that evening. It seemed wiser to wait and chat with him in person, but by quarter to three Kate had hit a brick wall and needed to take a break.

Knowing Tenoch was picking her up for their outing that evening gave her the perfect excuse to bike home; taking the longer route through the hills had the added benefit of allowing her to burn off some of the nerves she seemed to be experiencing over spending time with someone she'd all but assumed would never be a part of her life again. Making matters worse, she couldn't deny that something deep inside her wanted desperately to reclaim what had once existed between them, despite the undeniable connection she now had with Ocelot. Sorting out her feelings over the two men was something she wasn't entirely ready to do, so she set it all aside to focus on getting the most from her workout. As she sailed around the final corner of her neighborhood and slowed to turn into her driveway, she had the strangest sense of wry laughter over her gossamer connection to Ocelot. Pulling up in front of her garage, she let her eyes focus on something she couldn't really see and tried to reach for him.

What's so funny?

There was a long moment, long enough that she thought maybe he hadn't heard her; then, clear as a bell, his voice whispered back to her: *I had no idea the two of you were a thing. Now it all makes sense.*

Startled, Kate frowned. *Are you listening in on my thoughts, now?*

Not intentionally, he said gently. *I try to ignore your unguarded moments, but occasionally it's impossible to do so. Strong feelings lower your barriers.*

Oh shit, she thought. *How much...?*

There was a gentle chuckle. *Enough that I now consider him the competition. I might have to kill him so I can make sure I have you to myself...*

Surely you're not serious, she replied with a touch of fear.

Of course I'm not. And don't call me Shirley.

Kate blinked. *Did you... did you just quote a movie?*

Maybe, he laughed. *Are you going to be late for our meeting at ten?*

I don't think so, but I'll text you if I am.

That sense he was chuckling came across the connection again. *No need for phones now, is there? Just reach out and let me know if you're running late.*

Okay, she replied. *Sorry - this is going to take some getting used to.*

I have no doubt you'll soon get the swing of things — you're defelinely a quick study.

Kate groaned. *Cat puns? Really?*

It's a work in progress, he laughed. *Looking forward to seeing you later,* he replied with such feeling that her body suddenly reacted as though he had gently run one of those claws of his over a particularly sensitive spot.

Gasping slightly, she took a moment before replying. *Did you just—?*

Just a reminder of what I have in store for you tonight, he whispered sensuously. *So you won't forget whose heart you already hold in your beautiful hands.*

Kate felt her face flush as a significant part of her began to ache for release. *You are playing dirty.*

This isn't a one-way street, Ocelot laughed. *One of the many benefits of our connection.*

She thought about that for a moment. *You mean—?*

Yes, though it might take a bit for you to learn how to—

Kate felt more than heard the guttural moan that reverberated across their connection; apparently, simply visualizing what she wanted to do to Ocelot was enough to trigger the reaction she'd hoped for. The confused jumble of emotions that washed over her from his side confirmed that Kate had shocked him. Badly.

Like that? she asked innocently.

Daaaaaaaaamn, was the drawn-out reply. *I think I'm going to need a shower now.*

Sorry.

No, you're not, he replied with a rueful chuckled. *I had that... coming, if you'll pardon the pun.*

Maybe you did, she laughed. *Still, I'm sorry...*

Don't be — it's also a vivid reminder about which one of us is truly in control. I've got to go — see you tonight.

Ocelot—?

Though she could still feel him, Kate understood intrinsically that he was in a spot where he couldn't spare the focus to communicate; sighing, she waited for her body to calm down a bit before putting away her bike and then hitting the shower herself. The hot water did little to wash away the sexual tension coiled deep within her gut, nor the reminder of the last time — and the last person — who had once drawn such sensations out of her. She could still vividly remember her first time with Tenoch the summer of their senior year; it had been an insanely warm July day, and he had been hanging out with her on the patio beside her parent's in-ground pool. Kate hadn't read into his seemingly innocent verification that they would have the house to themselves, nor did she immediately understand his nervousness when he'd arrived mid-morning. The tight Speedo he'd changed into before joining her at the pool connected a few dots, along with how he'd carefully slid onto her lounge chair under the blazing sun. Promises were made that day, promises that were shattered several months later on the night of their Senior Prom; still, the gentleness of that first time was something she fondly remembered, along with just how deferential Tenoch had been. He made it clear from the outset that her happiness was his only concern, and that he would go only as far as she wanted — no further. It had made their sudden split all the more heartbreaking.

Shutting down the shower, Kate hurried through the rest of her preparations; knowing where they were eating that night, she selected a light blue pantsuit and a white blouse, then put her hair up in a fancy bun. As she was reapplying her makeup, Kate realized the shade of lipstick she still wore was the one that Tenoch had loved; she decided she didn't want to know *why* she'd chosen that moment to remember. Kate was just shrugging into her suit coat when she heard the low growl of an expensive sports car turning onto her street. When the noise crescendoed in her driveway, she felt an eyebrow go up; walking to the living room, she pulled back the curtain and saw the sleek lines of a Dodge Charger sitting there, and the *GQ* figure of Tenoch walking up the pathway to her front door. Stuffing her phone into one pocket and her small billfold into the other, she barely made it to the door before the bell rang out.

The first thing she noticed when she pulled the door open was the brilliant smile that appeared; the second, the fact he was wearing the cologne he'd favored while they'd been dating. She tried to ignore how her heart did a funny skip as a result. "Kate," Tenoch said. "Ready to go?"

"Yes," she nodded.

Tenoch waited for her to lock the front door, then extended his arm in a gentlemanly fashion; intrigued, she accepted the gesture. "I'm glad we found the time to do this," Tenoch said as they walked down the short path to the driveway. "Given the circumstances."

"To be honest, I could use a break," she replied. "I've been looking at computer screens all day; I think my brain is slowly reformatting itself into a spreadsheet."

"Welcome to my universe," Tenoch chuckled as he guided her around to the passenger seat. Pulling the door open for her, he ducked away so she could slide in and then gently closed the door. A moment later, he was buckling himself in behind the wheel. "Traffic looks like it's in our favor," he said as he started up the engine. "We should make our reservation with plenty of time."

"Nice car," Kate said as he eased the Charger into reverse. "It... suits you."

"Thanks," he smiled. "It was a present to me."

"For what?"

"For surviving," he replied enigmatically. "How's your mom doing?" he asked smoothly.

"Fine," she said, aware that he had deftly changed the subject.

They spent the drive to Giovanni's Ristorante in companionable conversation, though it hardly made a dent in covering all that had passed since they'd last seen each other. As they pulled into the very full parking lot for the popular establishment, Kate realized Tenoch had managed to deflect many of her questions about his time away from Santa Marcel; it wasn't lost on her that she'd been far more open and wondered why her friend — *supposed* friend — was being so coy about what had happened to him. He again extended his arm to her after giving the keys to the valet, and she wasn't the least bit surprised when the *maître d'hôtel* immediately took them to a quiet table in the corner well away from the subdued but sizable dinner crowd. Menus appeared, a bottle of wine selected and in short order Kate found herself staring into a set of green eyes that felt every bit as bewitching as they once had. The warmth from within began to creep outward; in an attempt to stop the strange tide that appeared to be rising of its own accord, she downed her glass of ice water and made a healthy dent in the fragrant red Tenoch had selected. It took every bit of willpower she had not to start fanning herself with her napkin; glancing at Tenoch, she was surprised to see his face was just as flushed as she felt — and that a small bead of sweat had appeared along the edge of his hairline, partially hidden by his curls.

What the...? she thought.

The response was immediate. *What the what?*

She knew something flickered across her face at the unexpected response from Ocelot, for Tenoch's eyebrows had gone up. *Not now,* she hissed across their connection.

What's going on? was the concerned question, followed by a gentle probing along their connection. *Are you okay? Do you need me—*

Tenoch appeared to be frowning. "Kate? Are you all right?"

I'm having carnal thoughts about my old boyfriend, she blurted out. *While attempting to have dinner with him. I think this is your fault for getting me into a state earlier.*

There was a moment of quiet, followed by the sense of being slowly hugged. *Take a moment to center yourself,* Ocelot said. *Let me help you get there.*

Kate nodded, which made Tenoch frown even more. "What is it?" he asked.

You'll feel more like yourself in a moment, Ocelot said. *One... two... three.*

Almost like she had suddenly burst to the surface of a pool, Kate felt entirely normal once again. *What did you do?*

I've redirected your emotions, Ocelot said. *It won't last more than a few hours, but you should be able to get through dinner.* There was a soft chuckle. *The unfortunate side effect is that they will all come crashing back later with far more force.*

That sounds unpleasant.

Not in the right hands, was the teasing reply. *Enjoy dinner.*

"Kate?"

She blinked and only then realized that Tenoch was kneeling

beside her chair. "I'm sorry," she said, smiling slightly. "I didn't mean to check out there. I guess I'm more tired than I realized."

"Do you want me to take you home?" he asked, his face creased with concern. "We can do this—"

"No," she shook her head. "No, I'm fine now."

"Are you sure?"

"Yes," she smiled. "But thanks for being concerned."

Tenoch eyed her for a moment, then slowly nodded before returning to his seat. They'd barely begun another banal conversation about the weather when their appetizers appeared; snarfing down one of the crab-filled mushrooms seemed to steady her even more. Once their salads had been cleared, Kate finally felt capable of letting herself enjoy the moment; perhaps it was the wine, or maybe the general atmosphere, but even Tenoch seemed more relaxed, enough that she decided to venture into dangerous territory. At the risk of destroying the moment, she gripped her wineglass and then took a deep breath, preparing to plunge into the one question that had been bothering her for, well, decades.

"Tenoch—"

"I think I found something that might be helpful to your investigation," Tenoch said, seemingly unaware that Kate had begun to speak. Slicing off another piece of his prime rib, he dabbed it into the small container of horseradish sauce before placing it into his mouth. Chewing thoughtfully, his eyes never left her face. "Are you interested in tracking shipments from Oaxaca?"

Toying with her baked ziti, she nodded. "Obviously, though I'm having some trouble getting what I need."

Placing his fork and knife on the edge of his plate, Tenoch reached into his suit jacket and retrieved a letter-sized envelope. Sliding it across to her, he waited until she was holding it before continuing. "These are the transponder codes for the GPS trackers on the next wave of containers coming north."

Her eyes went down to the light-yellow envelope. "That's *exactly* what I needed," she said, looking back at him. "How on earth did you know?"

Tenoch smiled slightly as he picked up his fork. "Part of what they teach in business school is how to forecast future results based on past performance," he said. "My mother informed me last night that someone broke into Vasquez Industries; whoever it was, they got in and out without a trace but seem to have also accessed a certain former employee's computer."

Kate felt her face flush again, though this time it was more out of embarrassment. "I see," she replied carefully as she looked at the envelope again. "Was, uh, anything taken?"

"For some reason, the I.T. department has been too busy to do a full forensic analysis," he replied, his eyes dancing with merriment. "So, we really don't know." He nodded toward the envelope. "Considering the favor you asked me yesterday, it wasn't hard to figure out what, exactly, was being sought. And," he smiled faintly, "that it might not have been in the files that were accessed."

She looked at him for a moment. "We're coloring a bit outside the lines here," Kate said quietly. "I appreciate what you've done for me so far, but if I take this from you, there's no going back." She paused. "For either of us."

Tenoch put his fork down again and leaned across the table. "Whatever is going on at Vasquez Industries needs to be stopped," he replied softly. "I'll be damned if I allow our family's company to be used as a front for something illegal. It *must* stop. I'd prefer to do this with your help, with the full weight of the law behind us, but I *will* stop it — by any means I have at my disposal."

Kate's eyes widened slightly at the quiet malice behind his words. "You're sure? There's a real possibility we may only get answers, and never any justice."

"Justice will *always* be served to those who deserve it," Tenoch said with a coldness that literally made her shiver. "*That* I can guarantee."

Nodding slowly, Kate wondered a bit at this strange side she'd never seen of Tenoch as she reached for the envelope. "That must have been a top-tier business school you went to," she said as she slipped the envelope into the interior pocket of her suit jacket.

"Not many survive the experience," Tenoch replied as he straightened up in his chair. "How do you like the wine?"

"It's good," she said, her eyes dropping for a moment to the vibrant red in her glass. "Very good." Her eyes came back up to his. "Are you *sure*?"

"More than anything," he said without hesitation.

Kate nodded again. "Have you looked at the... information?"

"Slightly," he replied. A shadow of a smile appeared. "Enough to know that actually tracking those containers will require access to a computer within the Vasquez Industries network."

"Shit," she breathed. "Then I am back to square one."

Those green eyes danced with merriment again, confusing her for a moment. "That depends."

"On what?"

"On whether you're open to a nightcap after dinner," he answered. "I might happen to have such a computer in my possession."

Kate wasn't sure if it was the wine or the aftereffects of whatever Ocelot had done, but she was relatively certain she was picking up on a particular undercurrent with Tenoch's offer. "I might be," she said neutrally as she folded her napkin and put it onto the surface of the table. "Would you excuse me for a moment?"

"Of course," Tenoch smiled.

He stood as she did, and she couldn't help but feel that his eyes were on her the entire way as she threaded a path through the restaurant toward the restrooms. Mind spinning, Kate pushed open the door to the women's section and then found the first open stall; locking the door, she pressed her hands against its cold metal surface and tried to sort through what was happening. It was clear Tenoch had just offered her access to *exactly* what she needed; less clear was whether she was correctly intuiting what the possible cost for gaining said access might be. The Tenoch she had fallen in love with all those years ago would never have swapped favors in that manner, but the coldly calculating version she'd glimpsed that evening, *he* seemed like one who might.

Who was this man? Did she even *know* him?

Maybe thinking she could trust him based on her past relationship had been a mistake out of the gate; as she stood there, hearing the sounds of all that went on in a bathroom, Kate felt the cold shiver of realization that in just those few short days of his reappearance in Santa Marcel, she had nearly run away from a life spent upholding the principles she had sworn an oath to protect. Worse, she found herself seriously considering paying the price Tenoch was implicitly asking of her; despite it having been her idea to schedule the dinner, she was now seeing the evening through a different prism, and found herself hating the corner she seemed to have painted herself into. Nearly lost in all of it — but not entirely — was the realization that Tenoch clearly still had feelings for her. Deep feelings. Feelings that she was loath to admit she, herself, might also be harboring.

Shit, she thought. *What the fuck have I gotten myself into?*

The response across the link was almost immediate. *You still love him?*

Startled slightly, Kate took a moment before responding to Ocelot. *I... I guess I do. But I can't, right? Because of... us?*

It's possible to hold two truths at the same time, he replied.

She thought about that. *I've not had time to even* consider *whatever truth this is between us. Regardless, he has no claim to my heart, not after what he did.*

There was a long pause. *Have you ever stopped to think that maybe it was never his choice to exit your life the way he did?* Ocelot asked. *You of all people should know that there can be hidden forces at play.*

Kate frowned. *For someone who claims to have lost his heart to me, you seem to be cutting the competition an amazing amount of slack.*

The pause was longer the second time. *Let's just say I might be able to identify with his situation.*

What the fuck does that mean? she asked.

I had a life elsewhere, he replied, his whispery voice in her head taking on a slight tone of regret. *I left people I cared about to come to Santa Marcel. People I can never apologize to.*

The sudden pit in her stomach was nearly physical. *You... loved someone else?*

Is it such a surprise? he asked with a slight chuckle. *We do what we must.*

I'm not sure how I feel about that—

Let him tell you his *truth,* Ocelot interrupted. *And let the evening progress as it needs to. When you are ready for me, reach out and I will be there.*

Kate felt his presence diminish across their connection, and with it, a sense of reluctance to respond should she try to pull him back. The conflicting signals were hard to reconcile, especially since she was certain there was no small amount of sadness at the other end that she might be favoring Tenoch over Ocelot. It had been years since multiple suitors had fought over her hand; as flattered as she was at the apparent competition, she had no intention of being *anyone's* prize. Unlocking the door to the stall, she ran some cold water over her face, washed up and then headed back to the table she shared with Tenoch.

Their dinner plates had been cleared by the time she returned, replaced by coffee in fine china that quietly steamed into the air as she took her seat. Tenoch seemed strangely reserved as she took a sip of the robust brew; holding the mug in the air for a moment, she took a second sip and then gently placed the cup back on the saucer. She let the silence linger for another moment before finally speaking.

"Your place, or mine?"

FIFTEEN

For whatever reason, the moment Kate agreed to accompany him back to his beachfront condo had Tenoch suddenly thinking about the summer of their senior year in high school and a particularly sultry July afternoon forever etched in his soul. None of his many late-night fantasies had come close to equalling the reality of being with her for the first time; as they'd basked in the afterglow under the hot sun, entangled in each other's arms, Tenoch had found it easy to promise Kate he'd be with her forever. He could still feel the softness of her skin against his as they slowly — and repeatedly — sealed their commitment to each other that day; had he not run out of condoms, Tenoch was certain they would have continued long after the sun had sunk below the horizon. The next nine months had been the happiest of his life — a happiness that his mother had shattered just a few hours before he took Kate to the Prom. Getting through that evening as well as the final days of their senior year had been excruciating; being forced to disappear without a trace shortly after graduation had nearly killed him.

As he unlocked the door to his condo, Tenoch wondered if there was any way for him to channel his overconfident inner eighteen-year-old, the one who'd thought nothing of appearing on Kate's doorstep wearing a Speedo small enough to clearly telegraph his intentions while toting a backpack full of condoms to back them up. Stepping aside to allow her into his space, he caught a faint whiff of her perfume as she passed and realized whatever control he *thought* he had was tenuous at best when it came to Kate. Trying hard to steady his breathing, he carefully closed the door behind him and had begun to put his keys on the side table when he felt her hands at his waist. The touch was electric, owing perhaps to the deeper connection the two shared already — the one that was taking more effort than he could let on to prevent her from discovering. Focusing on her while simultaneously trying to shut her out, mentally, was an exercise he'd never trained for while in the jungle; the faint warnings in the back of his head about what would happen should she discover the truth were shoved further away as he turned toward her. Kate's hazel eyes, barely visible in the semidarkness of his living room, were soft as she reached a hand to his face, allowing her to pull him close enough to gently press her lips to his. Pulse pounding dangerously in his ears, Tenoch leaned closer and allowed a bit of his suppressed passion into a kiss that had her breathing hard when they finally parted.

His already heightened senses made him hyperaware of every-thing, from the sound of the ocean as it pounded the surf far below his condo to the way the thin fabric of Kate's blouse hugged her torso. Leaning closer again, he carefully kissed a spot just above her collar, then gently shifted his hands beneath her blazer so he could push it off. Taking the hint, Kate reached up and undid his tie; his jacket was next, which dropped to the ground in a soft *whoosh* of expensive fabric. He felt more than saw her fingers at his shirt, first tentatively then more aggressively unbuttoning it; Tenoch shrugged out of it before leaning back down to press his lips to hers once more. He wasn't expecting her to suddenly press into him, brushing her not-yet-free breasts against his exposed chest with just enough friction to elicit a soft moan from Kate; smiling slightly, he made short work of freeing them from their prison, then dipped a bit lower so he could run his tongue exquisitely slowly around one nipple, then the other.

Hands were suddenly at his waist, furiously fumbling with the Gucci belt; it didn't help that he'd begun to walk the two of them toward his bedroom as he continued his assault on her soft bosom. Somewhere close to the couch he felt his pants slide down his thighs, followed by a quick tug at his boxer briefs; stepping out of them, he then knelt so he could undo her slacks, his hands intentionally sliding inside her waistband to help them down. His enhanced sense of smell immediately told him just how ready she was; that didn't stop him from slowly — ever so slowly — removing the last barrier between them. The fever of needing her began to take over, and he pressed her back against the wall beside the doorway to the bedroom so he could devour her delicious lips more thoroughly; she responded by wrapping one leg around his ass, then surprised him when she reached down to guide him into her willing depths. Tenoch felt his eyes widen and he tried to pull back; as much as he loved Kate — and dear gods, he knew now just how *deeply* he cared for her — he shared a measure of responsibility for ensuring whatever was about to happen between them didn't have any unexpected consequences. Granted, with his abilities the rules were a little different; still, he wasn't one to take chances and leave his fate to the whims of magic.

Kate sensed his resistance but continued to pull him into her. "Let it happen," she said, her voice husky.

"I've got condoms in the bedroom—" he said, gasping slightly as he felt himself slide into her.

"Got it covered," she whispered as her leg pulled him completely in.

The sensation of her depths fully embracing his member short circuited what was left of his sanity; it took him a long moment to realize the moan of ecstasy was his. More animalistic urges shoved aside what was left of his humanity; he growled slightly as he began to grind against Kate, each movement creating a delicious friction that had her arching against him. The fever intensified to the point where he lost track of time; Tenoch's world shrunk to the singular focus of the beautiful woman in front of him, and the need to ensure she achieved the release that her quivering body appeared to be craving. He rained kisses down on her now damp skin, then tasted the salt of her sweat on his tongue as he nibbled around her breasts and then buried his nose in the deep valley between them. His slow but steady rhythm morphed into something far more urgent; she began to meet him halfway, pulling him impossibly deeper with each stroke. The twinge deep within his loins that told him he'd gone too far presaged a massive shudder that had him rearing his head toward the ceiling, loosing a guttural growl that would have sent the birds of the jungle fleeing to the heavens; Kate was a fraction of a second behind him, shuddering into his chest as wave after wave of pleasure washed over her.

When the world reformed around him, Tenoch found himself gasping for air and completely wasted. Kate was still pressed up against the wall and was breathing equally as hard; looking down into her hazel eyes, he smiled slightly before reaching to push a sweat-soaked strand of her hair away from her forehead. "Hey," was all he could think to say.

She smiled back at him. "That was rather intense," she said.

He smiled wider. "I have a lot to make up for," he whispered softly.

Kate ran her hand through his curls. "Do you?" she asked. "We're not the same two teenagers we were, Tenoch. A lot has changed since you dropped off the face of the planet a decade ago."

Isn't that the truth, he thought a fraction of a second before realizing his mental shields weren't fully up. The look on Kate's face confirmed his fear, so he attempted to distract her by leaning in for another deep kiss. Pulling back, he smiled his most disarming smile before continuing.

"But not everything," he said. "You still have my heart wrapped around your little finger."

Kate's face softened. "Still the incurable romantic," she said.

"I don't expect you to feel the same way," he continued, carefully trying to walk the thin line between his two personas. "I'm sure there's someone else in your life now."

After a long moment, Kate slowly nodded. "There is, yes."

"Good," he smiled, inwardly breathing a sigh of relief. "I get that and completely understand; I have no right to magically appear in your life again and expect that you'd want to pick right up where we left off."

Kate arched an eyebrow. "All evidence to the contrary," she smiled.

Tenoch ran a finger along her chin before kissing it gently. "This is just a reminder of what once was," he said softly. "And what might be again if either of our circumstances ever change."

"It might be a while," Kate said. "I can't ask you to wait that long."

"I don't have a choice," he said more truthfully than she knew. "You own my soul and have from the moment I met you; I'll go to my grave before loving anyone else."

"That's terrifying! I won't let you—"

He put a finger to her lips. "What's done is done," he whispered softly. "I've made my choice."

She eyed him, then slowly nodded again. "I suppose you have," she said, then paused thoughtfully. "I'd feel far better about this if I knew more about what happened to you."

Tenoch groaned inwardly; Kate's innate investigative skills were never far from the surface. "It was a family obligation I thought I had gotten out of," he answered after a moment. "Or at least had put off until I was finished playing soccer. Events conspired to move up the timeline more than I expected."

"What sort of obligation?" she asked. "Was it related to your father passing?"

"Yeah," he said.

Thinking about the past killed what was left of his libido, so he slowly unwound Kate's leg from his waist and then gently pulled away from her. It seemed oddly appropriate to bear his soul to her while standing naked in his living room; glancing toward the sliders that led out to his balcony, he wondered just how much he could say without raising her suspicions — or inadvertently making a connection that would lead her back to Ocelot. Seeming to sense his shift in mood, Kate reached for his hand and squeezed it slightly in silent support; keeping her hand in his, he carefully led her across the debris of their clothing in the living room to the sliders, opened them, then helped her into the small hot tub huddled in the corner of his balcony. After turning up the jets, he joined her, sinking low enough to allow the water to cover his shoulders. Kate snuggled in beside him, running a hand behind his back before leaning her head against his. Composing his thoughts, Tenoch took a deep breath and plunged ahead.

"My *padre* was a complicated, private man," he began. "Growing up, I knew in general terms what he did; I was also taught from an early age that I'd be expected to take over for him when the time came." Tenoch smiled slightly. "I didn't realize that would happen at age eighteen."

"Take over?" Kate asked. "As in run Vasquez Industries?"

"Among other things," he replied generically. "I'd naively thought I could pursue my dreams before those family obligations kicked in; his unexpected death threw all of that out the window."

"He passed the spring before graduation, right?"

"President's Day Weekend," he answered softly.

"I didn't know he had health issues," she said after a moment.

"He didn't," he replied carefully. "*Padre* was traveling in Mexico and was killed by operatives from a cartel that didn't like our expansion into their area."

Kate sat up. "I had no idea."

"The company kept the details vague intentionally," he continued. "Our market cap would have suffered had it become widely known a penny ante drug gang had taken out the head of Vasquez Industries."

"Shit," she breathed. "Did the authorities ever bring them to justice?"

"After a fashion," he answered.

Tenoch had been with his mother when she'd wreaked her revenge on the souls that had taken out the patriarch of his family; when she'd finished, both the cartel — and the small mountain village that had housed it — had been erased from existence. It was his first true exposure to the power his family wielded — and the first time he'd fully understood what it had meant to take over the mantle from his *padre*. The flight back from Mexico to Santa Marcel on their private jet had been when *madre* had informed him of the training he would begin in the jungle after graduation, as well as her expectation that he'd cut ties with Kate as a result. He'd chafed at both demands, but in the end hadn't had much of a choice.

"I was too young to run the company," he continued, "so *madre* took over while I completed my education. That was followed by spending a few months at each of our facilities worldwide, learning the inner workings of Vasquez Industries. As geographically diverse a portfolio as we have, you can probably guess how long it took for me to complete what passes for a management training program in our company."

"I'm beginning to get the idea," she replied, and then looked at him thoughtfully. "Why is your mother still running things? Shouldn't you be the one in the top job now?"

Tenoch frowned slightly. "Apparently the terms of succession were... adjusted... while I was away," he replied carefully. Telling Kate he'd been the victim of a bloodless coup didn't feel appropriate. "My time will come," he added icily. "Eventually."

Kate reached for his hand and squeezed it. "Either way, you could have reached out — told me what was going on."

"Maybe," he replied. "Honestly, I didn't see the point; at best, we'd have had a long-distance relationship that wouldn't have survived the separation. It seemed best to just... disappear and let you get on with your life."

"I would have preferred to have had a vote in that," Kate said pointedly. "We made a promise to each other."

"We did," he sighed, "and I broke it. And I will be forever sorry for having done so."

"You didn't need to go through any of that alone."

Tenoch looked at her. "I know that now," he said. "Teenage version of me wasn't that smart."

"None of us were at that age," she sighed. "You do realize you're the reason I went into law enforcement, right?"

He frowned. "I didn't."

"Yeah," she said. "I became obsessed with finding out what happened to you, and becoming a cop felt like the only way to do it. Once I landed at Santa Marcel P.D. after the academy, I started poking around and located exactly *nothing* that explained where you went. I think there was a period when I visited your headquarters building enough the guard at the gate knew me on a first name basis."

"He probably still does," Tenoch laughed. "He never forgets a face."

"Regardless, Vasquez Industries ultimately leaned on our Chief and forced me to back off. And, as time passed, other cases with more current victims took over my life; while I still wondered, I'd actually written you off as dead." She paused. "Or worse."

Tenoch frowned. "What's *worse* than death?"

She looked at him. "Those women in the container, for one," she replied. "That, and I've seen far too many movies where people are plucked from the street and sold into a modern version of slavery in some faraway Eastern European country."

"Yeah," he said after a moment. "Yeah, I see your point. I am truly sorry to have worried you that way."

"You're here now," she smiled. "That's what counts."

Thinking it was a good time to shift the conversation, Tenoch picked up the thread that Kate started. "Speaking of containers," he said with a slight smile, "I'm thinking we might want to decode those GPS transponders before we begin round two."

Kate's eyes widened slightly, but he could also see her smiling. "That's a bit presumptuous, isn't it?"

"Maybe," he replied. "My computer is in the bedroom."

She chuckled. "Like you didn't plan *that*."

"Cross my heart," he laughed as he stood and exited the hot tub.

Reaching for the towels he had admittedly pre-positioned by the tub, he handed one to Kate as she joined him, then quickly dried off as much as he could before wrapping it around his waist. After a brief detour through his kitchen for two glasses of wine (also pre-positioned), they wound up at his small desk in the bedroom; he sat down and logged into his laptop, then brought up the VPN software that would allow him to connect to the data center back at the office. Kate hovered at his shoulder, watching intently as he navigated the somewhat complicated interface for their various systems; eventually, he finally landed on the page he needed.

Looking up at her, he asked: "Do you still have that list of codes I gave you?"

"It's in my jacket," she said. "One second."

Kate disappeared for a moment, then returned bearing the small envelope he'd given her at dinner; he felt his guilt at using the list to essentially lure her back to the condo warm his cheeks slightly, making him thankful for the low light in the bedroom. As he carefully opened the envelope and slid the list of transponders out onto the surface of the desk, he couldn't help but laugh at the insanity of Kate falling for his alter ego while still apparently carrying a flame for Tenoch; when she ultimately found out they were the same man — and he knew her well enough to know it was just a matter of time before she did, no matter what subterfuge he employed — there was going to be hell to pay. Assuming, of course, he survived the wrath of Tezcatlipoca.

One problem at a time, he thought.

"This part will be tricky," Tenoch said. "Technically, my position allows me access to the tracking system, but if what I suspect is true, the moment I key in these transponder codes, alerts are likely to be triggered."

Kate leaned in. "How much trouble will you be in?" she asked.

"Nothing I can't handle," he replied, though it took some effort to drive from his mind the image of his *madre* tossing him into his bookcase less than twenty-four hours earlier.

She put her hand to his chin and turned it toward her. "You don't have to do this," she said quietly, her eyes full of concern. "We can do this a different way — let me make you a confidential informant. Then I can get a warrant and do this properly."

"That will take time," he argued. "Time those women don't have. It's this or nothing."

Kate looked torn. "Are you certain? I won't be able to protect you, legally, if this goes sideways."

He looked deeply into those hazel eyes and felt the pang once more of what he'd been forced to give up in order to take his place with Tezcatlipoca. "Let me do this for you," Tenoch replied softly. "As part of my ongoing apology for leaving you."

"I'd prefer a box of chocolates," she chuckled.

"Oh, I have that too," he said. "Along with some champaign — as part of our second course."

Kate arched an eyebrow. "You put a lot of planning into this chance invitation, didn't you?"

"Years worth," he admitted.

She considered him again. "All right. But cover your tracks if you can."

"Way ahead of you," he replied as he turned back to his computer. "Here we go."

Taking a deep breath, he opened the tracking software and carefully transcribed the three codes into the entry window, then waited for the system to decode the transponders; now that he had all of the proper pieces in the same spot, it took but a fraction of a moment for the live map to pop up, showing in realtime the location of the containers in question. His joy at finally making *some* sort of progress was short lived, though, for to his horror he quickly realized he'd been misled: only one of the shipments was headed for Santa Marcel. The other two were headed in diametrically opposite directions with one bound for Singapore and the other en route to Cairo. As he clicked into the manifests to confirm what he was reading on the map, a warning popped up in the corner of the screen, alerting him to a cross-connected shipment; the feeling of dread deepened when he tapped on the alert and discovered three *additional* containers were being prepped in Oaxaca for follow-on shipment to the same destinations.

Shit! he mentally screamed. *This is worse than I thought.*

Kate's thoughts were immediately in his head. *Ocelot? What's wrong?*

Trying to keep his face impassive, he replied mentally. *I've... just come into some information,* he said. *How soon can we meet?*

I'm... currently tied up, was her tactful response. *I'll reach out when I'm home?*

"Good," he said aloud.

"Good?" Kate echoed.

"Good *God*," he hastily amended. "There are *six* containers, and only two are headed here. The other four are split between two other destinations: Singapore and Cairo. Getting to them won't be as easy as I thought."

"I have a contact that could help," Kate said after a moment. "Can you print out a copy of those coordinates? I can touch base with... them... and let you know."

Having a sense of what she was planning, Tenoch nonetheless played dumb. "Your network in the international law enforcement community must be quite broad," he said. "Especially if it can span such disparate authorities."

"You have no idea," she said. "I'll need to reach out right away, though."

Her voice was in his head almost immediately. *I think I have some info as well. I'm going to leave for home soon, but we definitely need to talk. The situation is graver than I realized, and time is of the essence.*

I guess that means our night of mad, passionate sex is out; I'll leave now and meet you at your place, he replied mentally as Ocelot before turning toward Kate. His brain began to hurt at trying to keep both conversations going. "I take it this means our second helping is going to have to wait."

"I'll make it up to you," Kate said as she leaned in for a kiss.

"Promise?"

"Promise," she smiled.

"I may not survive until then," he said plaintively as he sent the coordinates to his printer.

"Somehow, I doubt that," she laughed.

SIXTEEN

Witching hour traffic was light enough Tenoch made good time getting Kate to her house in Santa Marcel; after the evening they'd had, she found herself somewhat disappointed that he left her with a rather chaste kiss on her cheek before backing his Charger out of her driveway. Despite the feelings that seemed to be bubbling up within her over Tenoch — and her continuing surprise that she still had them — her heart was already spoken for, even if it was still a mystery as to who, exactly, she'd given it away to. Pulling her key from her pocket, she unlocked the front door and then slipped inside; as she flipped on a light in her living room, she felt the first of what she suspected would be many pangs of guilt over having slept with Tenoch. She couldn't deny how conflicted she seemed to be, nor just how easily she'd allowed herself to be seduced by her former boyfriend. Dropping her purse to the couch and wandering toward the slider and the shadowy figure that might be waiting for her beyond it, she laughed at the irony for hadn't she done the exact same thing to Ocelot not two days earlier?

I don't even know who I am any more, she thought as she pulled the slider open. *The world has gone mad.*

The night air greeted her as she stepped out onto her patio; it took a moment for her eyes to adjust to the darkness, but when they did, she felt herself smile when she immediately caught sight of the two slightly glowing eyes carefully watching her from her rear wall. "How long have you been waiting?" she asked.

"Not long," Ocelot replied as he leapt down from the fence and into what she was now considering his customary crouch; slowly, he moved toward her and into the pool of light cascading out from the living room. "How was your evening?"

"Full of surprises," she replied. "You changed your costume again?"

Ocelot sighed as he slowly stood. "Not intentionally, no," he answered. "The ears and the tail are courtesy of Tezcatlipoca, a sign that I'm getting close to being able to transform into my *nagual* form."

"*Nagual?*" she asked.

He smiled at her. "Sorry. My, uh, animal form."

Kate felt her eyebrows go up. "Animal form? Like, you can turn into a giant cat?"

"Jaguar, in this case," he smiled wider. "Though that's just one form I can take; there are others."

"Just when I thought this relationship couldn't get any weirder," she sighed.

"That's what you get for falling in love with me," he chuckled.

"Well, the ears are kind of cute," she admitted. "And I like your hair curly," she added, though she couldn't shake the sense it made him seem more familiar than before.

Something passed across his masked visage. "I'm not sure why I can't control the hair any longer," he said. "I fear Tezcatlipoca has some ideas about what my final look will be."

Kate frowned. "That's your *actual* hair?"

"God no," Ocelot replied with a smile. "This is so totally not my style; we're going to have words the next time I see Tezcatlipoca."

She'd been an investigator long enough to sense when someone was trying to mislead her; that Ocelot's tail chose that moment to twist slightly didn't help his efforts. He was clearly lying, which gave her great pause — but not enough to pursue it further. Yet. "That might be a rather one-sided conversation."

"Likely, yes," he laughed. "Now, what did you find out?"

"We have a problem," she began as she led him into her home. "Tenoch was able to decode the transponders and that opened a bigger can of worms than I expected."

Ocelot, ever the gentleman, had closed the slider but was still standing beside it; Kate belatedly realized he was waiting to be invited to take a seat. At her nod toward the couch, he smiled, leapt over the coffee table and somehow managed to gently land on a cushion before speaking. "Let me guess: there are more containers than we realized?"

"Yes," she nodded. "There are six in play at the moment, and not all of them are headed to Santa Marcel. Two are routed toward Singapore, while the rest are destined for Cairo."

Ocelot slowly nodded. "That fits with what I found," he said. Kate watched with fascination as he raised one of his claw-tipped hands and quickly snapped his fingers; the whorl of energy appeared just in front of him, and as he reached in for something, she wondered what it meant that she was getting used to seeing his virtual hiding spot. "I know it's in here," he murmured as his masked face frowned slightly.

Kate couldn't help herself. "Even high schoolers clean out their locker once a term, Ocelot."

His brown eyes shifted to her face. "Hah hah," he muttered as he continued to reach around.

It *was* a bit odd that Ocelot's arm had essentially disappeared up to the elbow. "How big an item can you store in that little fold of space-time of yours?" Kate asked.

"I dunno," he replied absently. "I've never tried anything beyond a laptop. Why?"

"Just curious," she said thoughtfully. "Could you have stuffed me in there the other night? Seems like it would have been a handy spot to hide me instead of trying to send me home."

Those brown eyes flicked to hers again. "I'd never stash a living thing in there," he said quietly. "A slightly different version of this spell is what was often used to banish those who had crossed one of our gods — or worse, whatever king was in charge at the time."

Kate's eyes went wide. "Like an actual purgatory?"

"One without the concept of entropy," he nodded. "Where there is no death, only endless, unrelieved existence."

"Remind me never to get on the wrong side of your deities," she breathed.

"Ah — here it is." Ocelot withdrew a small binder bearing the logo of Vasquez Industries and handed it to Kate. "I went back through the data Sebastian provided me originally and discovered some odd financial transactions with our subsidiary in Macao."

"Macao," Kate repeated as she flipped open the binder. Pages of spreadsheets were inside, most having some sort of highlighting on them. "It wouldn't be the first time that place would be a haven for financial shenanigans."

"I've not had time to fully trace them other than finding a tentative connection to Oaxaca," Ocelot continued as he settled back on the couch. "That alone seemed like enough proof we were on the right path."

"Everything keeps pointing back to Oaxaca," Kate said as she leaned against her breakfast bar. "Why there? What's so special about that location?"

His masked visage frowned again, which, oddly, was quite endearing; it made him look like a far younger teenager trying to wrestle with a tough Calculus problem. "Beyond the obvious — as a shipping hub, it connects Central America to the outside world — I have some theories," he began.

Kate eyed him for a moment. "Your opposite number," she said as she slowly. "You mentioned before that while you're in ascension, someone else out there was at their apex."

"Exactly," he nodded. "It's not an accident that Oaxaca is where this all seems to be starting."

It took a moment for Kate to connect the dots. "The jungle?" she asked. "*Your* jungle? It's there?"

"Well, technically the jungle is everywhere," he said with a smile, "but one of our most sacred places is less than a hundred kilometers from the hub."

Kate nodded toward the small amulet just below his throat. "I thought your power came from your pendant?"

Ocelot looked at her for a long, long moment, long enough that Kate realized he was deciding how much he could reveal to her. She was about to wave him off when he began to speak once more. "The stone *channels* whatever power Tezcatlipoca chooses to share with me," he ultimately corrected. "That, in turn, allows me to work my magic, though much depends on the environment I'm currently in."

"That explains your coffee-making exercise a bit better," Kate said. "So what's so special about this place close to Oaxaca?"

Her companion looked uncomfortable for a moment. "The... best explanation is that it's the fabled center of our beginning," he explained. "The birthplace of our gods." He tapped a claw tip against the small obelisk. "It's also where all of these enchanted beauties come from."

"You make it sound like some sort of forge — like something out of Greek mythology."

Ocelot smiled. "One of the adepts I was training with years ago told me there's a school of thought among the most learned of their order that *our* deities appeared to other humans around the globe in whatever form was most suited to *that* culture. I've done enough research into it myself to recognize the similarities between rituals in my codex and those carved into the stones at Thebes or painted into frescos in Rome millennia ago."

Kate felt a wave of astonishment wash over her. "Is it actually true?" she asked. "I mean, before I met you, I'd always assumed God was an artifact of our own need to know that there's something beyond death. Seeing as though you *work* for one, my perspective has shifted slightly."

He smiled. "I can imagine. I actually asked Tezcatlipoca about it; being the wily deity they are, the best I got was oblique confirmation the images of Sekhmet — the Egyptian warrior goddess — never quite captured their actual likeness."

"Your patron appears to be gender fluid," Kate frowned.

"Don't I know it," Ocelot laughed.

The very idea that he was working for an entity that had literally been around since the creation of humanity was a bit sobering; no small amount of Kate was hoping she'd wake up soon from whatever dream she was trapped within. When that didn't immediately happen, she forged onward. "So, your pendant was forged in this so-called 'sacred place?'"

"Yes," he nodded. "And before you ask, no, being closer to the source doesn't give us *more* power — save for one specific situation."

Kate started to slowly nod. "When you're in declination?"

"Exactly," Ocelot smiled. "And this indirectly tells us something: it's significant that whomever we are up against *needs* such help to channel every last ounce of their fading magic. This is the rare, singular case when proximity actually helps."

"To do *what*, exactly?" Kate felt herself frowning. "You don't need magic to cram humans into an overweight cargo container, and unless we're missing something, those are still being shipped using traditional freight methods. I feel like I'm missing a connection between *that* and whoever killed Sebastian."

"Same," Ocelot sighed. "I think it's too much of a coincidence to ignore, though."

"We've got to get down there, then."

"I agree," Ocelot replied. "But stopping those containers takes precedence over uncovering that link."

"Please tell me you have some magic up your sleeve that will help us deal with this,"

Ocelot held up an arm. "Well, seeing as I don't have any sleeves—"

"You *know* what I meant," Kate huffed.

"I do. And I might have a plan that will work."

"*Might?* I need something a bit more solid," Kate replied. "Especially since I slightly exaggerated the extent of my international connections to Tenoch."

Ocelot canted his head slightly and smiled. "You lied? To your former boyfriend?"

"It was either that or tell him about you," she sighed. "The latter didn't seem wise."

"Yeah," Ocelot agreed before looking a little uncomfortable. "What I've come up with so far involves a spell or two I've not entirely mastered," he admitted. "The results could be unpredictable."

"You're not instilling me with much faith."

"Then you'll just have to trust me," he said. "We don't have time for anything else."

"I'm afraid you're right," she replied. "What's the plan, then?"

Ocelot's tail started to twist again, a sign that she was beginning to dislike; she wondered for a moment if he even realized it was telegraphing his emotional state. "I'll use a portal to get to each unit," he said. "Once I reach them, I'll use another portal to bring them directly to Santa Marcel; after they are safely in California, I'll call another anonymous tip into your station and your team can take it from there."

Kate knew she looked skeptical. "That's a lot of portal wielding in a short space of time," she began. "Can you physically take that?"

"Yes," he said confidently, though his tail continued to betray him.

"All right," she said, though she was far from convinced. "That solves the containers already in motion, but not the original problem of them using the Vasquez Industries shipping network in the first place."

"I think it's a good bet that the base of operations for this scheme is Oaxaca," he said. "My final transit will be there to deal with that."

Kate frowned. "As a *solo* operation?"

"You don't want to be around when I finally get down to business there," he said darkly.

"I suppose not," she said after a long moment. "Still, you might need backup—"

"Unless you've suddenly developed a talent for magic, I'm not sure you'd be able to do that," he interrupted. "Besides, I need you to be safe; that means staying here in Santa Marcel and taking care of this end of things. I can handle whatever I find in Oaxaca, I assure you."

"Even if you bump up against this nemesis that is more powerful than you?"

"Timing will be everything," Ocelot replied. "I'm coming into my full abilities any day now, which means theirs are quickly waning. Besides, the jungle is my home turf — I've not been away as long as they have. The advantage will be mine."

Kate caught something in his response. "How long have you been in Santa Marcel, exactly?" she asked.

Ocelot seemed to sense he'd revealed something he shouldn't have and just smiled. "Long enough to have fallen in love with you, *princesa*."

She folded her arms against her chest. "That's not an answer to my question, flattered as I might be."

"It's all you're going to get from me for now," he smiled wider. "A cat's gotta have a few secrets."

Despite wanting to argue the point — and the nagging feeling at the back of her head that it was important — Kate decided to put it aside. "When do we leave, then?"

Ocelot's smile faltered. "There's no 'we' in the traveling aspect of things," he reminded her. "I need you to stay here and oversee the recovery of the containers once I send them back."

"My team can handle that," Kate said, stubbornly unwilling to concede the point. That, and she couldn't entirely discount a visceral need to accompany him. "I have a sense you're going to need me."

"I don't think—"

"I'm going, and that's final," she said. "When do we leave?"

Ocelot seemed torn, but when he finally hung his head, Kate decided she'd scored a victory. "Are you certain about this?" he asked as he slipped off the couch and moved over to her. "It *will* be dangerous. I'm not certain what we're getting into, and the chance you might get hurt scares the living daylights out of me."

"I'm a trained police officer," she said reassuringly as she reached out to him; her heart did a funny *pitter-patter* when he slipped under her arms and then held her to his costumed body. "I'm not worried about holding my own."

He smiled and reached up to brush a strand of hair away from her forehead. "Clearly you aren't," he said softly. "You have enough faith to support the both of us, don't you?"

The gentle touch of the tip of his claw had her closing her eyes; she'd not realized just how sensual it could be. "With reason," she replied as she reopened them and gazed deeply into his beguiling brown eyes. "Besides, how are you going to explain this outfit of yours if we run into anyone?"

Ocelot arched a masked eyebrow. "Far better than you waving your Santa Marcel badge at someone in Cairo," he countered. "Unless you are, in fact, a super spy with multiple identities working for the CIA."

"I'm not," she smiled. "That sort of work has never appealed to me; I never liked the idea of living a lie."

Something crossed his masked face. "It's not much fun, to be sure."

"Oh, shit," she breathed. "I didn't mean—"

"I know you didn't," he smiled. "But it does sting nonetheless."

"Would a kiss help make it better?"

He smiled wider and closed the distance between their lips. "Maybe. Might take more than one."

"Okay," she smiled.

Leaning into him, she pressed her lips to his and was immediately engulfed in such a deep sense of warmth that it took a full minute for her to realize something was wrong; despite how good it felt, she began to fight against the waves of contentment washing over her, instinctively understanding their true purpose. Within moments, she knew it was a losing battle, almost as though she were a trout attempting to swim upstream against a current infused by the spring melting of snow atop the mountains. Still cognizant of her body, Kate felt herself easily lifted off her feet, followed by being gently carried; the softness of the pillow behind her head seemed like nothing she'd ever experienced before, and it was hard not to actually purr contentedly when her blanket was pulled up to her chin. Only when his voice finally appeared in her head did the faintest notes of anger creep in around the edges of her consciousness.

I'm sorry, princesa; *I need to keep you safe, and that means ensuring you stay in Santa Marcel. I'll be back before you know it.*

What... she managed to get out. *What... do?*

Sleep, princesa. *You can be angry with me later.*

Oblivion overtook her at that point, but not before she had the sense that he'd leaned down one final time to kiss her...

SEVENTEEN

The portal deposited him inside the unfinished floor of a high rise in downtown; crouching on the concrete floor, Ocelot took a long moment to scan the space with his enhanced senses before creeping toward the massive floor-to-ceiling glass at the edge of the building. Given the time difference, he'd arrived in what was essentially the early evening in Singapore; while the great city didn't entirely keep to Western thoughts around work hours, the traffic on the streets below told him the day had definitely shifted into the wilder nightlife it was well known for. Pressing closer to the glass, he felt the faint chill of the slightly colder air that far up; being a creature of the sweltering jungle meant that climes such as Santa Marcel were far preferable, but that didn't stop him from forcing a claw into the glass and then starting to carve out a chunk. Not more than fifty meters away was the tower housing the offices of the subsidiary Vasquez Industries ran in Singapore, offices that held the specific security codes he was going to need before he hit the shipping staging area on the water-front. If he'd learned anything from the painful lesson doled out to him less than twenty-four hours earlier, it was the need to account for every possible method of discovery, large or small, and have a plan in mind to counter *all* of them. The codes were one key to that, codes that his alter ego had no way of obtaining without setting off a ton of alarms that would have found their way to his mother; staying off her radar for as long as possible was the entire game now, especially once he understood the link to Oaxaca. As he slowly pulled the glass from the window — and braced himself against the sudden gust of wind as he did so — Ocelot smiled wryly at how he'd not shared that *particular* portion of the plan with Kate; while the codes would allow him to disable the monitoring system at the docks, even with the magic he was planning on casting, he was far from certain his escapades would go undetected for long. He was starkly aware it wouldn't be difficult for his mother to deduce his movements once the alarm was raised over the missing containers, so time was most definitely not on his side; the sooner he got to Oaxaca and ended whatever it was his mother had begun, the better.

As he carefully pulled himself through the hole he'd carved in the glass and into the stiff breeze whistling between the buildings, Ocelot still felt like he was missing a key piece as to *why* his mother would risk all that Vasquez Industries had become in allowing their network to be used for such nefarious purposes; worse, he couldn't understand how she could break the sacred pledge the family had taken to protect the innocent on behalf of Tezcatlipoca. The two most likely explanations were both terrible: either she was under some sort of strange duress and being forced to do it, or she had willingly betrayed everything they had fought for over the course of fifteen generations. Digging his claws into the soft glass of the window at his back, Ocelot realized it was a question Kate's keen insights would have likely quickly answered. Thinking of her brought an immediate pang of regret, for contrary to what he had said to her, Ocelot would have appreciated her calm company by his side.

Oh, Kate, he thought as wind continued to buffet him. *You don't yet know how much you mean to me — and how you are now far too important to risk on something like this. Not yet.*

He didn't expect an answer, for the somnambulant spell he'd cast on her was designed to last for at least an hour — just long enough for him to do what needed to be done and, hopefully, return to her side. Whatever anger she'd likely feel at his transgression was something he would be willing to live with for the rest of his life in the name of keeping her safe. Putting aside his substantial guilt, Ocelot slowly made his way along the razor-thin metal frame of the window to the edge of the building, then carefully turned so he could face the one opposite; as strong as the winds were at that height, the strange mop of curls Tezcatlipoca now seemed to feel should be part of his costumed persona whipped around his face with an unexpected fierceness. While he rarely spoke against the desires of his patron, the new look wasn't really working for him, underscored, perhaps, by the strange look of dawning recognition he'd seen in Kate's eyes. Unless the deity had changed the terms of their agreement, it was far too soon for his beloved to discover who was beneath the domino mask.

Looking across the wide gap, Ocelot narrowed his eyes so he could scan the office that was his destination; after what had happened back in Santa Marcel, he'd grown suspicious that using a portal to go directly inside would have been a far too dangerous step to take, though the longer he spent on the outside of the high rise, the more he wondered if his judgement had been faulty. Taking a deep breath, he yanked one claw from the glass behind him and made a quick casting motion; small circles of green-black energy appeared one after another, creating a floating pathway across the chasm. Pushing back his anxiety, Ocelot leapt to the first glowing disc and then quickly bounded across the rest, landing on the slightly larger ledge for the other building in mere seconds. When his night vision confirmed the office on the other side of the glass was empty, he snapped his gloved fingers three times to allow the glowing pools of light to fade away into the night, then quickly set to work carving out another slice of glass. True to form, the window was slightly thicker than the last one, just enough that he felt each precious minute ticking by as his claw tip slowly completed a nearly perfect circle. Pressing his shoulder to the spot, the glass fell inside with a soft *clunk*, and he immediately threw himself through the open space.

Arcing through the darkened room, he landed in a crouch on what turned out to be a significantly thick carpet; pausing again, he extended every one of his heightened senses to determine whether he was completely alone or not. Save for the faint heartbeat of the security guard two floors below him, his feline hearing confirmed he was safe for the moment; a quick sniff of the air told him the last occupant had departed some hours earlier, though he found himself wrinkling his nose in disgust at the heavy notes of their expensive cologne still hanging in the space. One of the worst side effects of his abilities was a growing intolerance for the panoply of fragrances humans seemed predisposed to douse themselves in; his time in the jungle had given him a unique perspective on the true scents from Mother Nature, flavors no chemist had ever been able to mimic to Ocelot's satisfaction. To his displeasure, he'd been unable to locate a spell in his codex that could help ease the situation, mostly because he was expected to *use* his enhancements, not block them.

Maybe if I survive this, he thought as he carefully crept toward a canted glass desk centered in the space, *Vasquez Industries will launch a sub corporation specializing in such things. Or,* he smiled, *maybe I'll hire a smart scientist that can whip up something to block the worst of the smells for me.*

Crouching once more to make sure he was below the angle of the web camera he'd spied on the front of the flatscreen computer sitting on the desk, Ocelot belatedly realized he was looking at a nearly identical version of his mother's office back in Santa Marcel, right down to the hidden cocktail bar behind the desk and the set of mysterious doors on opposite walls. The similarly was so acute, in fact, that for a moment he fought back a strange sense that he'd been there before — when he knew, in fact, he'd never once set foot in their Singapore office. Arching a masked eyebrow, he sat back on his haunches and considered how long the odds were that two spaces thousands of kilometers apart would be so similar. While it wasn't outside the realm of possibility the designer for the headquarters building had been used in Singapore, Ocelot intuitively knew there was more to it than that.

Feeling a surge of curiosity override the sense that he was losing precious time, Ocelot paused just long enough to throw a cloaking spell over the computer before leaping to the doorway to the right. Carefully, he reached a gloved hand to the knob on the door and pushed it open to reveal the executive washroom he'd expected to find, complete with the phone beside the toilet. Pulse pounding in his ears, Ocelot pulled the door shut and then gracefully leapt to the doorway on the left — the one he'd been long forbidden from entering for as long as he could remember. Reaching for the door-knob, he felt a sudden surge in that invisible magical blanket that always shrouded him; pulling back, he felt the sizzle recede.

Curious, he thought. *May it not kill* this *cat.*

Taking a deep breath, he pushed through the uncomfortable tingle and twisted the handle; instead of swinging into the space beyond, the doorway slid sideways, revealing a rectangular portal shimmering with the same energy as those he typically opened for transit. Masked eyebrows rising, Ocelot realized he was looking at what the adepts had long considered a myth: the dimensional doorway, a magical portal only a select few could conjure that connected multiple places simultaneously. Once cast, they took an immense amount of energy to keep open, energy that could only come from one source. With a start, he realized he'd seen the answer to this particular puzzle already; turning away from the doorway, he snapped his fingers again to open his prized fold-in-spacetime storage area, then reached into the whorl of energy to pull back the small stone he'd found in that first container days earlier. Holding sliver of flint up and in the direction of the doorway, his masked eyes narrowed when he saw the vein of quartzite light up and then begin to pulse in time with the waves of energy he could feel pouring off of the portal. Only then did the final piece drop into place.

She's not trafficking in humans, he thought. *I mean, she* is, *but she's using it to cover for getting this — whatever it is — to any destination that has one of these portals. But why?* He found himself asking. *Short of getting between our offices faster, I can't see how it would hel—*

All at once, the answer hit him with the force of the absolute truth he knew it to be.

My god, he thought as he glanced down at the small obsidian disk nestled into his costume. *It's the same stone! And with enough of them, and someone powerful enough to channel their power, I'd be willing to bet a skyscraper could be moved across the galaxy with hardly any effort.*

He looked up at the sizzling energy of the dimensional portal and slowly began to nod.

What was it Kate said? Overweight containers? he asked himself as he looked again at the flint in his gloved hand. *Between the stones required and the women, I bet they were; those poor souls were actually hiding the true purpose — but why? Why go to the effort of* shipping *magical artifacts instead of using the portals—*

Blinking, the answer dawned on him a moment before he tossed the stone into the glowing doorway. A miniature supernova exploded where it hit the shimmering doorway; he barely had time to leap sideways to avoid being taken out by the small but impressive wave of energy that sizzled across the office, singeing everything it touched. Crouched on all fours, Ocelot wrinkled his nose at the additional acrid odors now flooding the space before casting his rain spell to put out the flames before the fire alarms were triggered; as the deluge rolled off his costumed form, he turned back toward the door.

"This is what *padre* was doing, wasn't it?" he asked the empty space, hoping — but not entirely expecting — an answer. "How we became the apex predator in global shipping?"

Now you understand, mijo, a familiar voice said in the back of his head; it held an unusual note of tenderness that Ocelot rarely heard when speaking with Tezcatlipoca. *And now you know why I chose you for this purpose.*

"Is this some sort of retribution?" Ocelot asked, his voice shaking. "To punish me for the transgressions of our family? I had no part — no knowledge—"

No, was the immediate reply. *Not punishment. A reckoning, perhaps; and a restoration of the way things Ought To Be.* There was a long pause. *Your father understood this, but in the end was thwarted.*

"Thwarted?" he asked, puzzled. "By whom?"

You already know the answer to that question.

That shiver of recognition ran down Ocelot's spine once more. "*Padre* didn't die on a business trip, did he?"

My brethren are just as powerful, and just as deadly, Tezcatlipoca replied enigmatically. *They will do anything to keep me from reaching equilibrium. Until you arrived in the jungle, I feared for the future.* There was another pause. *Don't prove me wrong.*

"Good to know I'm on the right track," Ocelot sighed.

Save those women. And stop what is going on in Oaxaca before it's too late.

It became clear in the course of a few heartbeats he was alone again; his miniature thunderstorm had eased up to a gentle drizzle, allowing him to more fully survey the damage. There wouldn't be any way to hide that he'd been here now, not that he actually cared to at that point; while he knew more than a few spells to return the office to the state in which he'd found it, his inner teenager had begun to emerge, overwhelming him with just enough of a rebellious impulse to leave the damage as is. Unfortunately, that also meant the computer where he'd hoped to purloin the security codes was now nothing but a still-smoking melted pile of plastic and silicon; sighing, he closed his eyes and reached out into the office, pulling together all of the essential elements he needed to restore some semblance of order. The spell he chose typically took a lot out of him, but when he opened his eyes to find the space pristine and the computer back where it was supposed to be, he felt no worse for wear and chalked it up to being that much closer to his ascension.

Not wanting to waste another moment, Ocelot quickly cast the cloaking spell around himself and then leapt over the desk to gain access to the computer. As he'd correctly assumed, the light indicating the web camera was active was on, despite the screen itself being dark; given the angle, it likely hadn't picked up the supernova from the dimensional doorway, but he picked up the pace just in case someone *did* notice it had gone offline for a few seconds. Using a claw tip, he tapped at the spacebar and saw the login screen appear; his heart began to race as he realized he'd reached the point of no return. Under better circumstances, he would have crafted a fake employee for the Singapore location and therefore buy himself a bit more time, but that was the one commodity he was far short of. Taking a deep breath to steady himself, he tapped in his credentials and then held his breath while he waited for the system to authorize his access.

The few seconds' wait was excruciating, but ultimately the desktop appeared; knowing the clock was now truly ticking, he quickly dove in and accessed the security subsystem. A few heart-beats more and he had the seven codes he needed displayed on the screen; committing them to memory, he started to exit the security system before pausing; grinning slyly, he deftly opened a terminal window and then used the command shell to remotely log into several other offshore locations, triggering a series of breach alerts in the process. Sitting back, his sly smile widened at the thought the InfoSec office back in Santa Marcel would be slowed trying to deter-mine whether Tenoch had *actually* used a device in Singapore, or if his credentials had somehow been compromised and were now being used to hack the *entire* Vasquez Industries system. Deciding to muddy the waters further, he left his account active on the computer and then made a giant leap toward the dimensional doorway.

His original plan had been to open a portal to the docks, but as he eyed the shimmering energy, he wondered if that would be neces-sary; having never used such a device, he only had the tall tales told by the adepts to guide him, which made what he was about to do pretty damn risky. Hoping that Tezcatlipoca was still looking out for him, Ocelot closed his eyes, thought about where he wanted to go, and then boldly stepped into the whirling energy. The searing of the magic as it tore him from where he'd been and deposited him else-where took his breath away; dropping to his knees, Ocelot found himself taking in air in massive gasps as he tried to figure out if it had worked. The stacks of corrugated metal containers on either side of him confirmed he'd guessed right; a moment later, the salty tang of being on the waterfront hit his sensitive nose, along with the other myriad scents of a working port.

Having committed the map of the docks Vasquez Industries owned to memory earlier, he used the tall loading crane as his land-mark and took off at a full gallop for the security hut in the south-west corner of the yard. As he ran through the urban jungle, his predatory senses began to take over; a part of him was surprised he no longer needed to cast a spell in order to hear the heartbeats of the humans scattered across the yard. The sizable concentration of frantic beats on the northeast corner told him where his target container was; skidding to a stop at a natural intersection between stacks of containers, he decided it would be easier to avoid what he assumed were the rent-a-cops randomly patrolling around him and deftly leapt upwards. Driving his claws into the soft metal of the shipping container, he hurled himself further upward until he landed in a crouch atop the stack; barely winded, he immediately set off toward the security hut again, cloaking his advance with as much stealth as he could muster.

Leaping over one canyon between stacks, he crouched at the edge of another, then flung himself over the side; using a small gust of wind to slow him down as he fell, he dropped nearly silently on top of the modular structure, then leaned an ear to the roof so he could determine how many poor souls were beneath him. Only one set of heartbeats appeared to be present; without wasting another moment, he drove his claws into the roof below him and peeled back just enough of it to allow him to drop inside. The startled guard was halfway out of his seat, fumbling to get to the gun at his hip; Ocelot brushed him back into the chair with a quick gust of wind, forcing the gun out of his hand. As it clattered to the discolored industrial tile, Ocelot cast a secondary spell to twist the arms of the chair across the torso of the still-spluttering guard, pinning him in place. He ignored the string of curses hurled in his direction as he wheeled the guard into the small bathroom at the rear of the hut, then cast two more spells: one to melt the lock in the door, and a second to temporarily soundproof the room. By the time anyone heard the erstwhile guard's screams for help, Ocelot would be long gone.

Heading back to the console the guard had been stationed at, Ocelot scanned the controls for the set he needed; smiling when his masked eyes landed on it, he quickly used the codes he'd borrowed to create a blind spot just large enough to allow him to get to — and then remove — the containers from Oaxaca before anyone realized what he was up to. Glancing over to the monitor that displayed the rolling security bulletins from the home office, he wasn't surprised to see that the alert of a possible breach at the Singapore location had already gone out; what made his masked eyes widen was the immediate followup to lock down *all* shipping locations.

That didn't take long, he sighed as he leapt back up through the hole he'd made in the roof. *This is going to be tighter than I thought.*

Cocking his head, he noted where the concentrated heartbeats were and then leapt into the night.

EIGHTEEN

Her dreams were like being inside one of those classic Hollywood film noirs that her father had so adored; many a weekend afternoon of her youth had been spent alternating between the latest iteration of *Star Trek* and Turner Classic Movies, with a special emphasis on anything that had been shot during the Golden Age. *To Have and Have Not* was a particular favorite, one that had introduced her to the entire genre in the first place — and her father's strange obsession with the actress Lauren Bacall. She'd not fully appreciated how much of a fan he was until the year she surprised him with tickets for the annual film festival held at the old Chinese Theater in downtown Los Angeles; Bacall had been the headliner that year, one of her final public outings before her passing. Kate's father had insisted they drive up to LA hours earlier than needed just to ensure they got a good spot in line; it paid off when they scored seats fairly close to the stage — and the microphone where attendees could ask questions. After watching her father hang on every word spoken by the still beautiful actress, she'd recoiled in some horror when he immediately jumped up during the

Q&A portion of the program. Her embarrassment shifted to something more like awe when her father told an unexpected story of how he'd met her mother while watching one of the many movies Bacall had shot with Humphrey Bogart — and how their mutual love for the couple had led to thirty years of wedded bliss. Bacall, ever elegant, had laughed in her unique way and then related a tale of how nervous she'd been on set with Bogart for the first time, and how that had led to the now-famous Bacall stare. It had been a lovely moment, one that her father had treasured right up until his unexpected death.

Unlike *those* movies, though, whatever Kate was experiencing felt far more modern and brimming with malice. Tall skyscrapers surrounded her and reached for the overcast sky high above her, and the wind was cold against the thin fabric of her blouse. The Glock in her hand felt even colder, though *why* she had it out was a bit of a mystery. Whatever city she was in was massive, and yet completely devoid of activity save for the far-off sounds of some sort of clash. Pausing at a deserted street corner, she tried to get her bearings as small snowflakes began to fall; adding to the etherial nature, she could actually *hear* the full orchestra playing the soundtrack for whatever movie she was in. As she turned the corner and began to head toward the activity, it wasn't hard to miss how the string section had suddenly begun to wail, a non-subtle warning that the heroine was headed for danger.

Four steps in, the skyscrapers disappeared and were replaced by endless rows of stacked shipping containers; the tension in the soundtrack accompanying her movements became palpable, but she pressed on, the sound of some terrific battle becoming more prominent as she closed in. Flashes of light strobed against the overcast sky, one after the other, illuminating the thickening snowflakes. Trudging through the deepening snow drifts became increasingly difficult; in moments, her slacks were icy cold and sticking to her skin, an unpleasant reminder she'd not dressed appropriately for the callout. The sense that she shouldn't be there — that she should, in effect, be *anywhere* but there — became unavoidable as she rounded the final corner and found Ocelot standing in the middle of a small clearing; his hands were raised, and it *looked* like he was literally trying to push a container—

Sensing her presence, Ocelot turned; the expression on his face was one she'd never seen before, equal parts fear and exhaustion. "You can't be here," he said through gritted teeth. "Go back."

"I can help—" she started. The orchestra played some sort of lovely tune, something she realized was the strange music she heard in her head each time she thought of Tenoch. Or was that Ocelot?

"Go... *back*," he said forcefully.

Bolting upright from her pillow, Kate found herself nearly hyperventilating; her heart was pounding in her ears, making her worry that some sort of cardiac event had manifested. It took every last ounce of willpower to get herself back under control, but when she did, she found herself bathed in sweat and angrier than she'd ever been before. Without a second thought, she reached for and then yanked, hard, on the gossamer connection she shared with Ocelot.

Not the best time, was the immediate response.

Fuck that, she replied. *Where the fuck are you? And what did you do to me?*

How she knew he was dealing with something at the other end was a mystery to file away for later. *I'm nearly done in Singapore,* he answered after a long moment. *About to go to Cairo. You need to get your teams to the intermodal yard now.*

I can do that, she replied. Kate waited a moment and then continued. *Was I actually there with you? Just now?*

In a sense, was the terse reply. *This is taking... a lot of my focus, enough that you were able to sneak past my mental barriers for a moment.*

Are you okay?

For the moment, was his enigmatic reply. *Go to the yard. I'll be in touch once Cairo is complete.*

Ocelot —

Not now, he said with a finality that told her he'd ignore any further attempts on her part to reach out.

Tugging gently at the thread was enough to confirm he was still alive; it was small solace, but enough that she was able to roll out of her bed and find her abandoned iPhone to call Dispatch. After ensuring units were on the way to the Santa Marcel Rail Yard to intercept another batch of human cargo, she dashed through the shower then changed into her more standard attire as befitting a detective. Kate had made it as far as the front door when her iPhone rang; glancing at the number displayed, she smiled slightly as she answered.

"Tenoch?" she asked as she stepped out into the early morning chill; sunrise was still a few hours out, making her wish she'd grabbed something more substantial from her closet than her blazer.

"Kate," came the warm voice of her former boyfriend. "Can you come to Vasquez Industries? I think I've found something you need to see."

Unlocking the door to her car, Kate paused. "I'm actually on the way to a callout," she replied. "I can swing by afterwards, if that's okay?"

"It might not be," he replied. "Once my mother arrives, it'll be harder to show you. You need to get here now if you can."

"What exactly do you have?" Kate asked, concerned at his tone; it was unlike him to be so forceful.

"I don't want to talk about it over the phone," he said, lowering his voice as he spoke. "If she finds out I'm still speaking with you, it'll be my head."

Warning bells began to go off in the back of her head. "You're not alone, are you?" she asked carefully.

There was a long pause. "Can you come, Kate?" was his rejoinder. "I would be best to see you in person."

Kate paused again. It wasn't exactly confirmation, but it didn't make her feel any better, either. "I can have a deputy cover for me while I swing over," she ultimately replied. "I can't stay long; it's an active investigation."

"Understood," he said. There was a faint note of relief in his voice. "Park in the executive lot; I'll buzz you up the elevator when you arrive."

"All right—" she started to say when the line went dead.

Pulling the phone away from her ear, Kate looked at the now-dark display and frowned at her slight reflection. *Something's off about this*, she thought. *But I'll be damned if I can put my finger on just what it is.*

Tapping the screen to activate it, she speed-dialed the number Tenoch had given her and found herself immediately sent to voice-mail; her sense that Tenoch might be in real trouble intensified when her second and third tries met a similar end. Without hard evidence, though, she was reluctant to call out the calvary; the last thing she needed was to show up guns a-blazing at Vasquez Industries just to discover he was simply trying to hide the fact he'd reached out to her while wandering the halls of the building. Still, it seemed best to let Ocelot know plans were shifting slightly on her end, so after she updated the officer on scene at the rail yard that she'd be delayed, Kate tugged at that gossamer thread connecting her to the masked hero.

Ocelot? Are you there?

The stony silence at the other end didn't tell her much, so she tried again.

I've got to go to Tenoch; I think he's in trouble. I'll get back to the rail yard as soon as I can.

Kate wasn't entirely surprised that Ocelot wasn't answering, but it was also pretty hard to tell if he'd gotten the message or not; deciding to cover her bases, she dug through her satchel for the burner phone he'd given her a few nights earlier. Ignoring for the moment that the battery was in need of charging, she quickly tapped the redial button and left the same message as voicemail before tossing the device back into the depths of her bag. Sliding behind the wheel of her car, she started it up and backed out of her driveway, unable to shake her base cop instinct that she needed to tread carefully. Exactly *why* she had that sense was perhaps more troubling.

The drive across Santa Marcel was uneventful at that early hour; as she turned into the small driveway for the executive parking lot at Vasquez Industries, the faint glow of the pending sunrise had begun to color the hills around the building. To her surprise, the small guard station protecting the executive lot was empty, but that didn't prevent the arm from immediately going up at her arrival. Glancing at the bubble camera on a post high above the guard station gave a partial explanation, but it didn't alleviate the crawling sensation along her skin nor the sense that it might just have been wiser to have brought backup. Putting her car back into gear, she pulled through the gate; it took a moment for her to register that the lot was completely empty, another sign that perhaps all was not as it should be. Wondering now who might be calling the shots, Kate pulled into one of the many empty slots and then made sure the clip in her Glock was full — then reached into the glovebox safe to grab a spare clip, just in case.

I don't know if you can hear me, Kate thought across the connection she had with Ocelot, *but I am nearly certain something is about to go down at Vasquez Industries. My gut tells me it's connected to what you're currently doing, so under no circumstances are you to come back. Finish what you're doing. I can take care of myself.*

There was a strange twinge across the connection, just enough of *something* to tell her she might have gotten through to Ocelot. Not waiting to confirm that observation, she exited her car and slipped her Glock into the holster at her waist, then made her way in the cool morning air to the steel doors of the elevator. She wasn't surprised when the light on the small pad next to the doors winked from red to green at her approach, though she was somewhat more wary when the carriage doors snapped open nearly immediately. Every instinct told her not to get in; even harder was to resist the impulse to pull the Glock back out of her holster and hold it at the ready. More for the small camera she saw mounted inside the elevator than for herself, she calmly stepped inside as though she had no care in the world.

The doors snapped shut behind her, allowing the carriage to move upward into the building. It was a bit off-putting to find there were no controls on the interior, no way to stop her ascent nor call for help should she get stuck. Curious, she pulled her iPhone from her blazer pocket and confirmed that she suddenly had no signal — despite having had a full five bars a few seconds earlier in the parking lot. Putting the phone back into her pocket, she kept her blazer unbuttoned and her hand within easy distance of her sidearm. As the lift slowed to a stop, she tried to game out what might transpire over the next few moments; when the doors opened to reveal the empty elevator lobby on the executive floor, she frowned slightly at how that had confirmed one of her guesses.

Stepping out onto the expensive carpet, she let her eyes adjust to the semidarkness of the hallway; while the official workday had yet to start, Kate wasn't surprised to find herself in the shadows. Carefully, she made her way down the hallway, intuitively knowing where she was expected to be. Rounding the corner and entering the main hallway for the executive suite, Kate saw a small pool of light coming from an open office door at the far end — the office belonging to Tenoch. The invitation for the proverbial fly to enter the spider's den was clear.

And it felt incredibly wrong.

Pulling the Glock from her holster, Kate held it at the ready and slowly made her way down the hallway. "Tenoch?" she called. "It's Kate. Are you here?"

Her voice echoed in the emptiness. Cocking her head slightly, she didn't hear anything in response, confirming perhaps what her instincts had already been telling her. Holding the gun higher, she pondered for a moment trying to make a break for the emergency stairwell Tenoch had ushered her into earlier, then thought better of it; whatever she was about to face, better to do it now and get it out in the open. Besides, there was a good chance whomever was waiting for her in Tenoch's office thought she was going in blindly; maybe, just *maybe*, she might be able to turn that to her advantage, for whatever that might be worth.

The door for Tenoch's office was open about halfway. Kate pushed the door open fully with the toe of her shoe, then moved in, gun up, and cleared what turned out to be an empty space. "Hello?" she asked the air. "Is anyone here?" she continued as she slowly turned in a full circle for a second time, ensuring she was, for the moment, alone. "Tenoch?"

Continuing to slowly circle the room, Kate took the extra step of ensuring nothing was hiding behind the only other door in office; the washroom beyond was smaller than she would have expected for someone of Tenoch's stature, but then again, she wasn't up on Fortune 500 protocols in that area. Returning to the main space, her eyes fell to the desk and the vase holding a beautiful white-yellow orchid she was certain hadn't been there a moment earlier. That particular flower also seemed vaguely familiar; stepping closer, she flipped through her mental photos and realized a fraction too late where she had seen it before.

"It's good to see you again, Kathryn."

Turning at the familiar voice, she made sure to keep the gun up as she spoke. "Where's Tenoch, Ms. Vasquez?"

"Not here, as you well know." The matriarch of the corporation was standing in front of the only exit to the room and was wearing a fairly standard pantsuit; the telltale orchid was pinned to the base of her tightly wound bun. While she didn't appear to be armed, Kate got the impression Reyna Vasquez was far more dangerous than she looked. "Why did you come?"

"The better question, perhaps, is why did you *need* me to come?" was Kate's reply. "Tenoch is doing something you don't like, isn't he? And you need leverage to make him stop."

There was a whisper of a smile on her otherwise impassive face. "He spoke highly of your intellect," she said as she took a step closer. "I can see it wasn't hyperbole."

"No further," Kate warned as she held the gun steady on the woman. "I have backup on the way. We're going to have a nice conversation while we wait."

"I think not," Vasquez replied as she took another step toward Kate. "We have a general dampening field active at the moment — specialized tech that acts like a Faraday cage we can deploy during emergencies. Since we've been monitoring the movements of the Santa Marcel Police Department, I'm relatively safe in assuming you also know about the dampening field, too."

"We have protocols," Kate continued calmly. "I'm due at a crime scene soon, if I don't appear—"

"Your deputy is no longer expecting you," Vasquez interrupted.

Kate nodded slowly. "Another tech you have?" she asked. "Some sort of AI that can mimic voices?"

"Something like that," Vasquez smiled. "You are right about two things, though."

"And what would that be?"

"We *are* going to have a chat," Vasquez answered. "About what's

going on at the rail yard. You're going to tell me everything you know
— what you found, and how you found it."

"I'm surprised," Kate said, smiling as she played for time. "I
thought your son told you everything?"

"He's quite capable of keeping secrets," Vasquez replied darkly.
"From me. And you."

"I used to date him," Kate continued, unable to resist needling
the strong woman slightly. "He's kind of an open book to me."

"You might want to skip the final chapter then," she replied as
she took another step closer.

Kate waved the gun at her again, forcing her to stop. "Oh? Why?"

"Because you're not going to like how the story ends, my dear."

The pithy response she'd teed up died on her lips when she
caught movement out of the corner of her eye; she'd barely glanced
in that direction before the swarm of thick vines burst from the
formerly innocuous looking vase and began to wrap themselves
around her legs. Having seen far stranger things already in her short
time with Ocelot, the shock value of being attacked by an inanimate
object was somewhat lessened, allowing her to mount an unexpected defense. Training took over and she unloaded several rounds
from the Glock into the speedily creeping vines, freeing her legs in a
burst of greenery that flew across the room; diving over Tenoch's
desk, she landed with her back against the wall and blasted two
more tendrils that had quickly snaked around the desk toward her.
Kate spared a single look at Vasquez and found her still blocking the
only exit to the room and wearing a serene expression that was
extremely unsettling; the windows behind Kate were an option,
maybe, but only if she'd somehow figured out how to sprout wings
and fly. Since that was more in Ocelot's department than hers, she
went back to picking off more of the vines as they encroached on her,
trying to carve a path toward the door. It took longer than it should
have for Kate to realize she was fighting a losing battle against an

enemy capable of nearly immediately regenerating; as she neared the end of the clip in her gun, she knew she'd run out of bullets long before Vasquez quit.

Shit, she thought as she pressed herself into the bookcase holding Tenoch's Disneyland antiques. *Shit, shit and double shit. There's only one move here, isn't there?*

Slowly standing, Kate held her hands out in surrender; a fraction of a second later, the vines had completely encircled her from head to toe. Almost to emphasize how badly she had lost; the greenery slowly began to squeeze the air out of her. Eyes widening in shock, she turned toward her now captor.

"Are you ready to talk?" Vasquez asked.

Unable to even gasp, Kate just nodded. Vigorously.

"Good," Vasquez said as she waved her hands strangely.

Kate felt the pressure ease — but only slightly. Taking in as much air as she could, Kate waited for the stars to leave the edge of her vision before speaking. "Before we... begin, what was... the second item?"

The smile she saw sent chills down her spine. "You're definitely my leverage with Tenoch."

"He's... not going... to like that," Kate managed to get out, each breath still a challenge.

"I'm counting on it."

NINETEEN

He'd not bothered with stealth in Cairo.

The dimensional doorway hiding within the docks in Singapore had been something of a godsend, though it hadn't been easy levitating the shipping containers through them; up to that point, the largest item he'd attempted to move with magic had been a coffee cup he'd left in the kitchen. Scaling up the effort had taken a bit out of him, but not as much as he'd expected, another sign that his ascension was nearly complete. Once he'd ensured the containers had safely arrived in Santa Marcel, he'd stepped through the doorway himself and landed in the middle of a shipping yard more than ready for his incursion. Unleashing the ferocity inherit in his abilities, it hadn't truly been a fair fight; after packing the unconscious bodies into an empty container, he'd located the next batch of human cargo and then shoved them back through the doorway, acutely aware that he was now working on borrowed time. When replenishment forces didn't appear, it dawned on Ocelot that they were likely regrouping in Oaxaca, preparing to thwart his final effort to put an end to whatever machinations *madre* had in motion.

Leaning against a container that had been overturned during his battle with the locals, he paused to catch his breath; only then did he try to reach out to Kate to follow up on her last message to him over the connection they shared. Her timing had been exceptionally bad — he'd been up to his new feline ears fighting off paid mercenaries at the time — but now that he had a moment to find out more about whatever it was she had gotten herself into, he found he was unable to tug at the thread between them. Masked face frowning, he tried again, harder, and became increasingly alarmed that he wasn't able to feel her. There were only a handful of reasons Ocelot might not be able to reach her, and none of them were good; replaying what she'd said to him over and over again, he was sorely tempted to abort the final phase of his efforts and return to Santa Marcel.

Still, Kate had been firm that she had it under control and to finish what he started; tugging again at the now-silent connection to her, a significant part of his soul thought that was a lousy idea. The rest couldn't deny that now that the genie was out of the bottle, this might well be his only chance. Unhappy to say the least, Ocelot pulled himself together and then dashed through the still-glowing dimensional doorway.

The humidity of the jungle immediately brought him up short. Dropping into a defensive crouch, Ocelot quickly took stock of his surroundings and discovered the doorway hadn't deposited him where he'd expected. Instead of a thriving multimodal shipping port, he was instead in a small clearing deep within a dense rain forest kilometers from the coast.

Shit. She did the one *thing I didn't expect—*

Straightening, he turned and bolted for the glowing doorway and then took a massive leap toward it; his claw-tipped fingers had nearly reached the shimmering energy field before it winked out completely. Sailing through the now empty space, he deftly tumbled to the ground and came out in his defensive crouch once again. Grimacing slightly, he grudgingly acknowledged he'd been outfoxed; the real question now was *why*, for he was perfectly capable of opening his own portal back to Oaxaca. All he needed was a suitable reflective surface to work with, something easily found in the denseness of the jungle.

He gnawed on that conundrum as he stood and moved over to a sizable tree whose canopy covered a small portion of the clearing; leaping upwards, he dug his claws into the soft bark and pulled himself onto a large branch, then crept to the end and paused. Balancing easily in the slight breeze, he closed his eyes for a moment and allowed the scents and sounds of the jungle surrounding him to become known. Sniffing at the air, his keen nose told him he was in strangely familiar territory; that was buttressed by the familiar cacophony of the creatures who called that part of the world their home. The slight diminution in their noise told him only that they were aware he was now there; the arrival of an apex predator never went unremarked, especially one that depended on stealth as much as he did. Fortunately for them, he was neither in the mood for a proper hunt nor had the time to spare for one in the first place.

Sniffing at the air a second time, he confirmed that he was where he *thought* he was; opening his eyes, he caught glimpses of the cloudless blue sky through the canopy and wondered why *madre* had brought him here, of all places. It was one question among many that he would have to answer later; in the meantime, he swung off the branch and landed on his feet, then began to run through the heavy undergrowth, seeking the rushing brook where he'd taken cool refuge after finishing a hard day of training in the hot jungle. He smelled the water long before he pressed through the tall ferns protecting the bank; dropping to his knees in the mud, he quickly cast his reflective transport spell and willed the glowing circle to life in the clear surface. The portal appeared nearly immediately, and he thrust his hand into it — and found himself tumbling down from the sky, crashing through the branches of a massive rubber tree. Using his tail to flip around, he managed to whip up enough of a wind to slow his descent so he didn't slam into the forest floor completely at speed; still, the impact was hard enough that he felt like those little cartoon stars were dancing around his head. Pushing himself out of the damp, rotting carpet of leaves, he tried to ignore the blow to his ego, for it had been a long, *long* time since he'd blown the spell that badly.

Or had he?

Sitting up a bit straighter, he realized the tree he'd just fallen through was the same one he'd been in a few minutes earlier. Glancing sideways, he could make out the path he'd forged to the brook; looking upward again, he realized it might not entirely have been on him.

Huh, he thought.

Standing, he dashed back through the undergrowth and dropped to the side of the brook again; cautiously, he cast the reflective transport spell a second time and waited until he saw the port in Oaxaca appear. Bracing himself, he placed the tip of his claw into the glowing circle, and once more found himself in free fall. Having expected it that time, he immediately righted himself and flung his arms and legs out as wide as he could, giving himself more surface area; catching an updraft, he shifted his angle enough that he was able to grab the first branch that looked large enough to support his weight and did a giant one-armed loop around it before landing in a crouch atop it. That high up, he smiled slightly at the Ocelot-shaped depression far below, then flung himself downward, one branch at a time, until he landed once more on the floor of the rain forest.

She's got me stuck in a loop, Ocelot sighed. *I'm not going anywhere she doesn't want me to go. Should've seen* that *one coming, too. Some hero I am.*

Tugging at the connection with Kate again, he began to wonder if there was another explanation for why he wasn't able to get through to her; the nearly dead silence at the other end was highly unnerving. Granted, they'd not been tethered long enough for him to truly know the range their connection might have; still, as he stared upward at the tree he'd now fallen through twice, he suspected strongly it had nothing to do with the vagaries of the bonding magic. *Madre* was blocking his access to Kate, and he had an even stronger suspicion why.

She's far more powerful than I realized, he thought. *In a way that confirms everything, doesn't it? She's the one at her zenith, the one being pushed aside as I ascend; the stones, the portals — she was setting things in motion that would help keep the company at the top long after she lost access to her power.*

He looked down at his claw-tipped hands and wondered.

Does she serve Tezcatlipoca, like me? Or as a proxy for my padre *until I ascend?* he asked himself. *If she was, why didn't that ever come up during my training or time with them?*

Turning his hands over, he stared at the strange magical fabric covering them and wasn't all that surprised when the realization finally pushed its way to the top.

Her powers are different. She serves another deity — one in conflict with mine. And I think I know which one it is, he added with a frown as another piece clicked into place. *Shit. Madre has pulled us into a civil war that's been ongoing since the beginning times.*

Ocelot dropped to his knees, processing the enormity of the situation. *It all makes sense now,* he thought. *It's a fucking chess match among the gods and we're just the latest pieces on the board they're using*

— and I'll be damned if I'll let any of it hurt the people I care about. The people I'm supposed to be protecting.

The sizzle of that magical cloak he always felt hugging him ticked up a notch, then another; in mere moments, all of his already enhanced senses felt like they had kicked into a far higher gear than he'd known existed. Startled slightly, he closed his eyes for a moment and found he could *literally* see the entire jungle as it stretched away from him, along with every living thing within it. Scents became more nuanced, painting in a complex picture of the world around him; sounds from kilometers away reached his ears and were so distinct, he could hear a hummingbird drinking from a flower. Opening his eyes, Ocelot found his vision had changed as well; he watched with mirthless fascination as an army of leaf cutter ants carved up a rubber tree, then blinked and refocused on a small caterpillar creeping along a different branch, the vibrant rings of color along its body moving in and out of the sunlight as it went. Leaning back on his haunches, he felt a cold smile appear on his masked face.

There could be worse times for this to have happened, I guess. Oddly, I thought there'd be more razzle-dazzle when I ascended; regardless, madre *is not going to be expecting me to be in possession of my full abilities. I'll have to use that to my advantage.*

Flexing his now-stronger magical muscle, he reached across the connection to Kate once more and wasn't all that surprised that he could now feel — no, he could actually *see* — the barrier that had been erected between them. Beyond just preventing communication, he realized it was also shielding his ability to determine her location; oddly, that told him more than his *madre* had probably intended. Putting aside for the moment his real concern she'd found out about their mating, he considered his next moves very carefully; probing the barrier, he knew intrinsically that he was now able to push his way through it if he wanted, though it would reveal more than he should at that moment. Pulling back, he realized there might be another way to communicate with Kate, one that might escape *madre*'s notice.

Refocusing on the jungle around him, Ocelot raised his gloved hand and held it palm-upward; within seconds, a small bird full of colorful plumage gently landed on it. Smiling at the irony, he nodded at his new little friend. "Find her," he said simply. "Tell her I'm on the way."

He wondered for a long moment if his magical message had gotten through; when the bird cocked its small head slightly, he let out the breath he hadn't realized he was holding. Lifting his hand up a bit more in encouragement, he smiled again when it spread its wings and then flittered off into the jungle, trailing a merry melody in its wake. That he was able to translate the tune into confirmation of cooperation — and was capable of tracking the small bird's path as it disappeared — underscored how rapidly his nascent abilities were manifesting. Keeping one mental eye (as it were) on where the bird was going, he slowly stood and readied himself for the next stage; fortunately, he'd spent long enough beneath the domino mask that he knew he'd be able to pull off the bit of legerdemain he'd need to convince *madre* he had yet to ascend. He took a few moments to build up enough rage within himself to make the next few moments as convincing as possible; with Kate seemingly in danger, it wasn't actually all that hard to do.

Growling slightly, he looked to what he could see of the sky. "I know you want me," he said, barely able to keep the anger out of his voice. "Leave her out of this. Your fight is with me."

While he hadn't entirely expected an answer, when a brilliantly colored butterfly easily six inches across fluttered down from the canopy above and then was joined by a dozen siblings, he smiled ruefully at having guessed correctly at least once. As the butterflies arranged themselves into a strange three-dimensional floating version of his mother's face, he wondered how much his *madre* knew about his relationship with Kate, versus what she suspected; throwing up as many mental barriers as he could, Ocelot prayed to Tezcatlipoca that she still thought of him as a smitten teenager. He could use that to his advantage if she did, but should she know — or even suspect — Kate's *true* importance to him, well, he might as well turn his immortal soul over to the gods then and there for all the use he'd ever be to them at that point. Leaning down into a crouch that spoke to how deadly he *could* be, Ocelot waited impatiently for the avatar to finally speak.

"*Mijo*," the strange face said. "I had no idea the very mole I was looking for was my own flesh-and-blood, nor that you had adopted such an irritatingly cliched persona in your attempt to thwart me."

"Of all people, I shouldn't need to remind you that our efforts on behalf of Tezcatlipoca are supposed to remain in the shadows, keeping truths ordinary humans forgot millennia ago safely hidden from view. People in *this* century are more likely to accept a super-hero than what we truly are, more likely to ignore the fantastical things we can do." Ocelot sneered slightly. "Perhaps I should have, though, since you seem to have a selective memory for what our purpose on Earth is supposed to be."

"Purpose?" *madre* laughed. "*Purpose*? Do you actually think we have *relevance* in this place?"

"I've never doubted that," Ocelot replied. "We've been given a gift—"

"We've been *enslaved*," she interrupted. "By our beliefs and an archaic duty to beings that no longer serve the greater good. Tezcatlipoca has been filling your head with lies, *mijo*; it's time you knew that."

"It's no lie that you've been trafficking in human souls," he replied coldly. "Nor that my pledge to protect such souls *required* me to intervene." Ocelot narrowed his eyes menacingly. "But you knew that, didn't you? You *needed* me to act in order to complete your design."

The avatar managed to look astonished. "Well done, *mijo*."

"Those souls — those *beings* — meant nothing to you?" he demanded. "Or so very little that they were suitable only for obfuscating what you were truly shipping in those cargo containers?" Ocelot paused again, then slowly began to shake his head. "This is beneath the woman I know as *madre* and sullies the collective sacrifice generations of our family made in order to serve Tezcatlipoca with honor."

There was a long pause. "I do not serve that bastard."

Ocelot felt his anger begin to boil. "No," he said tightly. "You only serve yourself."

There was another long pause. "What I have done has been for our family," the avatar said. "To cleave us from this mindless, senseless devotion to gods who no longer have a right to control our very existence."

"We have no right—"

"We have *every* right," she interrupted. "Even you have to see how untenable our position is! This world — this place that we're charged with protecting — it doesn't matter what we do! Or how we do it! These *people* you are so invested in saving are intent on destroying themselves, and I want no part of it."

"You cannot change our destiny," Ocelot said, his mind reeling slightly at how unhinged his seemingly buttoned-down mother was sounding. "That's something you drilled into me as a teenager — especially that day you sent me to the jungle."

"The situation changed," she replied.

He found himself nodding for it neatly explained why his *madre* had such unusual abilities with natural vegetation. "You realize," Ocelot started carefully, "that by making a deal with Xipe Totec, you just swapped one deity with a grievance for another, right?"

Ocelot took no solace in the second look of shock on the avatar's face. "We do what we must to protect family."

The gnawing dread of certainty in his gut told him otherwise. "You've thrown your lot in with the god of war, *madre*. And now you've spread dimensional doorways across the face of this planet, doorways they can use for their own purposes." He narrowed his eyes. "Did you *ignore* all of the training we were given? Or the pages in our codex that explicitly counsel against removing more than is absolutely necessary from the sacred location — in order to keep the balance?"

"Balance is a myth."

"I suppose you learned *that* fucking nugget from Xipe Totec," Ocelot sneered. "You were so blinded by the prospect of expanding our legacy at the expense of Tezcatlipoca that you never saw how you were being played."

Judging from the way the avatar's jawline suddenly set, Ocelot knew he'd hit a soft spot; he braced for the inevitable counterstrike, verbal or otherwise. "Not as blinded as my dutiful son," she replied hotly. "Your actions make you just as culpable."

"Hardly. Drawing me into this mess solely to sow division between the gods suits only your purposes, not mine. And certainly not Tezcatlipoca."

"If that lie is the only way you live with yourself, so be it," she replied. "I'm sorry that it has to end this way; you had such potential."

Ocelot smiled dangerously. "You *actually* think you have trapped me here? In the jungle where I trained — where I honed my abilities?"

"I *know* I have," the avatar laughed. "If not through magic, then by threat: try to leave, and the woman you love will pay for the transgression with her life. Stay, and you might just see her alive again."

"Hurt Kate in any way," he growled lowly, "and I cannot be held accountable for what I will do to you. Even if you *are* my mother."

"Big words," she laughed harder, "that only underscore how dangerous it is to have such a mortal connection as your weakness. You won't leave. You won't even try. Enjoy your solitude. Now if you'll excuse me, I need to undo the damage you've caused."

Seething slightly — and not just for show — Ocelot bit his tongue as the butterflies dispersed and fluttered away into the canopy of the jungle. After everything he'd been through, he shouldn't have been all that surprised that his own mother was more than willing to abandon him to the perils of the jungle with no pretext of a concern that he might survive; the fact that he knew he *would* gave him some solace, enough that his white-hot anger subsided into a dull ache that was far more manageable. Reyna Vasquez had long felt like a different woman after he'd returned from his training with the adepts; now he understood why. While it didn't wash away any of the pain, it did make him laser focused on what he now needed to do.

But first he had to save Kate.

Raising some of the mental barriers he'd pulled over himself while dealing with his *madre*, Ocelot immediately located the small bird less than twenty kilometers from his current position. The fact that Kate was right where he expected to find her was grim confirmation that his *madre* suspected he was far more powerful than he'd let on — and wanted to prove it by luring him to a trap deadlier than anything the jungle had to offer.

So be it, he thought as he slowly pulled himself to his full height.

Taking a deep breath, he drew as much energy as he could from everything around him and murmured the incantation he'd not dared try until that moment; the blaze of light that washed over his form was brief but brought with it a strange electrical tingle that felt as though it were ripping apart the very cells in his body one at a time. When the stars cleared from his vision, Ocelot spared no time to contemplate the luxurious golden fur dotted with spots of jade that now covered him from head to tail; instead, he coiled up and leapt into the canopy of the jungle, unleashing a roar that scattered a clutch of birds from the branches above him.

I'm coming, Kate, he thought as he bounded from tree to tree as fast as his *nagual* form could move. *Hang in there...*

TWENTY

Kate wasn't sure what was worse: the insanely high humidity or the fact that she was strapped down to a moldy stone altar she suspected had been previously used for human sacrifice. Yanking a bit at the vines that seemed intent on ensuring she not move so much as an inch on the slimy stonework, she figured it was probably an academic question at best given the gentle hiss she could hear from off to her left. There was no need to see the ancient artifact Reyna Vasquez had informed her was the Mesoamerican version of a sandglass; the rectangular rack of sharpened sticks that was slowly, inevitably, inching its way toward her had effectively telegraphed the message that her time on Earth was coming to a rapid close. *Why* an ancient civilization had thought to craft such an unmistakably horrific way to kill someone explained a bit about the deities Ocelot served, or at the very least, how they wreaked vengeance on their enemies. As the rack slowly ground downward another millimeter, Kate decided she could finally admit — once and for all — Vasquez was evil incarnate; while it was something she'd suspected even back when she'd first begun dating

Tenoch, having it confirmed deep in some Central American jungle seemed like a cruel joke she'd not been in on in the first place.

Shifting slightly, Kate grimaced at the clammy embrace of her sweat-soaked blouse; if she survived, there wasn't going to be a shower long enough — or hot enough — to wash the grime of her experience off her body. The bindings were tight enough that she could barely raise her head, not that it mattered; there wasn't much to see beyond the flames of the torches that were quietly blazing at the four corners of the stone. How she'd wound up there was something of a blur; about all she could remember was Vasquez toting her vine-wrapped body back to the CEO's office and then shoving her through a glowing portal that had been hiding behind an otherwise ordinary looking door beside her desk. Kate had the sense she was *inside* something, but it didn't feel like a cave; every now and then, she *thought* she could hear the cacophony one might expect from a jungle, though it was muted enough to speak there being something buffering the noise — like a wall of stone or a buffer of soil. The flickering of the torches seemed directional, enough that Kate was reasonably certain some kind of doorway was behind her.

Good to know where the exit is, she sighed as she yanked at the vines again. *For all the good it will do me.*

She'd long since stopped trying to reach out to Ocelot, for whatever magic Vasquez had used back in Santa Marcel appeared to still be dampening her ability to sense their connection; as focused as Vasquez's questions had been on what Tenoch had known — and what he'd shared with Kate during their clandestine investigation — Kate had become increasingly certain that the woman suspected her old boyfriend was *also* working with the superhero, which went a long way toward explaining why Vasquez had been compelled to spirit her away from Santa Marcel and thrown the magical equivalent of a disappearing cloak over her just for good measure. Kate doubted the subterfuge would prevent Ocelot from finding her, but as she watched the razor-sharp sticks edge closer again, she did find herself wondering if all he'd locate was a somewhat slimmer and far less lively version.

Going over their conversation again, Kate smiled grimly at how she'd been able to use fairly standard law enforcement interrogation techniques to prevent Vasquez from actually learning anything actionable. While she'd not entirely lied about anything, she might have led the woman to believe Tenoch had done very little other than provide her with some key pieces of data — data that he'd not actually correlated himself. She thought Vasquez had bought the slight stretching of the truth, but that's when the inquisition had been abruptly ended; Kate wasn't entirely sure how long she'd been left alone in that dank, dark chamber but thought it had been *maybe* thirty or forty minutes. Long enough that she'd become singularly focused on her current predicament.

I'm stuck in a fucking Indiana Jones *movie,* she thought angrily. *And I didn't even get a chance to look at the forbidden treasure. What's that all about, anyway? Aren't you supposed to* steal *the treasure before dying a gruesome death?*

The warmth she felt at the sudden appearance of a certain voice in the back of her head nearly had her in tears. *No one is dying today, princesa.*

Ocelot? she cried out. *My God! Are you actually here?*

Nearly, was the reply. She got the sense he was exerting a great deal of energy. *I couldn't risk reaching out until I knew I was close enough; what's your situation?*

Kate's eyes went to the rack of sticks. *Not good. I'm about to become a Kate sandwich.*

He swore in a language she didn't understand. *Let me deal with these guards. One second—*

Screams of intense fear echoed into her space, mixed with the feral roar of a creature she truly didn't want to meet even in the daylight. Shouts were followed by more screams, and then a sudden silence that felt more oppressive than the humidity. Feeling her own pulse as it threatened to push through her skin, Kate heard the *click-click-click* of something hard as it moved across the stone floor behind her; she felt more than saw a sudden burst of light, and then, like some sort of goddamned hero in a Marvel movie, the masked visage of the man she thought she might never see again appeared above her.

"Hey," he said with a slight smile. "Thanks for waiting."

It took a moment for her to connect the dots. "You ascended?"

"I ascended," he nodded before his masked eyes glanced upward. "I can hold these back—"

Kate's anxiety rose when his masked eyes suddenly widened. "What?"

"She's near," he said, his voice low. "There's not much time and I de*feline*ly don't want to fight her here in such close quarters."

"You can sense her presence?" Kate asked as he slipped away from her. "And this doesn't seem like a good time for a cat pun."

"I pun when I'm nervous," she heard him say from somewhere behind her. "*Fuck.*"

"That doesn't sound good."

"It's not." His face appeared above hers. "She's enchanted the damn mechanism; I can't stop it."

"Okay," she replied as she glanced meaningfully at the sharp sticks above her. "Then shred the vines and get me out of here."

"You likely know those are enchanted as well," he sighed. "They'll regenerate and repair the damage as soon as I claw them."

Kate felt her heart sink. "So you can't cut me loose, and you can't stop the gears?"

"Pretty much."

"I'm not hearing any good news in there."

"Well," he said as he started to climb onto the altar. "It depends on how much you trust me."

"What are you doing?" she asked with some alarm as he pressed his costumed body against hers. "There's barely any space between you and those sticks!"

"Tell me about it," he said, his voice loud in her ear. "Do you trust me?"

"Implicitly," she replied instantly. "Though I don't see—"

"Look into my eyes," he said softly. "Try not to blink."

"Okay," she said.

"Good," he said. "Keep looking at me," he said encouragingly as the rack clicked down again. It wasn't lost on her that a small grunt escaped him as the rods drove themselves into his back. "Good," he managed to say through gritted teeth. "Don't blink... good..."

It wasn't until she felt the tear begin to roll down her face — and the soft dragging of a claw tip to capture it — that Kate understood what he was trying to do; he grunted again as the rack pressed into him with more force, but he somehow managed to keep her from feeling it. His masked eyes went unfocused for a moment as he whispered something under his breath; an unseen breeze began to whirl around them, a welcome movement in what had been a very cloistered space. Ocelot continued to murmur to himself, then he looked at her directly.

"Close your eyes and hold on. This is gonna be rough."

No sooner had she followed his instructions than she felt the strange inward-out yanking sensation moving through one of Ocelot's portals often gave her; unlike past transits, though, she felt every square inch of her body as it was drawn into the magical portal. She tried and failed to keep from screaming at the intense pain of being twisted like a pretzel, then untwisted; the world blacked out for a moment before she came to with her face pressed into the damp moss covering what felt like a large slab of stone. Blinking — and trying to catch her breath — she found herself on some sort of wide, flat area atop something built tall enough to tower above the oldest trees surrounding it.

My god, she thought before turning the other way.

Roughhewn blocks of stone taller than her rose to another terrace above her current position, which in turn led to several more ever-smaller versions before ending in some sort of ornamental carving. While it wouldn't be impossible to scale the blocks, someone had thoughtfully carved steps into the stones at the exact center of the wall. While it was clearly very old, Kate was surprised that the structure hadn't been reclaimed by the jungle, then realized that if they were *truly* at Ocelot's most-sacred-of-the-sacred locations, it had yet to be abandoned.

I'm really on one of those pyramids I read about in the Smithsonian magazine — fuck, I was just inside *it a few seconds ago! And this one is* huge; *oh, yuck, what did I just put my hand into —*

Looking down, she realized the dampness in the moss wasn't from the humidity of the jungle; recoiling slightly, she followed the trail of blood back to what might have once been multiple humans but were now nothing but a pile of body parts whose entrails were slowly oozing all over the place. The violence with which the unfortunate guards had been shredded spoke volumes; despite being a seasoned detective who had seen a thing or two, the bile rising in the back of Kate's throat was a palpable reminder that some things were better left to your imagination.

Holding back the urge to retch, Kate tried to stand but found her knees too weak to obey her; halfway back to the hard stone, she felt a careful hand around her waist arrest her fall and turned to see the concerned expression of Ocelot as he helped her to her feet. While her heart did that now-familiar two step when she was that close to him, something deep inside of her was struggling to reconcile the man she *thought* she had come to know with whatever he had become in order to rescue her. Those deep brown eyes searched her face, and for a moment, she thought she saw a slight look of sadness wash over his masked visage before it vanished back into one of concern.

"Not one of my finer moments," he said softly as he brushed something from her cheek. "Are you injured?"

It wasn't lost on Kate that his eyes remained on her. "Other than being stiff, no."

"Good," he said. "She'll be here any moment, and we need to be ready."

"Can't we just leave?" Kate asked. "Open a portal and go back to Santa Marcel?"

Ocelot released her and shook his head. "I'm not able to transit beyond the jungle," he replied. "And, as you might have noticed, there's a significant lack of reflective surfaces around here."

Kate nodded slowly. "You told me before that you can *use* any element from the environment in your magic – but you can't actually *create* them, can you?"

"That's part of the deal," he smiled wryly. "Hence using your tear." He looked over at the pyramid behind them. "I wasn't entirely sure I'd be able to get you out of the ceremonial chamber."

Kate risked a glance back at the pile of remains and the doorway just behind them. "Thanks for not sharing that little tidbit before you tried."

"My pleasure," he laughed mirthlessly. "You might want to hang onto something; I'm going to set the mood just a bit."

Glancing at the smooth stone of the pyramid's surface, Kate frowned. "That could be a problem."

"Then we go to plan 'B'," he replied, before adding with a slight chuckle. "Or plan 'T'."

"Plan *what the fuck*—!"

Ocelot's tail moved so fast, Kate had no time to react when it deftly encircled her waist and then quickly brought her over to his side. Exactly *why* he'd wanted her anchored in place quickly became evident as the light breeze she'd been feeling against her damp skin became something far more forceful. Holding his arms out, he closed his eyes and then began conducting an orchestra only he could see; the sky began to boil with foreboding clouds that flashed regularly with bolts of lightning. Debris from the jungle lifted into the air and then swirled around them, creating a curtain of leaves, dirt and moss that made seeing anything more than a few feet in front of them nearly impossible. The jungle was plunged into darkness as the thickening layer of clouds blotted out what was left of the sun; the rising whine sounded like something out of an old Celtic myth she'd once read, one where spirits announced their presence with an ear-splitting shriek loud enough to wake the dead. Glancing around them, Kate hoped with everything she held dear that Ocelot wasn't in fact summoning his late ancestors, but then again, maybe he was; not much would've surprised her at that point.

Higher, ever higher Ocelot brought the tempest; Kate's hair escaped what was left of the ponytail she'd tied it into and whipped around her face, pelting her painfully. The force of the wind became strong enough that Ocelot had to lean into the gale in order to keep their balance; Kate risked putting her arms around his torso when she felt her feet beginning to slide across the slickness of the stones. He responded by wrapping his tail even tighter around her. A massive clap of thunder rolled across the jungle, hundreds of times louder than anything she'd ever heard in her life; it was followed quickly by an even stronger one that shook the very foundation of the pyramid itself and quite nearly knocked both of them down. Whatever magic Ocelot was using kept them firmly rooted in place, but Kate could feel how his muscles were beginning to tremble beneath her; despite what he had told her, while he may have fully ascended, it was clear his body wasn't yet ready to handle the incredible power that came with it.

She'd barely thought the thought when she heard him in the back of her head. *I'll be fine. She's here. Stay close.*

I'm not going anywhere, she assured him. *Where—*

Ocelot's faster-than-human reflexes suddenly took over, allowing him to wrap the bulk of his form around her before diving sideways to narrowly avoid something massive that had been hurled in their direction. Some part of Kate's brain managed to register that it was one of the sizable blocks of stone that made up the structure of the pyramid a moment before they landed, hard, then tumbled together until Ocelot rolled off Kate and into a crouch just in front of her. She found herself on her hands and knees, slightly behind him, and staring at what Reyna Vasquez had become. The matriarch of the family company had been completely transformed; gone was the business suit, replaced by some sort of leather outfit covered in the colorful plumage of birds Kate was certain had been extinct for thousands of years. Her long hair had been tied into a tight club that ran down to the small of her back; despite the hurricane-force winds, Reyna floated serenely some ten feet off the ground, watching them with eyes that had become a painfully bright white color. Behind her, a dense thicket of vines roiled and twisted almost as if they were a living creature; unlike the ones that had captured her back in Santa Marcel, these were studded with angry looking thorns that looked capable of taking out a mere human such as herself in a single blow. Vasquez had her hands up, palms facing them; when they began to glow, she tried to gauge which way they were going to dive. Fortunately, Ocelot seemed far better at that game; when the second onslaught came their way — this time, a patch of the seemingly sentient vines, thorns outward — he grabbed her and leapt high into the sky, far higher than she'd thought possible and easily beyond the reach of the flailing vines.

Letting the wind carry them allowed Ocelot to land on the next higher terrace; without missing a beat, he leapt again, this time sideways and around the far edge of the level, neatly avoiding not one but *two* massive paving stones that had been lifted from behind them and sent in the direction they didn't go. Changing tactics, he scrambled up the stairs cut into the face of the pyramid, with Kate right on his heels; rain had begun to fall from the heavens in a downpour that made the annual monsoons seem like a spring sun shower, quickly drenching her to the skin. Upwards they climbed; she risked a glance over her shoulder and saw Vasquez was in pursuit, with her vine army close behind. Looking up again, she wondered what Ocelot was planning for each successive level they reached grew ever smaller, reducing the amount of space and therefore any options they had to mount a counterattack. Lightning flashed above them repeatedly, with a few strikes landing dangerously near them; the higher they went, the more exposed they were becoming — and then her eyes went to the strange ornamentation that sat at the very apex of the structure.

You're not serious, she blurted out mentally.

It's the only way, he replied instantly.

How—

I don't have time to explain. This will work, but you must do exactly what I tell you to do when the time comes.

We are going to have to have a long *conversation about our communication skills when this is over*, she groused.

I welcome that, he laughed slightly. *Now hush and hold on.*

Kate wasn't sure she needed an explanation, actually, given how the artifact was shaped. The real question was how Ocelot would get the angle he needed in order to make it all work; when they finally reached the last terrace, she barely had time to take in the small stone altar positioned just beneath what she'd begun to think of as a fancy lightning rod when it hit her what he was planning on doing.

Oh fuck *no,* she nearly screamed at him.

Trust me, was his response. *And stay in that corner.*

She should've expected the small burst of magic that brushed her across the terrace, and the one immediately behind it that essentially glued her to the stone; that didn't stop her from trying to fight it as she watched Ocelot turn and face Vasquez. It took a moment for her to realize it was her voice screaming, not the howling of the wind; Vasquez barely spared her a glance, and Ocelot was pointedly ignoring her. Slowly, Reyna crossed the stones, throwing whatever her magic could pull from the surroundings at him; stones, vines, parts of trees — it would have had a comical quality to it had the stakes not been so deadly serious. Ocelot seemed able to deflect the fusillade with some sort of magical shield he was able to throw up in front of him; it sparked each time something hit and was deflected off into the jungle far below, but Reyna's relentless attack had the net effect of slowly forcing Ocelot backwards one brutal step at a time. He made a good show of seemingly doing so unwillingly, but it was clear now to Kate he was subtly attempting to line himself up with the lightning rod. The closer he got, the more the altar and the strange ornament perched above it began to glow; her skin began to crawl as the very air around her began to take on a slight charge, all signs that Ocelot was really, truly going to do what she feared.

Playing up her role as a furious bystander therefore wasn't all that difficult; struggling against the magic binding her to the stone, she couldn't ignore how her heart was pounding, nor how each new bolt of lightning sizzling across the sky above her felt many multiples more powerful than the last. Whether Ocelot was responsible for that or if he was getting help from another source was hard to know; what she could tell was that Reyna was nearly an even match to him, a reminder that — for the moment — they were both at their apex of their powers. Just when she thought she couldn't take the rising tension any longer, she heard Reyna's voice as it easily cut through the tempest raging around them.

"*This* is the path you have chosen?" she asked.

"I never chose this path," Ocelot said just as clearly. "Your actions put me on it."

"My actions?" Reyna laughed. "My *actions* will ensure our line will survive the upcoming scission. My *actions* will protect the empire we've built, allowing it to endure well beyond any of us." She glanced at Kate. "*Your* actions, on the other hand, have gone a long way toward undoing all of that effort."

"Kate is not your concern," he said, tensing slightly.

"Clearly she's yours," Reyna smiled. "I suspected she meant more to you than you'd let on, that it wouldn't be hard to use her as bait to lure you here." She paused. "Your connection to her will be your undoing. It's a soft spot that your enemies will use against you."

Ocelot actually bared his teeth. "I'd like to see them try."

Reyna's eyes widened. "And there you go proving my point for me," she said before shaking her head sadly. "What a disappointment – a waste of time and resources. You could have had everything. The entire world would have been at your disposal."

"The cost would have been my soul," Ocelot replied. "You've betrayed everything — for what? Financial gain in a world that values *possessions* over true wealth?"

"Our world is dead and has been for centuries. It's time to move on. Make a new path."

"And make *new* gods?" Ocelot demanded angrily. "For that's pretty much what you're doing."

Vasquez actually smiled at that. "*This* world is willing to worship at the altar I'm creating," she said before looking at the stone one behind Ocelot. "We can use that to rule over *everything*."

"No," he replied icily. "We can't."

Reyna looked to reply, but didn't get the chance; Ocelot shifted the position of his body and a fraction of a second later, a brilliant white explosion slammed into the ornament just above the altar. Boiling energy leapt down and forcefully struck Ocelot in the back, pushing his chest forward and flinging his arms out wide. His head lolled backwards, and Kate felt her pulse race as his eyes rolled; before she could even process what was happening to him, the energy burst out of Ocelot and slammed directly into Vasquez, hundreds of times more powerful than what had struck the hero initially. Reyna's screams of agony were amplified by the magic as her body was lifted from the stones; Kate watched in fascinated horror as Reyna writhed in agony, her body slowly glowing brighter and brighter shades of pure white that became too painful to look at. Kate was forced to close her eyes against the glare and turn away, but the light was so brilliant it was almost as though she were still staring at it. Then it winked out, leaving behind only the fading echoes of Vasquez's final screams. Slowly, the wind began to lesson, and soon she felt the warmth of the sun on her still-soaked skin.

Not quite trusting it was over, Kate waited until she felt the gentle hand at her shoulder before opening her eyes. Ocelot was there, looking haggard but otherwise unharmed. "Are you okay? Is it over?" she asked, her voice hoarse from all of her yelling.

"Yes and almost," he replied. "Vasquez used magical artifacts from this pyramid to create portals across the globe. We still need to shut those down, and then we can go home."

"Portals?" Kate asked before nodding. "Like that weird doorway in her office?"

"Exactly. Except far, far larger."

"Like, large enough to ship stuff?" Kate asked. "No wonder Vasquez industries was dominating everyone. Can you really turn them off?"

"I just need to collect all the stones and bring them back here," he replied. "That will close the doorways and return some balance to the system."

"Oh," she replied. "That seems... anticlimactic."

"Sorry to disappoint," he laughed. "You want to go home?"

"Fuck *no*. I want to help."

His masked face smiled. "I was hoping you'd say that; I think I'd appreciate the company."

"Good," she said as she hugged him close. Pulling back, she looked at him for a moment. "Don't take this the wrong way, but once this is all over, if I never saw another jungle, it would be too soon."

Ocelot smiled. "That makes two of us."

EPILOGUE

"I appreciate you doing this."

Kate had taken the second guest chair beside him and reached over to hold his hand. "We could have done this at your office," she said gently. "There was no reason for you to come to the station."

Tenoch smiled slightly. "I'll be honest, Kate. I've been avoiding the office since *madre* disappeared."

"I can understand that," Kate replied. "I did the same thing right after my father passed away — he had a small workshop in our garage, and for months, I couldn't go in there because all I could see was him."

"Exactly," Tenoch nodded before sighing. "I can't avoid it forever, though. In her absence, I'm the acting CEO. Sooner or later, someone's going to have to start signing checks."

"I can't think of anyone else I'd rather see in that position," Kate replied. She searched his eyes for a moment. "It's only been a few days, Tenoch. Are you sure she didn't just take a cruise or something and forget to tell you?"

Despite having doubled his mental barriers, he worried she might hear what his heart was actually thinking. "It's unlikely," he said, which was, to a point, true. "I can't recall her ever taking a sick day, let alone a full-fledged vacation."

Kate shook her head. "Well, we'll do what we can in these sorts of missing person cases, but honestly, nine times out of ten the person who has disappeared generally *wants* to fall off the face of the planet. Without any clear evidence of a kidnapping, it's pretty hard not to conclude your mother has opted for a permanent change of scene."

It was colossally difficult not to arch an eyebrow at what he thought was an intentional double entendre. "Perhaps. If she finally answers the phone or sends me an email, I'll let you know."

"Good."

They looked at each other for a moment.

"About those cargo containers," Tenoch began. "Did the data I provided you help in any way?"

"It did," she nodded. "With some help from our... international connections, we shut the entire operation down at its source."

This time, he did arch an eyebrow. "I remain in awe of your network."

"Yours is probably far better," she laughed as the stood. She looked at him again. "I'm... really glad you're back in town."

"Me too," he replied, before smiling sadly. "While I'm sorry I was a day late and a dollar short, I am honestly quite happy you've found someone."

"I have," she said. "But I hope you'll continue to be a close friend, Tenoch."

"I will *always* be there for you, pr—Kate," he said, barely saving himself a major faux pas.

"We should do dinner again," she suggested as she showed him to the door of her office.

"With or without the extra curricular activities?" he asked.

She bopped him on the bicep, though he still managed to catch the slight shading on her cheeks. "You know the answer to that. See you around, Tenoch."

He wandered through the small but busy police station and then out to his waiting Charger in the visitor parking lot; making the Missing Persons report was the first step in formally wiping away his *madre's* legacy in Santa Marcel, a long process that he'd grimly begun the night he and Kate had returned from the jungle. Getting behind the wheel, he paused before starting it and stared out across the parking lot to the busy street beyond, but didn't see the early afternoon traffic. Instead, his mind replayed the events of the last seventy-two hours, including those final moments facing his *madre* atop the sacred pyramid. Taking her on, not to mention having to take her *out*, wasn't something he'd expected when he'd begun his sleuthing of the questionable shipping practices at Vasquez Industries. Despite their differences — of which there had been many — he found a sizable hole had appeared in his heart at her absence in his daily life, one nearly as big as that which had been created when *padre* had met his fate years earlier.

Sighing, he thought about the road ahead. Destroying the portals his mother had been using to dominate the shipping industry would set the company back a bit, though the new CEO had some ideas about spinning off that portion of the portfolio and focusing on other parts of the business — or developing something entirely new. Like, say, a professional private investigative arm that could offer highly specialized and somewhat unique consulting services to local law enforcement agencies. Glancing over his shoulder at the squat edifice housing the Santa Marcel Police Department, he had a sneaking suspicion who their first client might be.

Reaching for the start button of the Charger, Tenoch felt his world suddenly fade away; blinking against the darkness, he found himself standing once more in that strange in-between space where he often met Tezcatlipoca. The mists were just as thick as always, and as he waited for his patron to materialize, he looked down and discovered he'd somehow donned his magical costume so he could appear for his audience as Ocelot. And yet, as he turned his arms over and stared at his outfit, he found the color had shifted slightly; no, it hadn't changed so much as small, iridescent spots in a lighter green had been woven into the magical fabric. Holding his arm to the watery light in that space, he smiled slightly at the realization that it was a subtle testament to having completed his ascension.

Well done, mijo, the unique voice of Tezcatlipoca boomed in his head.

"I think we both know I had a little bit of help," Ocelot smiled.

None that wasn't deserved — or earned.

"Thanks, just the same." Ocelot paused, peering into the mists but still failing to see Tezcatlipoca. "Might I ask a question?"

Always.

Ocelot doubted that. "Were you aware that *madre* had forged an alliance with Xipe Totec?"

Yes, was the answer after a long wait.

"How long were you aware of it?"

There was another long, somewhat uncomfortable pause. *You are only aware of your father's connection, aren't you?*

Ocelot began to nod. "Not any longer. I presume the match of my parents was made to preserve some sort of balance?"

As has been done for generations.

He nodded again. "Except my *madre* didn't want to adhere to generations of tradition, did she? And found a willing ear in your brethren?"

As has happened multiple times in the past. And will happen again in the future. There was a short pause, and Ocelot felt like Tezcatlipoca was actually smiling. *Just not during this* next *generation.*

"Kate will be glad to hear that, I think," Ocelot replied, unable to smile himself. "Once she knows the truth—"

She cannot, Tezcatlipoca interrupted. *Not until her powers manifest.*

He felt his masked eyebrows rise. "That will take time, and you can't honestly expect me to continue my relationship with her as a masked hero with a secret identity."

That is exactly what I am expecting; you must be patient. Reveal yourself too soon and all will be lost.

"I thought we just *fixed* that kind of a problem," Ocelot persisted. "How does my mating affect any of this?"

All will be revealed in the proper sequence. Do as I ask.

Ocelot frowned. "It's not like I've got a lot of choice, is there?"

Until next time.

Tenoch blinked again and found himself back in the Charger, his finger halfway to the start button. Sighing as though the world were literally on his shoulders, he started the sports car with a loud rumble, backed out of his spot and then pulled into traffic, just one more cog in the strange mechanism of the universe in which he lived. The fact that he would be forced to hide in plain sight for the foreseeable future was something he could live with, albeit temporarily. Being forced to hide from Kate? *That* was something he wasn't sure his heart was capable of doing. Not now, not after what they had been through.

Time was not on his side.

ACKNOWLEDGMENTS

Close to two years ago, I had a strange idea to try and marry the traditional police procedural with some elements of conventional or urban fantasy; I wanted to discover if I could tell my kind of story, grounded in the sort of recognizable world we all lived in while still sprinkling in the concept of a magical world hidden just out of view for most mortals. I decided to try my hand at writing such a novel during one of the NaNoWriMo quarterly sprints, got halfway through it, and... lost my nerve. I shelved what I had done (all 50k words of it) and moved on over the next year to complete three more books and two novellas for my existing series before guiltily eyeing the manuscript I had literally left hanging. So I pulled it down, tinkered with it, and then set it aside *again* for another full year.

Two years later, I found myself at loose ends after writing the hardest of the Sean Colbeth stories, *Belie*. Darker and more tied to current events than normal, I needed a change of pace and pulled out this manuscript with a renewed interest in finally finishing the novel. It wasn't easy, for my two *usual* main characters were never far from my thoughts, trying to guilt me into dropping this side project and retiring to the comfortable universe I had already created. I very nearly gave in to that, too, save for a few inspirational words whispered into my ear from my beautiful wife, **Paula**.

"You'll never be free of this story," she said. "If you don't write it down now — get it all out — it will haunt you forever."

As always, she was right.

I've left myself some wriggle room to add additional novels to what could be a third series, but honestly, I'm probably going to let these two settle for a bit before I tackle them again. Kate and Tenoch are an interesting pair, to be sure, but for now, I think I will scurry back to safer territory and complete some of the other long-gestating ideas I have for Sean and Vasily Korsokovach.

At least, until I decide I need another change of pace... :-)

—C

January 30, 2025

ABOUT THE AUTHOR

Born and raised in Maine, Chris has spent nearly three decades as an IT nerd, writing just about everything other than a novel in the process. That changed in early 2019 when he was advised to find a way to wind down from his day job; sifting through his options, he recalled a childhood ambition to become a writer and quickly found himself weaving an entirely new world from the comfort of his laptop. *Reflection in the Shadows* is his seventeenth book and the first in a new series featuring Kathryn Oliver and Tenoch Vasquez.

Despite his love for the Northeast, the author escaped the cold for Arizona, where he currently resides with his beautiful wife and a Staffordshire Terrier rescue that insists on being walked regularly.

For all of the latest information, including hints about upcoming books and an exclusive reader newsletter, please visit the author's website at https://chrisjansmann.com.

- amazon.com/author/chrisjansmann
- bookbub.com/authors/christopher-h-jansmann
- goodreads.com/chrisjansmann
- mastodon.coffee/@chrisjansmann

www.ingramcontent.com/pod-product-compliance
Lightning Source LLC
Chambersburg PA
CBHW052033240626
47153CB00006B/2067